Trans

V Plague Book Five

DIRK PATTON

Dirk Patton

Text Copyright © 2014 by Dirk Patton

Copyright © 2014 by Dirk Patton

All Rights Reserved

This book or any portion thereof may not be reproduced or used in any manner whatsoever without the express written permission of the copyright holder except for the use of brief quotations in a book review.

Published by Reaper Ranch Press LLC

PO Box 856

Gilmer, TX 75644-0856

Printed in the United States of America

First Printing, 2014

ISBN-13: 978-1511504713

ISBN-10: 1511504714

This is a work of fiction. Names, characters, businesses, brands, places, events and incidents are either the products of the author's imagination or used in a fictitious manner. Any resemblance to actual persons, living or dead, or actual events is purely coincidental.

Transmission
Table of Contents

Author's Note 6

Also By Dirk Patton 8

1 12

2 25

3 33

4 42

5 49

6 58

7 67

8 76

9 85

10 91

11 97

12 105

13 113

14 124

15 130

16 138

17 148

18 156

19 165

20	175
21	184
22	193
23	204
24	212
25	219
26	227
27	238
28	249
29	259
30	272
31	282
32	293
33	302
34	310
35	321
36	327
37	336
38	345
39	358
40	368
41	377
42	383

Transmission
43 391

Author's Note

Thank you for purchasing Transmission, Book 5 in the V Plague series. If you haven't read the first four books, you need to stop reading now and pick them up. Otherwise, you will be lost as this book is intended to continue the story in a serialized format. I intentionally did nothing to explain comments and events that reference book 1 through 4. Regardless, you have my heartfelt thanks for reading my work, and I hope you're enjoying the adventure as much as I am. As always, a good review on Amazon is greatly appreciated.

I'm learning that as an author's fan base grows, there are more and more people that need to be thanked for their contributions to a novel. Some are significant, such as my beta readers Jess and Scott. Some may not spend nearly as much time, but are just as important because they offer suggestions that trigger ideas I might not have had. I would try to name everyone, but without fail I'd miss someone, so I'll leave it as a Thank You to all my fans that have corresponded with me either via email or Facebook.

I'd also like to respond to several comments I've received from people who admit they haven't served in the military but feel that

Transmission
sometimes I unfairly pick on branches other than the Army.

Yes, I do!

And anyone out there who has served understands completely, and can probably tell as many disparaging Army jokes as I can Marine, Navy or Air Force jokes. In all seriousness, whether Air Force, Navy, Army or Marines (and Coast Guard, too, though you're part of Homeland Security) the US military is just one big dysfunctional family. We snipe, berate and denigrate each other endlessly, but at the end of the day, if you mess with one, you mess with all of us. I just hope my Air Force readers can forgive me for making Roach an Air Force officer.

Finally, as always, my heartfelt thanks to Katie for putting up with me and being a good sport about her husband off running around with a stripper while she's left to the designs of a psychopath. Yet another reason I'm glad you married me!

You can always correspond with me via email at dirk@dirkpatton.com and on the internet at www.dirkpatton.com and if you're on Facebook, please like my page at www.facebook.com/DirkPattonAuthor or Twitter @DirkPatton.

Thanks again for reading!

Dirk Patton

Also By Dirk Patton

The V Plague Series

Unleashed: V Plague Book One

Crucifixion: V Plague Book Two

Rolling Thunder: V Plague Book Three

Red Hammer: V Plague Book Four

Transmission: V Plague Book Five

Days Of Perdition: V Plague Book Six

Indestructible: V Plague Book Seven

Rules Of Engagement: A John Chase Short Story

Recovery: V Plague Book Eight

Precipice: V Plague Book Nine

Anvil: V Plague Book Ten

Merciless: V Plague Book Eleven

Fulcrum: V Plague Book Twelve

Hunter's Rain: A John Chase Novella

Transmission Exodus: V Plague Book Thirteen

Scourge: V Plague Book Fourteen

Fractured: V Plague Book Fifteen

Brimstone: V Plague Book Sixteen

Abaddon: V Plague Book Seventeen

Cataclysm: V Plague Book Eighteen

Legion: V Plague Book Nineteen

The 36 Series

36: A Novel

The Void: A 36 Novel

Other Titles by Dirk Patton

The Awakening

Fool's Gold

Dirk Patton

Transmission

Transmission

Taught me how to shoot to kill

A specialist with a deadly skill

A skill I needed to have to be a survivor

It's over now or so they say

Well, sometimes, it don't work out that way

Huey Lewis And The News – Walking On A Thin Line

1

It was turning out to be a long morning. I had landed at Tinker Air Force Base a couple of hours ago, delivering less than the total quantity of backpack-sized nuclear bombs than had been expected. In all fairness, I'd run into a few problems and some game-changing news while recovering the devices from Los Alamos, but there were a couple of senior military officers who weren't very happy at the moment.

They weren't too happy with me for not having delivered, and even less happy with the news I had brought back, courtesy of a renegade Russian GRU officer. I've pissed off senior officers before and knew they would get over it. What was irritating as hell was the woman sharing the screen with the Admiral.

Kathleen Clark had been the Secretary of Energy. She was on vacation in Alaska with her husband, an avid salmon fisherman, and her personal aide when the attacks had occurred. For several weeks, she had stayed at their remote fishing cabin with a small security detail. Satellite phones had allowed her to stay in contact with the President and the two members of her staff that had survived and were bunkered with the White House staff.

Transmission

But as the federal government quickly began losing its ability to govern, there was less and less for her to do other than call in to meetings and listen to the desperation in the voices of the men and women in Mount Weather and Cheyenne Mountain. Then, her calls had gone unanswered. She couldn't receive a response from either location and concern pushed her out of the safety of the Alaskan wilderness.

A six-hour flight in a small bush plane, piloted by her husband who was a retired Coast Guard pilot, and they arrived at Fort Wainwright in Fairbanks. No one, including the General in command of the post, recognized her. But she maintained her composure as the Army went about verifying her identity. Once they were satisfied she was who she said she was, she was briefed on the current state of affairs and placed on a conference call with Admiral Packard, the ranking US military officer still alive.

It was the Admiral who had recognized the situation as soon as he realized whom he was talking to. The Secretary of Energy was legally in the line of succession for the office of the President. He had a list of everyone in civilian leadership positions that had been in either of the bunkers when they were destroyed by the Russians, and there were only two names not on that list. One was Jeremy Smyth, the Secretary of Education, and the other was Kathleen Clark.

No one had any doubt that every person that had been in Mount Weather and Cheyenne Mountain were dead. That left two potential cabinet members to ascend to the Presidency. One of them was missing and one had wandered in out of the Alaskan bush. After several frantic hours of talking to any lawyer he could find, the Admiral acknowledged that per the Constitution of the United States, Kathleen Clark should be sworn in as President without delay.

That led to the next round of consultations with the lawyers. Who could swear in a President? Admiral Packard was very surprised to learn that there is no requirement or provision in the Constitution for *who* officiates the swearing-in. In fact, the only requirement is that the individual being sworn, recite the oath of office. Technically, all Kathleen needed to do was say the words and she was President. But, the military likes to stand on ceremony and the base commander at Wainwright, Brigadier General Carey, officiated and was the first to congratulate the new President of the United States.

"And you felt you had the authority to make this decision?"

Transmission

The new president glared at me from half of a huge, high definition panel attached to the wall of the conference room we were borrowing from the base commander. President Clark was what could be described as a handsome woman. She had probably been a head turner when she was younger, but age had caught up with her.

Admiral Packard took up the other half of the screen. The Admiral was CINCPACFLT, Commander In Chief Pacific Fleet, or the commander of all US Navy ships, aircraft, and personnel assigned to that half of the planet. He was a handful of years older than me, iron-grey hair in a severe brush cut and had those washed out, blue-grey eyes you see on old sailors. The image was so good I could even see a couple of errant eyebrow hairs, which were distracting as hell. If you ever saw the actor, Larry Hagman, in the last few years of his life, well, that kind of errant eyebrows.

We were communicating via a secure satellite video link and he was on board the aircraft carrier USS George Washington, somewhere in the Pacific Ocean. The Washington had led one of the US battle groups that had fought and defeated the Chinese invasion fleet a couple of weeks ago. Talking to the Admiral, I had little doubt he was one of those leaders that had probably stood in the open air on the carrier's deck while a battle raged all around the giant ship.

"Madam President, yes I did. This was completely unexpected and I had no time to stop and make a phone call to ask for permission. So, I made the decision and can't undo it."

I wasn't exactly comporting myself in a properly respectful military manner, but I'd been being grilled for over an hour now. First by Colonel Crawford as soon as I stepped off the Stealth Hawk helicopter in Oklahoma City, and now by Popeye the sailor man and a woman I'd never heard of before an hour ago. I know, I know. Watch my ass before I wind up in the stockade. Wouldn't be the first time. That ship sailed a lot of years ago.

On the screen, I saw the Admiral's forehead crease a moment before the President's eyes flashed in anger at my response. Whether at my words, tone or both, I couldn't tell, and frankly didn't give a shit. Out of view of the camera focused on us, Crawford reached out and placed one of his big hands on my forearm. A "shut the hell up, you idiot" touch, if I've ever felt one.

"Gentlemen, I feel I need to get a better handle on this situation. I am going to be dispatching my Chief of Staff to Oklahoma as soon as General Carey can arrange a flight. I also want a supply of vaccine ready to be sent back to Alaska when that plane arrives. I will be staying here for the time being. Is there anything else?"

"Thank you, Madam President," Packard spoke up quickly.

A moment later, the President's half of the screen went blank. There was a flash as the display refreshed and when it came back, the Admiral filled the entire view. The frown on his face changed to a smile and a snort of laughter as his eyes shifted to look at my commanding officer.

"You're right, Colonel. He does have a big pair, and a mouth to match."

The Admiral's eyes shifted to me.

"OK, Major. I'm not going to Monday morning quarterback you. But for all our sakes, let's hope your gut made the right decision. I'm expecting a preliminary report on the analysis of the data from the flash drive within the hour. The analysis of the live vaccine will take a little longer."

The vials of vaccine I'd been given by Captain Irina Vostov were in the hands of the few surviving virologists who had set up shop in the University of Oklahoma Health Science Center near downtown. They were also pouring through the data on the small thumb drive and had shot a copy to a group of experts in Hawaii.

Hawaii had come through the nuclear, nerve gas and viral attacks completely unscathed. The Chinese had planned to use the island chain as a strategic base for an invasion of Alaska and the continental US, and had not wanted to deal with radiation or an infected and enraged population. When the Navy, with help from a few of our allies, had destroyed the Chinese battle groups and troop carriers, America's fiftieth state breathed a big sigh of relief.

Now they were dealing with shortages of just about everything. Hawaii produced very little of anything consumed by its residents, being dependent on uninterrupted deliveries of everything from fuel to food and clothing to diapers. I had overheard it mentioned that there had been a couple of food riots in Honolulu when the Governor declared martial law and seized all available food stocks to ensure equitable and rationed distribution to the population.

It was only going to get worse because there wasn't anyone left to produce, package and deliver food to the grocery store shelves. I really hoped there was someone over there taking charge and getting some crops in the ground before they literally started starving to death. You can live without power in Hawaii if they couldn't keep the electric grid going. It's not like a Minnesota winter or Arizona summer where the temperatures can kill you, several months out of every year. And there's plenty of water on the islands. But food...

"Oh, and Major." The Admiral leaned toward the camera and extended his arm, ready to hit the end call button. "Watch your mouth with our new president. You're an officer now. Act like it and don't make your Colonel look like an asshole."

"Thank you, sir," Crawford spoke.

I decided it was best if I kept my mouth shut. The screen went dark a moment later and the Colonel killed our connection to the satellite.

"I need a helo, sir," I said, dismissing the rebuke I'd just received.

"I've already got two out looking for them. What do you think you're going to do that isn't already being done?" He asked, rubbing his eyes, voice sounding tired.

"I think I need to be doing something and you don't need me here. I'm not a scientist, and there's no fighting to be done at the moment."

Dirk Patton

I was tired, but at least I'd gotten a few hours of sleep on the flight from Albuquerque to Oklahoma City. Granted, it was on a hard, vibrating steel deck and my back and neck felt like someone had tied knots in them, but there was no way I could just sit around as long as Jackson, Rachel and Dog were still missing.

Crawford looked at me with red-rimmed and bloodshot eyes. It was the first time I had seen him look tired since I'd met him in Tennessee. He leaned back in his chair, reached for a pack of cigarettes then glanced around the room and dropped the pack onto the table and his hands into his lap.

"OK. Go find Captain Blanchard and tell him I authorized it," he finally said with a sigh of resignation.

"Thank you, sir."

I got to my feet, ready to get out of there before he changed his mind or thought of something else for me to do.

"Oh, and Major." I paused with my hand on the conference room door and turned to look at him. "You did the right thing in Los Alamos. Do you think this Captain Vostov will be able to pull it off?"

Transmission

"I hope so, sir. If not, then the Russians win. There's not enough of us left to stop them."

After a moment's reflection, he nodded and waved me out the door.

It didn't take me long to track down Captain Blanchard. He was never far from the Colonel, and when I found him, he was standing next to a parked Humvee outside the base commander's office. He had a laptop open on the hood, typing with one hand while he held a satellite phone to his ear with the other. He nodded when I walked up and raised the index finger on his typing hand into the air, telling me he needed another minute. Leaning against a fender, I lit a cigarette and looked around the sprawling air base.

It was approaching late morning and the sun was shining brightly. The temperature wasn't that high, but it was humid as hell. Reminded me of Georgia. I was surprised, but when I thought about it realized I knew next to nothing about Oklahoma. My parents had been born and raised in eastern Oklahoma, near the Arkansas border, but had left for greener pastures in Texas soon after they married. I knew I had relatives somewhere to the east, maybe, but I hadn't seen or talked to any of them since I was a small child. I idly wondered if I had a clan of cousins hunkered down and trying to survive.

"What can I do for you, Major?" The Captain asked, bringing me back to the moment.

I told him what I needed and that the Colonel had authorized it. He nodded and turned to check a file on his laptop. After a couple of minutes of poking keys, he told me he'd have a Black Hawk ready to go in an hour. I thanked him, got directions to the base hospital and started walking. I wanted to go check in on Tech Sergeant Zach Scott, who had broken an arm and cracked his skull while we were in Los Alamos.

I walked along the side of a wide boulevard that ran across the northern edge of the base. Traffic was steady, Air Force vehicles passing me at sedate speeds. The last thing you ever want is to get a traffic violation on a military base. Pretty much guarantees you will wind up standing in front of your commanding officer. I've actually known a couple of guys that were passed over for promotion because they had speeding tickets on post in their records.

Still heavily armed, I was drawing lots of stares from passersby. I could have walked around an Army post without even getting a second glance, but the Air Force isn't used to filthy grunts with weapons strapped to their

Transmission

bodies wandering around. A Security Forces Hummer slowed to a stop, the driver looking at me with narrowed eyes. I turned and faced her, seeing her relax a notch when she spotted my Major's oak leaf.

"Can I give you a ride, sir?" She asked.

God, she was young. She looked like she should be worrying about who was going to ask her to the prom, not driving an Air Force Hummer with a pistol on her belt.

I took her up on the offer and was soon delivered to the hospital entrance. I thanked the Airman for the ride and strode through the glass doors, breathing a sigh of relief at the cool, dry air of the lobby. Another Airman was seated behind an imposing reception desk, looking me over when I walked up. I told him who I was there to see and was given directions to the room Scott was in.

"Major?" I had already started walking to the elevators when he called. I stopped and turned to look back at him. "There are no weapons allowed in the hospital. Sorry, sir."

"Don't be sorry, Airman. But I'm going up and I'm not leaving my weapons behind. And if you don't have a weapon, you should."

Dirk Patton

I turned and strode briskly to the elevator. There would either be a pissed off senior officer with a squad of Security Forces waiting for me when I came back down, or the Airman would ignore my breach of policy and take my advice. I didn't really care which at the moment. I stepped out of the elevator on the third floor, checked the sign to see which way to go, then whipped my rifle up when I heard the scream of an infected female.

Transmission

2

The screams were coming from my left. Opposite the direction to Scott's room. Rifle up and ready, I started moving in that direction, confused when I could see hospital staff moving about like nothing was wrong. Three nurses were seated at a round workstation, writing in charts.

An orderly was pushing a linen cart down the hall and a doctor stood at an elevated counter, typing into a tablet computer. He was the first to notice me, freezing in place and staring. One of the nurses looked up at the orderly, followed his gaze and stood when she saw me pointing a rifle in her general direction.

"What are you doing with that in here? No weapons in the hospital!" She shouted at me.

Thoroughly confused, I slowly lowered the rifle, looking around for the source of the screams. The doctor had heard the nurse's shout and turned from his work. He smiled a weary smile when he saw me.

"It's OK," he said, raising his hand, palm towards me. "She's restrained."

"Excuse me?" I couldn't believe what I'd just heard. Restrained? What the hell were they doing with a live, infected female in a hospital? If she got loose in their gun free zone, she'd rip through the staff and patients in minutes.

"We're trying to treat her, Major. These people are just sick. We shouldn't be killing them because they have an infection."

The doctor had approached as he spoke. He was wearing a white coat over blue scrubs with a Lieutenant Colonel's oak leaf embroidered on the chest above his title and name.

"Are you fucking kidding me?" I was too surprised to worry about rank. What the hell was this idiot thinking? "Have you seen what they do? One thing and one thing only. They kill us!"

"Major. This isn't your concern."

He gave me a look that I knew well. It was the look I usually gave to people that just didn't get it. I was more than a little irritated with this guy by now. The infected were dangerous as hell. Yes, I understand there's a need to study them and possibly come up with a treatment or a cure. That would solve many of our problems, but a patient floor in a hospital is sure as hell not the place to be doing that! The female I could still hear screaming should be safely locked away in a secure facility where the researchers themselves were the only people at risk.

Transmission

"Well, sir, I'm making it my concern. What happens if she gets free? There's no guard in the hall. Do you at least have one in the room with her?" I asked, peering over his shoulder in the direction of the noise.

"I assure you, there's nothing to be concerned about, Major."

He put a heavy emphasis on my rank, reminding me who was who in this conversation. Maybe I had been out of the Army too long, or just gotten old enough, but I didn't give a shit if he outranked me. He was putting a lot of people in danger and as far as I could tell, wasn't even taking basic precautions to safeguard them.

"Colonel," I said, stepping close and looking him in the eye. "We are going to go make sure that infected is properly secured, then I'm going to get a couple of Rangers up here to guard her until she is either moved to a secure location or is put down. Sir."

My tone and body language didn't leave any doubt that I was absolutely serious. He frowned and took a step back away from me.

"Where's your commanding officer and what's his name?"

"His name is Colonel Crawford and you'll be meeting him soon enough. Now, you can either walk me to the room the female is in, or I'll find it myself."

I moved forward into his personal space again. He looked me in the eye and I could see the anger and resentment in his, but also recognized he was smart enough not to keep pushing back.

"Fine. Follow me," he said, spinning on his heel and heading down the hall.

I noticed a small gesture to one of the nurses as we passed their work area. I had little doubt it was a 'call security' gesture. OK. We can play it that way. I reached to my vest and activated the radio that was connected to my earpiece. Blanchard answered almost immediately and I told him to grab the Colonel, a couple of Rangers, and meet me at the hospital. He had gotten to know me well enough to not ask why. Just promised they were on their way.

The doctor led me down the hall, stopping in front of a closed door at the very end of the corridor. I could hear the guttural snarls and screams coming from inside the room, the heavy wood of the door doing little to muffle them. He stepped to the side and made an 'after you' gesture. I reached out with my left hand and pushed on the handle that released the door's latch, placing my right hand on the hilt of my Kukri at the small of my back.

The door opened easily and the sounds from the infected ceased the instant the latch clicked open. I only had the man's word that the female was restrained, so I carefully continued to push the door, stepping forward as it swung into the room. There wasn't an immediate attack, so I kept moving forward, adjusting my grip on the Kukri and wiggling it slightly to ensure it would draw smoothly if needed.

Pushing the final few inches, I stepped through the opening into a normal looking hospital room. Normal except for the woman lying in the bed. She was young and attractive with long, brown hair. Dressed in a blue hospital gown, she was restrained across her chest and at each wrist and ankle with sheepskin lined leather cuffs. The kind of restraints normally used in a psychiatric ward to prevent the patients from hurting themselves or others.

I stood staring at the woman and she stared back at me with her intelligent, blood red eyes. If not for those, and the restraints, she would have looked like any other patient, but her gaze had locked onto my face as soon as I came into view. And she was coldly calculating how to get to me. This was one of the smart ones. I had no doubt.

Dirk Patton

There was movement from behind and I turned in time to raise a hand and grasp the doctor's wrist as he tried to stab a needle into my neck. Applying pressure and twisting his arm, I watched the loaded syringe fall out of his hand to the polished floor. Then his arm went limp as he collapsed to his knees and began sobbing.

"She's my wife. Please! Don't kill her. I can help her," he cried.

Scooping up the syringe, I turned to look at the woman. She lay there, staring back at me, still silent. I glanced at her left hand and saw a distinctive wedding ring. Looking down, I saw a matching band on the doctor's finger. His emotion and the whole situation took the anger out of me like it had been doused with a bucket of cold water.

What would I do if I found Katie and she was infected? I didn't know the answer to that, but I certainly understood the emotions this man was dealing with. Releasing his wrist, I pushed the plunger on the syringe, shooting a stream of whatever was in it onto the wall of the room before snapping the needle off and tossing the whole thing into a trashcan. Bending over, I grabbed his upper arms and lifted him to his feet.

Transmission

"I'm sorry," I said, looking him in the eye. "I truly am, but she's too dangerous to keep here."

"She's my wife," he said again, a pleading tone in his voice. "This just happened last night at dinner. One minute she was fine, then..."

He gestured helplessly at the infected. She chose that moment to scream, loud enough to make me involuntarily put my hand on my holstered pistol.

"No!" The doctor shouted, reaching out and grabbing my gun hand.

Normally that would get someone hurt or killed. But in this case, I just looked at him and nodded as his wife let out with another ear-splitting scream. From the hallway, I heard heavy boots running in our direction. A moment later, Colonel Crawford burst into the room, pistol in hand. Blanchard was on his heels, also with a pistol out and ready, two Rangers pushing in behind them.

"We're under control," I said calmly, raising a hand to slow down the charge.

"What the hell is this, Major?" Crawford asked, holstering his pistol and looking at the infected.

Dirk Patton

There was more noise from the hall, more running boots, then excited shouting. Air Force Security Forces had arrived. The two Rangers had spread apart and had their rifles up. It was the new arrivals doing all the yelling. I know they train cops to do that as it is a great way to create a moment of panic in suspects you're trying to capture alive. But Rangers aren't taught that. They're taught to shoot and get on with their day. Blanchard stepped into the hall to defuse things before some Air Force personnel wound up dead on the floor.

"This is the doctor's wife," I said, turning back to the Colonel. "And she turned when they were having dinner last night. I think that confirms what the Russian told me."

Crawford stood staring at the female. He nodded and let out a long sigh. The infected was silent again, watching us with those eyes. Eyes from a nightmare.

Transmission

3

I left the whole mess in Colonel Crawford's capable hands and went down the hall to check in on Scott. He was propped up in bed, arm in a fresh plaster cast and a thick, white bandage wrapped around his head. He was sleeping and, not wanting to disturb him, I turned and started out the door, but paused when I spied a black, felt-tipped pen clipped to a chart. Grabbing the marker, I crept to the edge of the bed and left a calling card on the pristine surface of the white cast.

Back in the hall, I held back when an Air Force Brigadier General, with half a dozen aides in tow, stepped out of the elevator and looked around.

"That way, sir," I said, pointing down the hall where Crawford stood talking on a satellite phone.

The General nodded and strode off. Captain Blanchard spotted me and trotted up before I could board the elevator.

"Your Black Hawk is ready," he said. "Waiting where you landed this morning."

"Thanks. What's he going to do?" I asked, nodding towards the Colonel. The General was standing looking at him as he continued his phone conversation.

"He's talking to Admiral Packard right now. Recommending we immediately start producing and administering the vaccine. If that woman turned last night, there's surely others that have turned as well and we just haven't found them yet. And there may be more that are about to turn."

I nodded, thanked him again for arranging the helicopter and stepped into the elevator. When I walked out the front doors of the hospital, there were three Hummers angled into the curb, obviously parked in a hurry. They all had Security Forces markings on them.

Looking around, I didn't see any other transportation, so said the hell with it and got behind the wheel of the closest one. I was sure someone would be pissed off when they came out and found it missing, but annoying an Air Force cop was at the bottom of my list of concerns at the moment.

It only took a few minutes to drive to the waiting helo, an older man leaning against it when I pulled up. I recognized him as the pilot that had plucked me out of the Mississippi and participated in the dogfight with the Russian helicopters. He was twenty years my senior, if he

Transmission

was a day, but still looked in good shape. Tall and thin with a full head of iron grey hair; he was dressed in cowboy boots, jeans, and a white T-shirt with mirrored aviator sunglasses. If the guy hadn't been on a recruiting poster when he was younger, he should have been.

"Major," he stepped forward and stuck his hand out. "Tom LaPaige."

I shook his hand and followed him around to the far side of the Black Hawk. He introduced me to an Air Force Staff Sergeant, who would be coming along to man the door mounted minigun. Meet and greet out of the way, we all climbed on board. There wasn't a co-pilot available, so I settled into the left seat, strapping in as Tom hit the starters for the two engines. They spooled up quickly and as I got my helmet settled in place, he scanned the instrument panel to make sure everything looked good. A minute later, satisfied with what he was seeing, we lifted off.

Tom was a retired Army CWO4, or Chief Warrant Officer 4. A warrant officer is the typical rank for Army pilots. The Army wants them to be officers, but doesn't want them burdened with the administrative duties of say a Captain or Major, who command a lot of soldiers. A warrant officer is typically only in charge of his aircraft and whatever crew is assigned to it. Actually, a pretty sweet deal. The pay and benefits of officer rank with only a fraction of the crap that comes along with management.

He had learned to fly his father's helicopter in the oil fields of west Texas when he was growing up, volunteering for the Army as the US was just starting to escalate its involvement in Viet Nam. By the time the war was in full swing in the late 60s, he was flying twenty medevac missions a day. He did that for two years before rotating back home and training new pilots. I wasn't surprised at the amount of combat flights he'd made. The way he'd flown when we fought the Russians had told me this was a guy who had been there and done that.

We talked for the first hour of the flight, then ran out of things to say as we kept making our way east. Tom followed Interstate 40 and we flew at fifteen hundred feet. High enough to let us have a great view for miles in every direction, low enough to see details that we might want to investigate. We flew slow, cruising at about a hundred knots, and I had too much time to think.

Captain Blanchard had told me that Jackson, Rachel, and Dog had gone to help with loading evacuees onto the train when they had to move because of approaching storms. They had then gone into town, West Memphis, for reasons he didn't know. The last communication he'd had with them was when Jackson called to say he was coming back with a total of three souls and was ten minutes away.

They hadn't been able to wait. A massive storm was bearing down directly on the area, and they had to get the civilians and all the aircraft out of its path. Jackson was supposed to drive to Little Rock where the Colonel had ordered a Black Hawk to wait for them at Little Rock Air Force Base, but they never showed. That was all that was known of their fate.

I was heartened by the news that Rachel and Dog had both been found, alive and well. Part of me was prepared for them never being located, or worse, being found dead. In the last calm moment we'd had together, Rachel had professed her love to me, asking if I felt the same. My head started going down the path of exploring my feelings for her, but I quickly shut that down. The last thing I needed right now was emotions clouding my decision-making. I just wanted her and Dog safe, then I'd worry about what I was or wasn't feeling.

It's about three hundred air miles from Oklahoma City to Little Rock and we covered that in just over four hours. There had been numerous vehicles we'd slowed to check out. Vehicles that were either moving along the freeway or showing some indication of life.

Dirk Patton

Whenever we'd see one, Tom would swing wide, drop to a hundred feet and roar past to give us a good look at the occupants.

We saw frightened families crammed into cars and trucks, couples ranging from teenagers to elderly, and the occasional solo traveler. All were heading west to the supposed safety of Oklahoma. None of them was a large, black soldier traveling with a pretty woman and a dog. Lacking a photo, that was the description of our search target I'd been able to provide to Tom and the door gunner.

When we reached Little Rock, Tom contacted the base on the radio and received permission to approach and land. We were carrying external fuel tanks, but he wanted to top us off to maximize our time in the air. Our expectation was that if Jackson, Rachel and Dog were alive, we'd find them somewhere between Little Rock and the Mississippi River. We knew they hadn't made it as far west as Little Rock. If they had, there was no doubt Jackson would have gone straight to the base and from there would have found a way to contact the Colonel. That call had never been made.

While Tom oversaw the refueling, I wandered off in search of a latrine. That's the Army term for a restroom. Right off, I couldn't remember if the Air Force had felt it necessary to

Transmission

change that as well. Regardless, when I found it, I must say it was the nicest, cleanest, shiniest latrine I've ever been in. One thing about the Air Force, they live in luxury compared to the rest of the services. I still harbor resentment for time I spent in Panama.

My entire company was housed in tents at the bottom of a large hill. Being at the bottom of a hill means you damn near get washed away every afternoon when it rains. You live in mud, mosquitoes and whatever shit trickles down from above. At the top of the hill sat a large, modern brick building, complete with running water and air conditioning. This was where the Air Force was housed. Every night, we'd go to sleep hearing their AC units humming away and boom boxes blasting. If one of them had been dumb enough to wander down the hill, I doubt he would ever have been heard from again.

Needs taken care of, I headed back to the Black Hawk and kept an eye on the ground crew while Tom and the door gunner took their turn. While I waited, I spread out a map of the area. West Memphis was a hundred and thirty-three air miles east of us. The terrain was so flat and the freeway so straight, it was only a hundred and forty-two road miles. There were two other helos out searching, one to the north of I-40, the other south. I didn't see Jackson leaving the Interstate without a compelling reason, but I was still trying to figure out why the hell they'd gone to town in the first place.

"That is the fucking cleanest, fanciest, five-star shitter I've ever had the pleasure of smelling up," Tom said when he walked up. "Knew I joined the wrong goddamn service."

"Hell, I hear they have some openings. Maybe you should re-up and try life as a wing wiper," I said with a grin, not looking away from the map.

"Fuck that. I can't drink tea with my little bitty pinkie sticking out," he said, moving in next to me to see the map. "So, what's the plan?"

"We know they went into West Memphis. First stop is town. A couple of days ago there were still three cops left alive and working. I want to find them and see if they know anything. We'll follow the Interstate and keep checking vehicles. After that... let's see what we find out when we get there."

By now our door gunner was back and we mounted up. Tom had us in the air a few minutes later and we picked up I-40 and resumed our eastward path. A few miles to the north, a blot of greasy, black smoke stained the sky and I asked Tom to take us closer. As we flew over, I could see heavy equipment carving deep trenches out of the ground. A few hundred yards to the west

Transmission

was another, larger excavation which was where the smoke was coming from.

Tom went into a hover, positioning us in clear air with an unobstructed view into the pit. At first, it looked like deep piles of tree limbs were being burned and I couldn't understand why they were doing that. Then I made out more of the flaming shapes and realized it was human bodies. Thousands of human bodies.

"Christ on a cross!" Tom breathed. "What the hell are they doing?"

"Infected," I answered. "Probably the best thing to do with the bodies."

A small group of figures dressed head to toe in white, bio-hazard suits was standing at the edge of the pit, watching the fire consume the dead. One of them held what had to be a bible and looked to be praying over the departed.

"Let's go," I said, snapping Tom back to the mission at hand. He nodded and spun us around to head back to I-40.

4

Rachel had been in shock after shooting Jackson. Yes, he had turned and tried to kill her, but she had felt a small part of herself die when she pulled the trigger. She hadn't known him long, but he had become a friend. A friend that deserved better than to turn into one of the raging infected and get shot in the head. She couldn't even bury him. He was still strapped into the cab of the pickup, sitting in the bottom of a flooded ditch. Not a fitting way to go.

She didn't know how long she stood in the water in the bed of the truck after firing her pistol and ending his life. It was a long time, based on how high the sun had climbed in the sky. Slowly coming out of her shock, she looked around. It was a beautiful day after the storm. The air had been scrubbed clean, the temperature down after all the rain. It was still, the violent winds having denuded the countryside of all life.

Dog sat at the lip of the ditch, looking off into the distance, protecting her as he patiently waited. She forgot she'd left the Bronco running and it idled away. Forcing herself to move, Rachel stepped over the tailgate and started wading through the water toward the earthen ramp. She had only covered a few feet when she stopped and turned to look back.

Her rifle and pack were in the cab, next to Jackson's body. The last thing in the world she wanted to do was go back down into the ditch and climb into that cab, but the weapon and supplies meant a chance at survival. She knew she was extremely lucky to have survived this long and didn't want to go on with only a pistol and the clothes on her back.

Heaving a sigh, she holstered the pistol and trudged back through the water, climbing over the tailgate. Reaching the back of the cab, Rachel bent and looked through the window she had broken out. Jackson sat lifelessly in the driver's seat, seat belt holding his corpse upright. Her pack was next to him, sitting in half a foot of water. Cautiously, she reached into the cab.

Rachel's skin broke out in goosebumps as she extended her arms into the space next to her dead friend. She imagined him suddenly reaching out and grabbing her in his iron grip. Pulling her all the way into the cab before tearing into her throat with his teeth. Heart pounding, she forced her body forward, grabbed the pack's straps and yanked it through the opening.

Adrenaline gave her a boost of energy and the pack came easily and quickly. It was heavier than she remembered, and the fear-induced adrenaline didn't help her manage the weight when she straightened up and it struck her in the stomach. Rachel let out a whoosh of breath as she was knocked onto her ass in the bed of the truck. Sitting with the pack on her lap she looked hard at the cab, but the body hadn't moved. It wasn't coming after her.

"Stupid," she muttered to herself and spun onto her knees to see through the window.

She couldn't see her rifle, but knew it was in there. It must have slipped onto the floor and was under the muddy water. The only way she could retrieve it was to climb all the way into the cab and feel around in the water. Moving before her courage could falter, Rachel stood and slipped a leg through the opening, gently placing her foot on the submerged seat. Quickly working her other leg through, she followed with her hips and splashed onto the seat.

A quick check of Jackson, who thankfully still hadn't moved, and she started searching for the rifle. It only took a moment to find. She was concerned when she lifted it and water poured out of every opening. Would it still fire? Of course, it would. John had swum across a lake with a rifle strapped to his body when he'd rescued Dog back in Georgia. But had he stopped to dry something out or clean something when he'd reached the shore? That, she didn't know.

Steeling herself, Rachel squirmed through the window into the open air. With every movement, her skin crawled, expecting Jackson's corpse to suddenly reanimate and attack. But it didn't. He was dead and nothing was going to change that. This wasn't a cheesy TV show about zombies, she reminded herself. This was real, and nothing's more real than death.

Back at ground level, Rachel went to the rear of the Bronco and lowered the gate. As the sun warmed her chilled body, she opened the pack and spread its contents out to check and start drying. Her eyes fell on a plastic encased MRE and her stomach grumbled so hard it nearly cramped. Using one of her precious bottles of water, she prepared and wolfed down the meal.

It was tuna with noodles and nothing had ever tasted as good. She'd heard John and Jackson, and a few other soldiers, grumbling about MREs and how bad they tasted, but she was hungry enough to eat anything and enjoy it. Dog had joined her as she prepared the meal and she shared with him as she tried, and failed, to not eat too fast. Apparently he agreed with her assessment. The food was good!

Next, she set about trying to figure out how to dry out the rifle. The damn things came apart. She knew that. She'd seen John with one stripped down to more parts than she could count, but she couldn't figure it out. She settled for removing and unloading the magazine and shaking all the water out of it. Then pulled the bolt open and shook the rifle hard before holding it to her mouth and blowing into the opening to force out any trapped water.

Magazine reloaded, she pulled the charging handle and a round went into the chamber as smoothly as ever. So far, so good. Stepping away from the idling truck, she held the rifle out at arm's length, aimed into an empty field and pulled the trigger. It fired and cycled, loading a fresh round. Best of all, it didn't blow up. Satisfied with the results, Rachel worked the sling over her head and let the weapon hang down her back as she inventoried her supplies.

Finally satisfied, she loaded everything back into the pack and deposited it between the Bronco's front bucket seats. All she had to do was gesture and Dog leapt into the truck and moved to the passenger seat. Climbing behind the wheel, she checked the gauges and looked up when Dog growled softly.

A vehicle was approaching. It was far in the distance, coming from the east, and had just come over the horizon. Rachel's heart immediately started beating faster. Her experiences with other survivors did not have a good track record. They might have seen her, but then they were far enough away that if her vehicle wasn't moving it should just blend with the environment. Did she start driving and try to outrun them, or was it better to hide until they went past?

Rachel only thought about it for a moment before shutting the engine off, grabbing her pack, taking the keys out of the ignition and jumping down to the pavement. Dog followed her out of the truck and she ran in a crouch for the rice paddy on the north side of the road. The ground gradually dropped away from the Interstate, quickly transitioning to a short, steep embankment down into the flooded field.

Rachel ran until her feet were in the water, then turned and threw herself onto the mud. She was facing the truck, seventy-five yards away and well concealed by the terrain. Raising the rifle, she looked through the scope. She had intentionally left the door swinging open on the driver's side of the Bronco and it made it look more like an abandoned vehicle. As long as no one stopped and felt the heat from the recently running engine, it would seem as if the truck had been sitting there for weeks.

Dirk Patton

The hiss of the approaching vehicle's tires finally reached her ears. It seemed to take forever before she also heard the engine and exhaust, then an old station wagon flashed by without slowing. Rachel let out the breath she hadn't realized she was holding, listening to the car speed farther and farther away. The farther, the better, as far as she was concerned.

After a few minutes, she could no longer hear any sound from the vehicle and decided it was safe to move. Picking herself up out of the mud, she glanced around and walked back to the Bronco, Dog staying close by her side. Behind the wheel, she inserted the key into the ignition and reached out to ruffle Dog's ears. He dipped his head toward her, enjoying the contact. With a wan smile, she grasped the key and turned it to start the engine. Nothing happened.

Transmission

5

We were following I-40 again, nobody in a talkative mood after witnessing the communal funeral pyre outside of Little Rock. Each of us was lost in our own thoughts as we flew. I was scanning through a hundred and eighty degrees to our front, my head on a constant swivel. Other than a very occasional car fleeing to the west, nothing moved. There weren't even any birds flying below us.

The thought occurred to me that maybe the virus had jumped from humans to birds. Why couldn't it? How many times had there been bird flu scares over the past several years? Obviously, that virus could mutate and infect humans. I wasn't a scientist, but I was pretty sure the eggheads that were working on this had already thought to check. Even so, I made a mental note to ask the question. All I needed was a bunch of enraged ravens attacking when I least expected it. And I wasn't talking about the football team from Baltimore.

I dismissed the thought, not sure whether to chuckle or get really concerned. Maintaining my scan, I let my mind drift and it went right where I didn't want it to go. Rachel. OK, fuck it. Time to deal with this. I missed her. Very much. With a start, I realized that maybe it was more than just missing her. Something was missing without her around. The same thing that was missing when Katie wasn't around. Then why was I out looking for Rachel instead of heading for Arizona?

Because I didn't have a clue where to start looking for Katie when I got there. The only shred of evidence I even had that she might still be alive was my truck missing out of the garage of our burned out house. But, so what? It could be missing for a hundred reasons. If one of those happened to be that she had taken it and escaped, then where had she gone? It had been over a month since the attacks by the Chinese. In that amount of time, she could be anywhere.

A thousand miles to the south, safe on a white, sandy beach in Mexico. She could be holed up in a cabin somewhere in the Arizona mountains, or could have headed north into Montana or Canada. Hell, enough time had gone by that she could be almost anywhere in the world by now. And as I thought about it, I remembered that three doors down the street lived a retired airline pilot that had his own twin-engine plane. If Katie had gone with him, she could truly be anywhere in the world.

Was I making excuses? Justifying my decisions? No. I was just trying to analyze what I knew. If she was even alive, my wife could be

Transmission

anywhere on the planet and I didn't have the first clue where to even start looking for her. On the other hand, Rachel had been alive less than twenty-four hours ago and I had a very good idea where to start looking for her. That didn't mean Rachel meant more to me than Katie. It just meant I had a reasonable chance of finding and saving one of them.

Sitting there, looking out the Black Hawk's windshield, my heart ached. It ached deep and hard. For Katie, and for Rachel. I made a conscious effort to not hit something in my frustration, clenching my fists tightly in my lap. Hitting things inside the cockpit of an aircraft in flight is generally not a good idea.

"You OK?" Tom asked over the intercom.

I glanced over and noticed him looking at my fists.

"Fine," I answered, forcing my hands to relax and making myself think about anything other than the two women I cared about.

"Good. Don't need you losing it up here," he said, then pointed out the windshield to the east. "Another car coming."

Spotting it, I nodded. Tom followed his normal pattern and swung us off to the side and descended. Turning when we reached one hundred feet, he flew by the car that was speeding west. It was an old Oldsmobile station wagon, originally blue but now mostly rust. Three small, white ovals stared out of the back windows. Children looking up at us. A man and woman were in the front seat. He wasn't Jackson, and she wasn't Rachel. Tom didn't need to be told the vehicle was a negative. He climbed back to our previous altitude and got us back on our heading.

We had only been flying for another few minutes when an alarm started sounding, accompanied by two red lights on the instrument panel. Tom reached forward and silenced the alarm and cycled the power to the warning lights. They blinked out, were dark for a couple of moments, then one after the other started flashing red again. He thumped an analog gauge a couple of times, but the needle was in the red and didn't move.

"What's wrong?" I asked.

"Over temp warning from the rotor shaft. Lots of false alarms in these things. We'll just see what happens," he answered, but didn't sound as confident as I would have liked.

When Rachel and I were fleeing from Atlanta, we'd encountered a downed Air Force flight crew and their crashed Pave Hawk

Transmission

helicopter. I was almost sure they'd told me that there had been an over temp warning from their rotor shaft that the pilot had ignored. Then they'd crashed.

"Put us down, now. Let's check it," I said.

Tom looked over at me to protest but saw something in my eyes that made him bite back his words and start descending. He landed on the eastbound lanes of I-40 a minute later, the big rotor spinning down as we unbuckled and got out. The door gunner was still strapped in and I told him to grab a rifle and get out to keep watch while we were on the ground. Tom was already climbing up the outside of the helicopter to reach the rotor shaft maintenance access panel. While he worked, I circled the area, making sure there weren't any infected about to crash our party.

"Told you!" Tom shouted a moment later.

I looked over my shoulder to see him holding up a part of the helicopter that was connected to a thin electrical cable.

"You could show me that all day and I still wouldn't know what it is," I shouted back.

"It's the primary temperature sensor for the shaft housing. It came loose and was lying next to where the exhaust is routed. It was reading the heat from the engine, not a hot rotor shaft," he said, turning back to return the sensor to its correct location.

He never completed the turn. The smooth, leather soles of the cowboy boots he was wearing slipped as he shifted his weight. A Black Hawk has shallow foot and handholds made into its surface, but they weren't intended for maintenance crews wearing shoes with slick soles. When Tom's foot slipped, his hands weren't gripping anything other than the temperature sensor. As he fell, his other foot's purchase caused his body to rotate. He hit the pavement head first. From forty feet away, I heard his neck break.

I rushed to him, but knew he was dead before I touched the body. The door gunner ran up behind me and looked down.

"Oh, my God! Please tell me you know how to fly this thing, sir."

"No such luck," I replied. "Keep an eye out. I'll see if I can raise anyone on the radio."

Leaving Tom where he lay, I climbed into the Black Hawk's cockpit and slipped on a headset. The radio was still on the frequency that had been dialed in when he contacted the Little Rock air controller, and I wasn't surprised when I couldn't get a response. The radio

Transmission

antennae in aircraft are designed and located to optimize the ability to reach other radios at a lower altitude, or at best, the same altitude. With the helicopter sitting on the ground, I didn't expect our signal was getting out very far.

Switching to the guard channel, reserved for military emergencies, I tried again. I hoped I would have success in reaching one of the other Black Hawks that was searching for my missing friends, but again I only received silence in response to my hails. Checking to make sure the Sergeant was watching the surrounding terrain for any approaching threats, I powered up the internal navigation system to find out where we were.

It only took a few seconds for the system to lock onto enough GPS satellites to accurately pinpoint the spot where I was sitting. Being an aviation system, it didn't show roads and cities, but did display major geographic features as well as both military and civilian airports. Little Rock Air Force Base was one hundred and fifteen miles to the west. The West Memphis airport was eighteen miles to the east. Powering the Black Hawk completely down, I climbed out and buttoned up the aircraft as tightly as possible.

"Looks like we're walking," I said to the Sergeant as I moved to stand next to him.

Dirk Patton

I couldn't remember his name and took the opportunity to glance at the tape on his uniform. Gabbert.

"Where are we going, sir?"

He looked and sounded frightened. I reminded myself that he was just a regular Air Force Staff Sergeant. His world had been inside aircraft up to this point, and being on foot in hostile territory was probably terrifying for him. I'd give him a little latitude so I didn't wind up with a basket case on my hands.

"West Memphis," I said, pointing east down the perfectly straight blacktop. "Little Rock is more than a hundred miles behind us. There're still a few civilians in West Memphis, plus there will be plenty of abandoned vehicles for us to choose from."

"How far is it?" He asked, swallowing nervously.

"A little over ten miles. Not far. We should be there well before dark."

I smiled, trying to exhibit some confidence for the man to pick up on, but I didn't think it worked.

We started walking, leaving Tom's body where it was. There wasn't anything else I could do with it. Putting it inside the helicopter would have prevented scavengers from feeding on it, but would also have made a hell of a mess as it started decomposing. I didn't have an entrenching tool – small folding shovel – with me, so digging a grave wasn't an option either. So, I regretfully decided to leave him where he was and try to get to West Memphis so I could do something to help those of us that were still alive.

6

We had been walking for about an hour and hadn't seen a sign of any other survivors. The countryside was eerily silent, even the birds having abandoned the area or were too afraid to make any sound. I was pretty sure they were just gone. The wind blew steadily in our faces as we moved eastward, providing the only environmental noise other than our boots on the asphalt.

Gabbert was jumpy as hell at first, constantly looking around and over his shoulder with his rifle held high and tight to his chest. I had to remind him several times to keep his finger off the trigger and indexed along the receiver of the weapon. Now, after a few miles in the hot afternoon sun, he was tiring. His eyes were only on the road directly in front of his feet and he'd let the rifle hang down his back on its sling. I'd made him move it to the side so it was at least readily accessible if he needed to fight.

The terrain around us was almost perfectly flat as we closed in on the river. We crossed the occasional small lake, but the pavement didn't even change elevation, just continued on concrete pilings that stuck up out of the water. Far to the south, I could see what looked like a cluster of small businesses and

Transmission

toyed with the idea of checking them for a vehicle. I don't mind walking, but I needed to be covering a lot of ground quickly, not plodding along at four miles an hour.

Making my decision, I motioned for Gabbert to follow me. Clear of another lake, we climbed over the guardrail and down a dirt embankment to the field below. It may have been a rice paddy at one time, but now it was just chest high grass and weeds. Ahead, maybe a mile away, I could make out the top of the sign for one of the businesses and assumed it was a truck stop. There had been an exit a quarter of a mile back, but I hadn't paid any attention to the signs that let travelers know what services were available if they got off the freeway.

We hadn't gone far, maybe a couple of hundred yards, when my little sixth sense started tickling the hair on my arms and running up and down my back on tiny mouse feet. Without breaking stride, I casually looked around, then checked over each shoulder, but didn't see anything. The feeling didn't go away and I came to a stop, holding a hand out to halt Gabbert.

"What's wr…" he started to ask, slamming his mouth shut when I glared at him and held a finger to my lips.

Dirk Patton

Rifle now up to my shoulder, I started a slow, three-hundred-and-sixty-degree scan. The wind was blowing harder, with occasional strong gusts, and the vegetation in the field moved in constant waves. Several times, I paused when I thought I'd spotted something, but it was just a larger weed or bush that wasn't moving perfectly in tandem with the surrounding grass. I paused again, a full circle completed without finding anything and was preparing to start a second scan when Sergeant Gabbert screamed.

He was a dozen feet behind, to my left, and was already vanishing into the tall grass by the time I swung my rifle in his direction. Before I could take a step, his scream was cut off as the vegetation surrounding the area where he'd disappeared started shaking violently. What the fuck?

I moved towards the spot but didn't make it before I caught motion out of the corner of my eye. Not one to normally shoot without knowing what I was shooting at, I spun and fired six fast rounds at the location where I'd seen movement. The grass shook in a way that wasn't from the wind. Then a faint grunting sounded briefly.

Not detecting any more movement, I turned to face where I'd last seen Gabbert. The grass was quivering, independent of the strong wind, and I could hear more grunting sounds. I

Transmission

wanted to put some rounds into the area, but if Gabbert wasn't already dead, I might finish him off.

Taking a step, I froze when the grunting stopped. There was a rustle in the grass and a bush shook as whatever it was started coming in my direction. Backpedaling, I focused in on the wake I could see in the waving foliage and started firing in burst mode. Nine rounds expended, my blood ran cold when there was a squealing scream, then it changed direction and moved swiftly away from me. I tracked the movement of its passing, and it was moving fast. A lot faster than I can run.

Moving forward again, I kept a close eye out for any more danger as I looked for Gabbert. I found him easily, and he was dead. Vacant eyes stared at the sky. The grass was pressed down under his body. Scanning the area again for movement, I didn't see anything, but that didn't make me feel any better. Glancing down at him in between checks of the immediate area, I could see damage to his right leg, abdomen and throat. His lower leg was slashed open to the bone. His abdomen also ripped open, intestines spilling out onto the ground, and most of his throat was torn out.

Fuck me! What can do that to a full-grown man in only a few seconds? At first, I thought it had to be an infected, but immediately dismissed that idea. The infected only had the teeth and nails they were born with. A human, no matter how enraged, simply cannot inflict that kind of damage on another, in mere seconds, with nothing other than bare hands.

Besides, even the smart infected scream once they start attacking and I hadn't heard a sound until after I had put some rounds into whatever it was. I wanted to go check the spot where I'd fired on the first movement, but the little voice in the back of my head was screaming at me to get the hell out of that field as fast as I could.

Now, if this had been a horror movie, I would have ignored it and gone stumbling around until something equally horrible happened to me. But this wasn't, and I like to think I'm at least a little smarter than film characters, so I started backing toward the pavement. Rifle up and constantly scanning, I moved carefully, expecting to have my legs slashed out from under me at any moment.

The wind continued to pick up, tossing the grass around like the surface of the ocean in a strong storm. If there was still anything moving in the field other than me, it had the perfect cover. I'd never spot a disturbance in the grass in time to defend myself. Glancing over my shoulder, I noted I was just under two hundred yards away from clear ground where I could see and effectively fight whatever this was. Walking backwards, I did a quick magazine change.

Wading through chest deep grass when there's something, or several somethings, that are most likely stalking you is not my idea of a pleasant stroll. I tried to watch in every direction at once. Continually, the wind would ruffle the top of the field and for a brief instant, I would think I was seeing the wake of an approaching threat. But nothing attacked and the ground finally started rising as the grass and weeds thinned. My instinct as I moved into a more open area was to dash for the road, but there was no way in hell I was going to turn my back on the field.

Finally at the guardrail, I swung a leg over without taking my eyes off the grass. Back on asphalt, I calmed my breathing and kept the rifle up, scanning across the large field. Whatever had attacked and killed Gabbert was either gone or being completely masked by the undulating surface of the grass. Shaking off the creeping feeling that was resting on my shoulders, I flicked my eyes up to the business that had been my destination.

There was a reasonable chance I could acquire a vehicle there, but I wasn't about to try crossing the field again. That meant a quarter of a mile backtrack to the exit. Glancing to my left, east, I looked for any sign of habitation. Nothing for as far as I could see, which was a good distance in this terrain.

Decision made, I stepped off to the west and headed for the exit. I kept the rifle up and ready as I moved, not relaxing until I had made it out over the waters of the small lake I'd crossed earlier. Continually checking behind me, I was moving slower than I liked, but when a predator is in the area, possibly stalking and waiting to strike, speed over caution is rarely the right way to go.

I reached the exit without incident, tempted to cut across a narrow arm of the field, but rethinking that idea and sticking to the pavement. The exit cut through a corner of the field, the pavement half the width of the main freeway I had been walking on. There were narrow, gravel shoulders on each side, the tall grass pushing right up to the edge. It was even taller here, nearly to the top of my head, and it felt like I was walking in a canyon.

Only a dozen yards down the exit road, I paused and surveyed my surroundings. Standing in the middle of the road there was maybe ten feet of clearance to either side, then the thick edge of the field started. Ten feet is nothing. I could cross that in less than a second. Depending on what the predators hiding in the field were, they might even be able to leap all the way from hiding to where I was standing.

Ahead of me, the road stretched out perfectly straight for what I guessed to be a half of a mile where I could make out two large structures. From my position, they appeared to be a truck stop and a cheap motel that probably catered to long haul truckers. I could also see the sun glinting brightly off of several vehicles parked around the buildings. But was the risk of running the gauntlet of the field worth it to maybe find an operable vehicle?

Eyes scanning up and down each side of the road as I weighed my options, I tried to come up with what kind of animal I might be facing. Unfortunately, I didn't know this part of the country well enough to even make a guess. Whatever it was had to be big and powerful to have killed Gabbert as swiftly as it had, and there just weren't that many large predators in North America that I could think of that were capable. A bear? Panther? No, those didn't fit. His leg has been taken out from under him first, then his stomach torn open and throat slashed as he lay on the ground. This was something built low.

Giving up on trying to figure out what it was, I decided I didn't really have a better option than to proceed and find a vehicle. Stepping off, I moved deeper into the canyon of tall grass, eyes constantly scanning, rifle up and swiveling back and forth in sync with my eyes. The wind was still ripping through, creating a loud sighing sound and rustling all of the vegetation in the fields. It was causing so much noise, I wasn't able to depend on my hearing to alert me to an impending attack. Frequent checks of my rear were consistently negative, but I also knew that without constant attention, something could emerge from the weeds and bring me down from behind before I knew it was there.

I covered half the distance to the truck stop when movement to the front brought me to a stop. As I watched, three low, hulking figures trotted out of the grass and onto the road no more than thirty yards away. They had massive shoulders with long bodies, narrow hips and were covered in a dense coat of black, wiry fur. Their heads were cruelly shaped and held well below their front shoulders. Gleaming, razor sharp tusks, several inches long, jutted up from their lower jaws and each animal had to weigh at least three hundred pounds. Razorback hogs. Oh shit!

7 Transmission

I didn't know much about razorbacks, but what I did know scared the hell out of me. They are faster and stronger than any human, generally nasty tempered, and with their sharp tusks I now understood how Gabbert had been taken down and eviscerated so quickly. But the question was, had we stumbled into them or were they hunting us? I didn't think the hogs were predators that would come after a human. As far as I knew, they would just defend their territory, but I didn't know enough about them to understand why they had killed him and come after me.

They stood there staring at me, blocking the road. The largest one was closest to me and his head was lowered as he made a popping sound with his mouth. I could see foam forming along his lips and splattering onto the black pavement. If this was a dog, my first thought would have been rabies, but I wasn't so sure that's what was going on.

Rifle sighted in on the leader's head, I reflected that I had the same problem now that I'd had with the bear I'd encountered in Tennessee. The M4 rifle does not fire a heavy bullet. Certainly wouldn't be my choice for trying to take down a three hundred pound wild hog. Or three of the damn beasts. With my thumb, I checked to ensure the fire selector was set to burst, then decided to try something a little more devastating.

Moving slowly, so I didn't trigger an attack, I reached into a pouch on my vest and pulled out a grenade. Carefully, I pulled the pin and let the spoon release into my hand rather than spin away and clank across the pavement. As soon as the spoon came off the actuator, I started counting. At three, I tossed the baseball sized explosive at the razorbacks. I was too damn close for this, but I needed a knockout punch on the half ton of pork that looked like it was ready to charge.

I followed the grenade with my eyes, trying to time my move with its arrival on target. I had tossed it underhand with a high arc so it would come down in the middle of them. If I had timed it right, it should detonate a couple of feet above the ground. Optimal placement for a fragmentation grenade. Unless you're standing within the damage radius of the metal fragments that would be propelled outward faster than the speed of sound when it detonated.

Dropping to the ground a fraction of a second before the grenade exploded, I successfully avoided the jagged metal that whizzed overhead, but was still pummeled with the concussion of the blast. And deafened. Popping up, I snapped the rifle on target. One of the razorbacks that had been standing to their rear had taken the worst of the damage and lay on the road dead. The grenade had apparently gone off just a few feet in front of its face, destroying the animal's head.

The second hog from the rear writhed on the ground, squealing in pain. I couldn't see the extent of his wounds from where I lay, but he was down and no longer a threat. The largest one, the one who had been foaming at the mouth, had damaged hips and rear legs, but was dragging his badly bleeding body in my direction with his front legs. I pulled the trigger and pumped three rounds directly into his face. He spasmed once before collapsing to the ground, dead.

One of the lessons I'd had beaten into me in training was to not relax just because the enemy in front of you is neutralized. That lesson had been reinforced more than a few times in combat over the years. Now it was automatic and I quickly got on my knee and scanned behind me. Finding nothing, I stood and walked slowly to where the last razorback was sprawled across the asphalt, writhing and squealing. I stopped a few feet away and looked at him.

Dirk Patton

Fragments of the grenade's casing had apparently severed his spine and also torn open his body on the side facing the blast. As he thrashed about, blood and body fluids gushed out of the rent in his abdomen. He saw me standing there looking at him and began trying to drag his shattered body across the pavement to attack me. As he moved, his head turned and the sun shone brightly on his face. For the first time, I got a good look at his eyes. Blood red. Just like an infected human.

I was stunned. Rooted to the spot in horror at the thought of the infection spreading to animals. I had idly wondered earlier about the possibility of birds being infected but hadn't thought about pigs. I should have. The swine flu has been a problem for as long as humans have been keeping and raising the animals. Now a virus has jumped the other way? That's just marvelous.

Firing a single round into the animal's head, I moved to check the other two. I was dismayed when I pulled back each of their eyelids and saw the same red eyes. What the hell did that mean? Were they going to hunt us the same way infected humans did? I still didn't know if this whole encounter was because we had stumbled into their territory, or if they had been stalking us.

Transmission

I didn't think an animal like this would stalk. They weren't predators the way a wolf, a big cat or a bear are, and hunting prey wasn't part of their nature. But was it now? And were these male or female? I stepped to the back of the biggest razorback and using the toe of my boot raised one of its rear legs. It, he, had an enviously huge set of balls. A quick check of the other two revealed they were both female. I guess slow and stupid was exclusive to males of the human race.

Reminding myself to not get caught up in over analyzing things, I stood and checked the area around me. Still clear. For the moment at least. Were there more of these waiting for me? Putting those thoughts aside, I resumed walking toward the truck stop. I was on high alert, moving slowly with my rifle ready to go, but I made it to the far end of the field without encountering any more of Miss Piggy's cousins.

I was downwind from the truck stop and could smell the bodies well before I got there. I reminded myself to not only watch for infected, but also keep an eye out for razorbacks and aggressive scavengers. It was to the point that I was ready to shoot anything that moved.

The truck stop was massive. In front were twenty, slightly elevated islands with four gas pumps each. To the side, ten islands with two diesel pumps each. The building was all glass, half of it shattered out and twinkling in the afternoon sun. Peering inside, I could see what looked like a slightly smaller version of a shopping mall. Aisle upon aisle of merchandise stretched farther into the structure than I could see.

Dozens of bodies littered the floor inside, several more lying on the concrete apron between the pumps. They all appeared to have died a violent death and were in various stages of decomposition. Some were bloated with gasses, others already having ruptured and spilled their gelatinous contents onto the ground. A few hadn't begun bloating yet and I guessed they had only been dead for a day at the most. Definitely no longer than that in this heat and humidity.

Insects were everywhere. Flies. Ants. Beetles. More than I had ever seen, all busily consuming or laying eggs in the rotting flesh. Checking closer, several of the fresher bodies showed injuries consistent with what the hogs I'd just encountered could do. Legs and torsos slashed open. Throats ripped out, ribs crushed under the weight of the heavy animal as they'd stood on their victims to finish them off.

Well, that answered one question. The razorbacks hadn't been defending territory. They were actively aggressive. I could only hope

Transmission

they'd be as aggressive with infected humans as non-infected. I made another slow scan of the area to check for any approaching danger. All I saw were more bodies in the motel parking lot.

Then the missing piece struck me. No scavengers other than insects. There should be crows and vultures and other birds. Coyotes too, and possibly even domestic dogs that had gone feral. None of the bodies showed any sign of having been fed on. Where the hell were the scavengers?

Deciding I'd seen enough, I started looking around for transportation. The first thing that caught my eye was a silver Shelby Cobra Mustang with a fuel nozzle sticking out of its filler neck. I took one step in that direction before stopping myself. I wasn't here to find a car that would be fun to drive, and I didn't need one that could go fast. I needed something practical.

I turned a slow circle, looking at vehicles, but also checking my surroundings. Nothing was moving and I spotted a ride that suited my needs. A brand new Lexus GX SUV sat at the farthest fueling island. Walking over, I took a second look around, but it was the only four-wheel drive vehicle in sight. Bending as I approached, I checked under in case something was lying in wait, ready to grab my ankles and yank my feet out from under me.

Looking in the window, I made sure there wasn't a decomposing body waiting for me. Seeing nothing, I opened the driver's side door, gratified when the melodic tone of an alarm started up. The keys were in the ignition. I took another look at the rest of the interior before reaching my arm in and turning the key. It started easily, engine noise barely audible even standing outside. The gas gauge read full. Thankful the owner had finished filling up before whatever had happened to him had happened, I hopped behind the wheel and pulled the door shut.

The seats were leather, as were most of the surfaces other than the thick carpet that was immediately stained by my filthy boots. Air conditioning came on automatically. A moment later soft jazz started playing. The luxury was almost surreal after weeks of running, fighting and surviving. Shaking my head, I played with the touch screen in the middle of the dash until the music was shut off, then found the navigation and brought up a street map. A dot pulsed in the middle of the screen, marking the big vehicle's location.

Shifting into drive, I pulled out of the truck stop and followed the map until I reached

Transmission

an entrance ramp that would get me back on I-40 east. The SUV accelerated smoothly and rode like there was only glassy smooth pavement beneath the tires. I had never driven a Lexus before, always having had an aversion to Japanese cars, but I had to admit this was nice. But, give me a kidney-busting Ford four wheel drive any day. This damn thing was far too nice to ever think about taking off road. Well, not anymore I guess.

Within a couple of miles after getting back on the Interstate, I saw a vehicle approaching. I slowed and rolled down the tinted window so I could get a good look at it and the occupants. It was an old Ford Bronco, filthy with mud. There were a couple of cleaner spots and it looked like it was painted orange. The Bronco slowed as well and I looked across the median, meeting the driver's eyes. He looked back at me, as did the man sitting in the passenger seat. The driver nodded a cautious greeting. I nodded back, then we passed each other and continued in our directions of travel.

8

Rachel tried the key a second time, but there was no response from the starter no matter how hard she turned it. Turning the ignition back to the off position, she pulled the key out and reversed it, reinserted and turned. Still nothing. The dash wasn't even lighting up. She sat back in the seat and stared at the gauges, finally pounding the steering wheel in frustration.

She didn't know what to do. Getting out and opening the hood wouldn't help her unless there was something incredibly obvious that was causing the problem. Something as obvious as a part dangling in front of her face with a flashing sign hanging from it saying, "I'm the cause of all the problems, and here's how to fix me."

"Shit!" She muttered under her breath, leaned down and pulled a release lever.

The hood popped up a couple of inches and she climbed down, Dog hopping out behind her to see what was going on. Rachel lifted the hood and peered into the dirty engine compartment. Never one to care about cars, other than as transportation that was supposed to work when you needed it, she had no idea what to check.

Transmission

She knew that cars needed electricity to start and run, and decided the best idea was to check every wire she could find. The Bronco had been working just fine, so she suspected something had simply vibrated loose. If she could just find the right wire, she felt confident she could reconnect it and fix the truck.

Rachel spent twenty minutes identifying and tracing wiring. But every wire she found appeared to be solidly connected or disappeared into a piece of the engine that she had no idea what function it performed. She gave it another ten minutes, then decided to try the ignition again. Not bothering to climb back behind the wheel, she reached in and turned the key. The vehicle was still completely dead.

Slamming the door, she turned and surveyed her surroundings. There was some heavy construction equipment that had apparently been used to dig the trench that had saved her from the tornado, and the same vehicles she had checked earlier when she found the Bronco were still sitting where they had been. The only possibility was the Mercedes. It hadn't had keys in the ignition when she'd checked, but maybe they were somewhere inside the vehicle.

Walking over, she opened the door and began searching. Looked under the seats, in the center console, the glove compartment, pockets molded into the doors. She didn't find them. Frustration growing, she slammed the door and kicked it, leaving a large dent.

Looking around again, she thought about trying to get one of the pieces of construction equipment started and use it to drag the truck out of the ditch. Once she got it back to ground level, it wouldn't be difficult to get Jackson's body out of the cab and she knew the keys were still in the ignition. Then she remembered that the truck was sitting in several feet of water, and even if she could manage to get it back up onto the road, it was most likely damaged beyond repair.

Frustration was starting to become despair when Dog bumped her with his muzzle and growled. Adrenaline surged and she looked in the direction his nose was pointed, but didn't see anything. Regardless, she wasn't about to discount his warning. If he was seeing or smelling something he didn't like, she was instantly ready to trust him.

Not knowing what to do, but certain that standing out in the open was a bad idea, Rachel hoisted her pack onto her shoulder and ran for the flooded field where she'd hidden from the car that had passed earlier. Dog ran next to her and in less than a minute they were back on the

Transmission

muddy slope of the field. Rachel lay on her stomach, only the top of her head visible above the edge as she watched the road.

She watched for a long time, but nothing appeared. A check of Dog kept her on edge as he was still on high alert, eyes glued to the east. Finally, Rachel saw several figures materialize on the horizon. At first, they were too far away, but after a few minutes of closely watching, she could tell they were approaching.

They didn't seem to be in any hurry as they calmly walked down the middle of the westbound lanes of the Interstate. Another couple of minutes and she could tell it was four men. A minute after that and she could make out the barrels of their rifles pointing skyward from where they were slung across the men's shoulders.

Rachel would have liked to trust them. To run out and meet them and ask for their help. But there wasn't anything she could think of that would make her trust a man that was a stranger. Not after all that she had seen and what had happened to her. When they were still two hundred yards away from the abandoned Bronco, Dog growled again.

Turning to look in the new direction, Rachel caught her breath when she saw two large animals moving across the muddy field directly to the east of her. She didn't know what they were, but they were big and moving fast. Their destination was the small group of men, and they were approaching at an angle, behind them. None of the men had seen them yet.

The animals had heavy front shoulders and big heads. Even from a distance, Rachel could see the gleam of white tusks or fangs protruding from their mouths. She couldn't be certain, but each of them looked to easily be twice the size of Dog, maybe even larger. Fear coursed through her as she watched the beasts swiftly close on the unsuspecting men. They were terrifyingly fast, covering ground at a ferocious pace. Frozen in place, Rachel could only watch the attack unfold.

One of the men walking at the back of the group finally heard something and looked over his shoulder. For a second he froze, gawking, then shouted and started to turn and pull the rifle off his shoulder. He never completed the turn, the lead beast charging in with head lowered. Reaching the man, it slammed into his legs and, using its powerful neck, slashed upward into his body.

The man screamed as he was torn open from groin to chest, then the razor-sharp tusks hooked on bone and he was lifted into the air and tossed over the animal's back. The second beast, running a few steps behind the leader, stomped on him with heavy hooves while slicing open his throat.

When the first man had shouted, the other three reacted slowly, looking to see what the commotion was before bothering to unsling their rifles. The first animal to arrive still had momentum on his side and slammed into another of the group, tearing into his body. Blood jetted from severed arteries and the animal squealed as it attacked. Rachel was stunned and terrified to her core by the speed with which two grown men had just been torn open and killed.

By now, the two surviving men had their rifles up and started shooting. The reports from the weapons were deep and loud, and Rachel could tell they were firing a much heavier bullet than she had in her rifle. Even with the heavier caliber hunting rifles, neither of the animals went down easily. From her vantage point, Rachel didn't think they went down until they were shot in the head.

Both animals on the ground, the men slowly advanced on them, rifles aimed and ready to fire if either one twitched. After a quick check, one of them slung his rifle and pulled a large revolver. He fired a shot into each of the brutish heads from only a couple of feet away. Rachel wanted to cheer his actions. She did not want to see either of these things get up again.

The two survivors checked on their friends, who were both apparently already dead. The men just stood and stared at the bodies. Rachel could tell they were talking to each other, but they were too far away for her to hear anything that was said. After several minutes, they pulled packs off the bodies and began rummaging through them, taking several items which were then stowed with their gear.

Ready to proceed, they took the time to raise their scoped rifles and scan their surroundings. Rachel ducked below the lip of the berm she was lying on, making sure Dog was also hidden from their line of sight. She gave them plenty of time to check the area before carefully sticking her head back up.

They had finished their survey and were just walking up to the Bronco. Where before they had been walking casually, rifles slung, they now moved with weapons in their hands. Both were constantly checking their surroundings, frequently looking behind to make sure there were no more surprise attacks.

"Let's check that one."

Transmission

She clearly heard one of them as he gestured at the Mercedes. They walked over and while one stood guard, the other opened the door. After checking the ignition he searched the vehicle for the keys, but didn't have any more success than Rachel. Except for the Bronco, all the other vehicles in the area were obviously disabled. Rachel had left the hood up, but that didn't deter them from checking.

Again, one stood guard as the other opened the door and leaned inside the vehicle. Rachel could see him reach in and, by the way his arm moved, knew he had turned the ignition. He didn't have any better luck. Stepping around the open door, he moved to the front and peered under the hood.

"What the fuck was that, Mike?" The man on watch asked. The near panic in his voice was clear to Rachel.

"Don't know, man. Never heard of a razorback attacking like that for no reason."

Mike reached deep into the engine compartment and grunted as he applied force to something. A minute later he straightened up and wiped his hands on grubby jeans.

Rachel had lived in the southeastern United States all her life and, while she'd never seen one before, she knew what a razorback was.

Her dad had hunted them when she was a little girl and she remembered stories about how dangerous they were when cornered. How they could tear open the dogs used to hunt them with just a single slash of their tusks. She shuddered and looked around to make sure there weren't any racing up on her, even though she knew Dog would warn her long before she could detect them.

The sound of a starter followed by the rumble of a big engine snapped Rachel's head back to the front. Son of a bitch! It had taken him all of a minute to find the problem and fix it, and her transportation was about to drive away without her. Did she approach them and ask for a ride? Was that less of a risk than being stranded out here with murderous razorbacks running around? She couldn't decide.

They looked OK. Looked like nothing more than survivors that were trying to make it to the safety of the west. Everyone couldn't be looking to hurt their fellow survivors. Could they? Rachel lay watching and her indecision became her choice as they got into the Bronco and drove off to the west without even knowing she was there. Dog looked back to the east and growled deep in his chest.

Transmission

9

Captain Irina Vostov stood in the shade of the hangar door and watched as a large crate was loaded into the belly of a giant Antonov AN-124 cargo plane. The three American SADMs were well packed inside, the wooden slats that made up the sides marked with severe warnings in Cyrillic against opening or tampering with the contents. The lid was held in place with a dozen large screws and tagged with a bright red GRU seal. If the warnings on the sides didn't discourage attempts at petty theft, the GRU tag certainly would. Perhaps the SVR, descendent of the KGB, might not fear repercussions, but Irina wasn't worried. GRU cargo was nearly sacrosanct in Russia.

Along with her crate were dozens of other shipping containers that held looted American technology, as well as a couple secured with Kremlin seals. She had no doubt these contained luxury goods that had been taken for President Barinov and his cronies. All of the crates and shipping containers loaded and secured, one of the American's Stealth Hawk helicopters was slowly wheeled up the ramp by a large tractor. Its rotor blades had been put into shipping position, all of them turned in the same direction to extend along the length of the aircraft where they were securely strapped to the tail.

She didn't understand the reason for taking the helicopter back to Russia to be disassembled, studied and duplicated. There were no adversaries left on the face of the Earth that could ever hope to stand against the Russian military. China and all of Asia was dead. India was dead. Western Europe still had some pockets of life, but they were few and far between.

Despite the best efforts of the Mexicans, with help from the Central and South Americans, the virus had jumped the quarantine zone and spread like wildfire, stopping only when it reached the southern tip of Argentina. Other than Russia, where the vaccine had been widely distributed to the population, only a few select islands remained untouched. The largest of these was the island continent of Australia.

Early on, almost as soon as the attacks on the United States had happened, Australia had sealed its borders. All inbound air and ship traffic had been turned away. And so far, it was working. The land down under had not had a single case of infection. What at first had been sharp criticism of the government for turning away refugees, in one case sinking a boat loaded with people that refused to reverse course, was now praise. But Irina knew that without the vaccine, Australia was on borrowed time. The virus was loose in the world and there was no stopping it.

She hoped the American soldier to whom she'd given the vaccine had made it safely to whatever his destination was, and that the Americans were even now feverishly producing and distributing the inoculations. Time was running out for them. She'd just seen a report that the Air Force personnel being held in the local jail were starting to turn. Only eight of them so far, but she knew this was just the beginning. The start of an unstoppable avalanche.

The helicopter made it fully inside the cavernous interior of the Antonov and the crew, under the sharp-tongued instructions of the loadmaster, set about securing it for the six thousand mile journey to Kubinka Air Base, just outside of Moscow. A flight of twelve Mig fighter jets sat at the end of the closest runway, waiting for the giant plane to be ready to go. They would escort it all the way to Moscow, ensuring that neither the remnants of the American military, nor any of its NATO allies, were able to interfere.

When the plane landed at Kubinka, at 0300 local Moscow time, a GRU Colonel would be there to meet it and take possession of the crate containing the nukes. Colonel Alexander Grishin was a childhood friend of her uncle and was risking everything to assassinate President Barinov and help seize control of Russia. He had already disabled the air base's radiation detectors with the help of one of Russia's most notorious hacker groups. Once the bombs were clear of the base, they would re-enable the detectors and were prepared to shut down the net that constantly monitored all approaches to, and the interior of, the Kremlin.

She had spoken with Colonel Grishin via encrypted satellite phone less than an hour before, and the man had sounded as calm as if he were talking to her about the weather. Her nerves were getting to her and she was sweating, even though it wasn't that warm of a day in the high, New Mexico desert. Watching the flight crew complete preparations for take off, she thought about her Uncle's plan.

One of the nukes would be armed and placed in the trunk of an official military sedan that would deliver him to a meeting with the president. This meeting would be attended by all the highest ranking military officers, as well as all members of the Duma, the equivalent of the American's Congress. Due to his rank and status, the vehicle would not be searched, and with the radiation detectors offline, the bomb would be driven right into the heart of the Kremlin. Early

Transmission

in the meeting, he would feign falling ill and excuse himself, returning to the car where his driver would have disabled the vehicle in a manner that would appear to be a normal breakdown of the notoriously unreliable Zil automobiles.

Another car would be called for, his driver telling security that a maintenance crew would be along presently to retrieve it. Her uncle and his driver would depart in the second vehicle and an hour later a nuclear detonation equivalent to one thousand tons of TNT would destroy the Kremlin, President Barinov and the entire military and political leadership of the country. So many things could go wrong with the plan, including Barinov refusing to excuse her uncle. If that happened, his driver, a trusted aide, would shut down the nuke's timer and they would have to look for another opportunity.

The flight crew was done and the cargo doors now closed. The pilot and co-pilot were performing a walk around of the aircraft prior to takeoff. They were dwarfed by everything about the plane, even the tires on the landing gear taller than they were. Despite their imminent departure with the crate safely aboard, Irina didn't budge from where she stood. The sharp burning pain from the bullet wound in her leg gnawed at her, but she stoically endured it. She was a Russian and could proudly handle pain.

Once the plane was in the air and she could no longer see it, she would alert Colonel Grishin that it was on the way. Only then would she leave the hangar and get some much needed rest.

10

Captain Roach worked throughout the day to get the steady stream of evacuees processed and entered into a simple Excel spreadsheet that was doing duty as the database of civilians that had made it to Tinker Air Force Base. He didn't like the work, but was excited at the opportunity to identify women for his and Synthia's games. Any girl or woman that caught his attention was marked on the list in a subtle manner.

When their names were typed into the spreadsheet, he would insert a period rather than a comma between their last and first names. Roach was pleased with himself for having come up with this idea on the fly. If anyone noticed, they would pass it off as a typo. He was confident it was nothing that could ever be attributed back to him as there were also two Sergeants entering data into the same spreadsheet.

So far, he had picked out four women. The first on his list was the woman he'd met when he first arrived at the processing station, Katie Chase. There was something about her that intrigued him, yet frightened him at the same time. He preferred women who were naïve. Sometimes their naivety was due to a lack of life experience. Others simply weren't smart enough to recognize danger when it looked them in the face and smiled.

Katie, however, was anything but naïve. He recognized the intelligence, and more. There was iron behind her beautiful smile and he had no doubt she knew how to use the large pistol she carried on her hip. He would have to be careful with her. He wasn't going to be able to trick or lure her the way he did other women. She would see through him, he was certain. But that just made him want her more.

She had been placed in an empty barrack not far from his new house, the other women and all the children who had arrived with her sharing the space. Seated at a folding table in the hangar that had been pressed into duty for processing civilians, he looked up from the laptop and through the open door at the large building to which Katie had been assigned. It was on the far side of a series of runways, but clearly visible. He thought he could see figures running around, chasing each other, outside the building. The kids playing.

Letting his mind drift, he fantasized about taking her home with him. Walking in the front door and surprising Synthia with her. Hitting her in the back of the head to subdue her before she could recognize the danger. Carrying her to the bedroom where he and Synthia would strip her naked, tie her to the bed, gag her and wait for her to regain consciousness.

When she woke, she would be confused for a moment, then terrified. Roach knew from experience that as soon as he saw the fear in her eyes, he would immediately achieve a rock hard erection that only the dispensation of pain could relieve. He pictured in his mind what he would do to Katie. What Synthia would do as he violently penetrated the bound woman. He could already hear her whimpers and moans as they drew their pleasure from her body.

Then the climax. The knife thrust to her heart as he pushed himself even deeper into her. Feeling her body spasm as the life force left it, at the same time reaching his orgasm. The sensation of her going still as his heart pounded out the last of his pleasure. The calming of his entire being as the desire, need, to take the woman's life as he deposited his seed in her was fulfilled.

"Sir?" Roach was startled, snapping out of his daydream and looking up at the Sergeant that was speaking to him.

How long had the woman been standing there? He realized he had an erection and was glad he was seated, the table concealing his tumescence.

"Yes. What is it?" He asked, his voice gruff with emotion. The Sergeant gave him an odd look.

"There's another group just clearing the main gate. They'll be here in five minutes. Just thought you'd want a heads-up."

"Thank you."

Roach nodded and dismissed her, watching her walk away. Not his type, he thought, looking back at the laptop.

Katie Chase. Chase. Why was that name familiar? Roach thought about it for a moment, but couldn't place why it rang a bell. Scrolling down the list to look at the other names he'd marked, he suddenly stopped and scrolled back up. Chase. That was that fucking Army Major's name! No, not possible. Or was it?

Leaning forward, he scanned across the spreadsheet, reading the details the woman had provided during processing. She was from a suburb of Phoenix, Arizona. In the column for next of kin, he read the name. John Chase. Was that the Major's first name? He thought hard, but couldn't remember ever having heard it. Scrolling far to the right, he checked the column

Transmission

that showed whether or not the person being processed had family in the military. It had an upper case N, for no.

Roach thought about what he knew about the man. He hadn't been in uniform the night he'd arrived at Arnold Air Force Base with the bitch and the dog. Had he been recalled by that damn Army Colonel that had interfered? That would explain why this woman had answered no to the question about family in uniform. Things had changed that she didn't know about.

Minimizing the spreadsheet, Roach logged in to one of the few military databases that were still operational. He didn't know the details about where it was or how it was still accessible. All he cared about was that he could still get in. Clicking in the search box, he typed in the name and hit enter. The cursor spun for a few seconds before the screen refreshed with the search results.

Staring at him was a younger version of the Major. The face was a little leaner and he had hair, though it was cut close to his scalp, but it was the same hard eyes. The same little sneer of the upper lip that silently communicated "I can kick your ass, and I know it". The nose was straighter, apparently having been broken at least once between the time of the photo and when Roach met the man, but it was without a doubt the same prick.

The record showed the Major had declined to re-enlist about ten years ago, leaving the Army as a Master Sergeant. Other than basic details such as date of original enlistment, his entire file was classified. But Roach knew there was a part that wouldn't be. Clicking a couple of links, he quickly found what he was looking for.

Four years ago, the Major had requested a copy of his DD-214, the paperwork showing a person's dates of service, type of discharge from the military and some other minor information. Roach didn't care about the dates, or whether or not he had received an honorable discharge. He wanted to know where the forms were mailed, and there it was. A street address in the same suburb the woman had listed as her home.

Roach felt energized. He had that fucker's wife! And the best part was, the Major, if he was still alive, would never know she was here unless Roach decided to tell him. With a smile, he scrolled back to the left, selected the entire row that contained Katie's information and pressed delete. She would be his little secret.

11

Dog growled a second time, raising his head higher and twitching his nose as he sampled the smells the strong wind was bringing. Rachel looked at him, then looked east again, but still saw nothing other than an empty horizon. Regretting her failure to approach the two men and be safely in a vehicle, miles away by now, she got to her knees to gain some elevation. Still nothing and Dog continued to growl.

Growing more concerned by the moment, Rachel finally stood to her full height and moved to the higher ground near the Interstate. Dog stayed next to her, between her and whatever had him worried, pushing against her with his body. He wanted her to start moving west.

Standing still, Rachel looked again. When she still failed to see any danger, she raised the rifle and peered through the scope, slowly scanning across the horizon. Her breath caught in her throat when she saw four razorbacks moving across the field no more than three hundred yards away. Their black coats blended well with the dark mud and when she looked without benefit of the scope's low power magnification, she couldn't spot them even though she knew where they were.

They hadn't seen or smelled her or Dog yet. The wind was from their direction and was gusting, so she wasn't concerned about scent. But did they have good eyesight? This she didn't know. Usually, the animals with the best vision were at the top of the food chain, and based on her limited knowledge of the wild hogs she didn't think they had evolved as top-level predators. As far as she knew, they were herbivores, but she wasn't about to bet her life on that.

She had witnessed a pair of them attack a group of men and kill two of them. But something about the attack hadn't felt right. There was no stalking of their prey. They had just charged straight in and attacked with no apparent concern other than killing. With a start, Rachel realized that she had just described an infected human!

Her mind went back to medical school classes. Learning about contagions and how they are transmitted from person to person. They hadn't delved into inter-species viral transmissions, that was training that would come after graduation depending upon specialization, but it had been discussed. The media had enjoyed frightening the public for years with speculative reports of bird and swine flu pandemics. Those reports contained enough fact to be scary, but also a lot of what ifs and occasionally outright bullshit.

Transmission

However, it was quite common for a virus to mutate and jump from one species to another. Birds, swine, primates and many other mammals could pass along an infection to humans. And it worked the other way, too. Rachel knew that and even understood some of the mechanics around how it happened. That knowledge didn't make her feel any better. In fact, it scared the hell out of her. Like infected humans running around wasn't bad enough?

Looking around, her eyes fell on the bodies lying in the middle of the westbound traffic lanes. Moving quickly, she walked over to the closest razorback and knelt next to its head. With a tentative touch, she lifted one of its eyelids and gasped when she saw the blood red eye. She jerked her hand back like she had received an electric shock and stood up to check on the hogs in the far field.

They were moving in her direction at a fast trot, but still didn't appear to be aware of her presence. That didn't matter. Their trot was faster than she could run and she remembered the speed they'd displayed when attacking the men. She never would have guessed they could move that fast, but they did have fairly long legs for their body size and were probably capable of running at least as fast as a dog.

Rachel turned, checking the area for shelter from the approaching beasts. She knew she couldn't outdistance them and had to find someplace to hide before they got close enough to see her. There were still the abandoned vehicles, but the only one that was still intact was the Mercedes. She could get in, but it was low to the ground and she didn't know if the razorbacks would try to break in if they detected her. They were certainly big and strong enough to smash out the car's windows.

Dismissing the sedan, she looked at the construction equipment. There was a big orange grader, but its cab was open to the elements. Even though the seat was ten feet off the ground, Rachel didn't like her odds of being safe in it. Behind the grader was an even larger backhoe. Its cab was also ten feet off the ground, but was enclosed. Calling Dog, she ran to the machine and, after a moment, found the obvious way to climb up and into the operator's seat.

Mercifully, the door was either unlocked or lacking a lock, and she quickly clambered aboard and took a seat. Dog stood on the ground, looking up at her and whining. He wanted to follow, but the ascent that was easy for a human was impossible for a canine. Rachel turned and checked on the razorbacks' progress. They were still trotting along, oblivious, and were now less than two hundred yards away.

Transmission

Frozen by not knowing what to do, she stared down at Dog. His whines were growing louder as the beasts continued to close. Looking over her shoulder, Rachel saw the hogs suddenly accelerate to a full run. They had been seen. Damn it!

Reacting, not thinking, she quickly slithered down the side of the backhoe, jumping the final two feet to the ground. Bending, she wrapped her arms around Dog's torso and lifted as he scrabbled with his front paws, trying to climb up the steel side of the machine. She gave up after only a couple of seconds. Maybe John could have lifted Dog and carried him up to the cab, but there was no way she could.

A quick glance over her shoulder and she knew she had less than ten seconds. Abandoning the backhoe, she dashed for the Mercedes, yelling for Dog. Arriving at the driver's door, Rachel imagined she could hear the heavy breathing of the razorbacks and risked a backward glance. They were passing the grader and almost on her. Dog was standing between her and the swiftly approaching beasts, legs spread and head down with teeth showing, but she knew he was way out of his weight class in that fight.

Yanking the front door open she screamed for Dog, who turned and leapt into the car. Rachel was right behind him, nearly slamming the door on her leg in her haste to reach the safety of the interior. Less than a second after she closed the door, the lead razorback slammed into it, rocking the entire vehicle. Rachel screamed and Dog hopped into the back seat and started barking at the window, frothy saliva flying onto the glass.

The remaining three razorbacks were close behind, the car continuing to shudder as they slammed into its sides. They began slashing, the wickedly sharp tusks making a horrible screeching sound on the sheet metal. When that didn't work, they started circling the car, occasionally slamming a shoulder or head into one of the doors.

Rachel got Dog back into the front seat, finally calming him to a degree with an arm circled around his neck. He was taut as a bowstring and primed for a fight, but she wasn't about to let him out of the car. As fast and strong as he was, the razorbacks would gut him in an instant and stomp him to death when he went down.

As she sat in the front seat, watching them continue to circle, Rachel was reminded of old movies about sailors lost at sea with sharks circling before attacking. The build of the animals kept their heads lower than their shoulders and she was relieved to see that they weren't trying to break the glass. The lead razorback was massive, his shoulders a good six inches taller than the bottom of the side window. He must have weighed close to four hundred pounds and was regularly slamming into the car, looking for a point of weakness to exploit.

Rachel leaned her head back against the leather headrest and took a deep breath. They seemed safe for the moment, but what the hell were they going to do? How long would the razorbacks keep trying to break in? And even if they left, what was she going to do? They would still be around and she didn't think either her or Dog would survive on foot for very long.

She started going over ideas in her mind, thinking about options. Equipment available to her. Anything that would help them escape, or kill the razorbacks. There were no vehicles within sight that were still functioning. It was a safe assumption there were none to the east. Otherwise, the men who had fixed and taken the Bronco would already have been driving. Had the tornados caused that much devastation?

She had already searched the Mercedes for its keys, as had the men, but out of desperation, she started another search. Slow and methodical. Even if she had checked a spot earlier, she looked again. Looked in spots that she knew were too small to hold even a single key, but not willing to risk overlooking something. After fifteen minutes, she hadn't found them and the hogs were still there, still slamming into the doors nearly every circuit.

Transmission

12

Marine Corps Gunnery Sergeant Michael Tate cursed what he suspected was the same fly for probably the two-hundredth time. The pest was about to start trying to crawl into his ear again, but he ignored it and stayed perfectly still. His cheek was resting against the stock of his M40A5 sniper rifle, right eye peering through the high power scope. He was dressed in a ghillie suit with multiple branches of sagebrush stuck through the weave to further break up the outline of his body. All but invisible, he lay on a sandy ridgeline half a mile away from Kirtland Air Force Base in New Mexico.

Tate had been in position for close to twenty-four hours, taking the occasional catnap, but had been awake far more than he'd slept. Next to him, equally well concealed, was Sergeant Michael Blaine. Michael T was white, and Michael B was black, but they had become as inseparable as twin brothers the day they met at the Marine's Scout Sniper Basic Course at Camp Pendleton, California.

Michael T had impressed the instructors from day one, many of them privately commenting that he could be the next Carlos Hathcock, arguably the best and most well-known American sniper in history. Certainly a legend within the Corps and any comparison to him was high praise. So when Michael T had spoken up after Michael B washed out of the shooting part of training, he was given what he asked for. Michael B became his spotter, joined to his hip for as long as the two were in the Corps.

The pair had been at Marine Corps Air Station Yuma, on the Arizona-California border when the attacks occurred. They had stayed there for the past month, helping defend against the infected that started stumbling out of Southern California. Until the Russians invaded.

Admiral Packard had been a busy man the past couple of days. There were still several intact military bases within the continental United States, and many more special operations units still able to fight. As soon as it was known which American bases the Russians chose to occupy, he had ordered Marine Scout Sniper teams into each area. Not to start picking off Russian officers, but to observe and report on what the invaders were doing.

Hedging his bet, he had also ordered a small team of Force Recon Marines into each location. These teams were equipped with a specialized Humvee, called an Avenger, that had pods of SAMs –Surface to Air Missiles – mounted on the back. The teams were under orders to

Transmission

ignore any Russian helicopter or attack aircraft, but to engage any transport aircraft that were believed to be taking American technology to Russia.

Michael T had been watching the previous night as an American MRAP had pulled up to the same hangar. What looked like a civilian female, two Russian Spetsnaz, a female US Air Force officer and a big guy that had to be SF had climbed out. They'd wheeled a Sci-Fi looking helicopter out of the hangar and, while the Air Force officer had fueled it, three packages, a full body bag and an injured man had been loaded into the aircraft.

When they were ready to go, the civilian woman had kissed the SF guy on each cheek, then he and the Air Force officer had climbed aboard. Moments later the helo had flown directly over his head at no more than fifty feet and he'd been amazed at how quiet it was. That was when he realized it was a Stealth Hawk.

"Badger two-five, how copy?" Michael T mumbled into his radio.

"Copy five by five." The reply was almost instant. Badger two-five was the small Force Recon team set up in a valley a few miles north and east of Michael T's location. In line with the main runway at Kirtland.

Dirk Patton

"Red force guppy in five mikes. Be advised, he will have twelve, one – two, guard dogs."

A large Russian cargo plane would be taking off in five minutes, and there would be twelve fighter escorts.

"Copy. Guppy in five. One – two dogs. Badger two-five ready."

Michael T watched as crate after crate had been loaded on a giant Antonov cargo plane, followed by another of the Sci-Fi looking helicopters he now was sure were Stealth Hawks. He had also kept an eye on the attractive blonde woman, barefoot and wearing a skirt, who had kissed the SF guy goodbye. She had watched the loading of the aircraft with a keen interest, not even taking her eyes off of it while speaking on a large, satellite phone.

The jet was taxiing to the main runway where six of the Mig fighters sat waiting. Once it was in place, the remaining six Migs would form up at a safe distance behind, all thirteen aircraft taking off within a minute of each other. Michael T watched them jockey around as all the pilots got into position.

The Antonov's pilot's face was large in his scope and he wished he could put a round through the man's head. The plane wouldn't go anywhere, and while they might look, the Russians wouldn't find him or his brother. But, his orders were clear. Observe and report, only. He could not engage any target for any reason, other than self-defense.

A moment later, the lead Migs throttled up and raced down the runway, quickly leaping into the blue sky. The Antonov had started rolling at the same time, but the much larger aircraft was heavily loaded and needed nearly the full length of the runway to get off the ground. As soon as its tires left the tarmac, Michael T notified the Force Recon team. The remaining Migs were in the air in moments, racing to gain altitude.

The Russian Air Force is neither incompetent nor stupid, but they are human and susceptible to human arrogance. Their mistake that day was thinking that the only possible threat to the lumbering jet was from other aircraft. They were well protected against that threat with a two hundred mile radius CAP around the base as well as the twelve escort fighters, whose only purpose in life was to protect the Antonov. What they didn't take into account was the possibility of a surface to air attack.

No routine ground patrols were occurring to prevent an enemy from setting up on the airfield. No low-level helicopter patrols, creating a safe buffer zone around the base. Nothing. This was good for the Marines. It had made their jobs much easier and increased the likelihood that they might successfully evade what was sure to be a swift Russian response once they shot the plane down.

"System is on automatic. Badger two-five bugging out." Michael T heard over his radio earpiece. Acknowledging the transmission, he wished them luck.

The Marines had set the Avenger's system to automatically track and shoot any aircraft that came within range of its sensors. Then they had gotten the hell out of the area. Hopefully, they would be able to put enough distance between them and the Avenger that the Russians couldn't find them. They would probably have five minutes at the most from the time the first missile left the pod mounted on the rear of the Hummer.

The Antonov pilot had never flown in a combat zone before coming to America. If he had, he likely would have gained altitude as quickly as possible. He also would have requested and been granted permission by the air traffic controllers to spiral up as he climbed, keeping his aircraft in vertical alignment with the air base. But he did none of this. Instead, he flew

Transmission

straight ahead, slowly gaining altitude. Civilian passengers would have appreciated the smooth and steady take off, but they wouldn't have liked the results.

One minute after the Antonov's landing gear left the tarmac, the giant plane had only climbed two thousand feet. Ten seconds later, it entered the Avenger's sensor range, the Boeing-made system locking on in a fraction of a second, analyzing the signature, and firing a missile. The Marines had programmed some additional instructions into the computer that controlled the weapon, and quickly the remaining seven SAMs rippled out of their pods and sped skyward. Each of them was locked onto one of the Migs, the fighters still below the missiles' operational ceiling of fifteen thousand feet as they loitered, waiting for the much slower cargo jet.

Five seconds later the first missile struck the base of the Antonov's right wing, the warhead detonating. The wing sheared off and thousands of pounds of jet fuel ignited, the plane vanishing in a thunderous explosion that blew out windows all across Albuquerque. Two of the Migs that had been targeted successfully evaded the SAMs, but five more weren't so lucky and met the same fate as their larger brethren.

Irina Vostov stood on the tarmac, staring northeast in horror at the massive fireball. The smoke trails from the missiles still visible in the clear air, she cursed the Americans. Had the Major betrayed her? Taken the vaccine and given her the nukes only to destroy them before they could be used? Was he mad? Didn't he understand? Anger overcoming her fatigue, she pulled out her satellite phone and punched in her uncle's phone number.

Transmission

13

I slowed when I saw the sign for the West Memphis Airport. Would Rachel and Jackson have gone back there, even though they knew it had already been evacuated? I didn't think so, but I couldn't ignore the possibility and fail to check. Taking the indicated exit, I rolled down the ramp, slowing to steer around a small, foreign sedan lying on its side in the middle of the road. There were no other vehicles around and I wondered if the tornados I had been told about had turned it over, or maybe even dropped it there.

The two-lane road at the bottom of the exit was obscured with muddy water that had washed onto it through a break in an adjacent dike. The heavy Lexus navigated the axle deep water without any drama, wrapping me in the luxury of its air conditioning and ventilated seats. This was the most comfortable I'd been in quite some time, but I'd trade it at the drop of a hat if I got to the airport and found Rachel waiting impatiently for me.

I drove past the airport before I realized I had arrived. The tall control tower was the landmark I had been looking for, and not seeing it, I hadn't recognized the area. Slamming on the brakes, I reversed and took the access road that cut across a muddy field. I could see the single runway, but there was nothing else remaining. No control tower. No hangars. Nothing other than some twisted steel and small piles of debris where the structures had been.

Coming to a stop, I sat and stared in awe at the total devastation. A tornado, or perhaps more than one, had literally wiped the airport off the map. Anything that was more than a couple of feet tall had been ripped away. Letting off the brake, I allowed the SUV to idle forward, steering onto the tarmac. I was looking at the damage, not where I was driving, and was surprised when first the right front, then right rear tire hit a big pothole. Stopping, I looked in the mirror. There was a chunk missing out of the asphalt! How powerful had these damn storms been?

There was little point in wasting any more time at what had been the airport. I could see for a very long distance in every direction and, other than debris, muddy fields and pools of dirty water, nothing was visible. Hooking a U-Turn, I left on the same road I had come in on, turning back to resume my eastward trek on I-40.

The total destruction of the airport disheartened me. If they had been caught by one of the tornados, they were dead. There was no getting around that. My only hope was they had somehow been able to either avoid the storms or find shelter. Maybe in West Memphis? If West Memphis was even still on the map. Time to find out.

Reaching the entrance ramp to I-40 east, I slowly accelerated onto the freeway, dodging big potholes where pieces of the asphalt were missing. Shaking my head, I avoided another wreck by driving into the median. The SUV's four-wheel drive came in handy. I was sure a two-wheel drive vehicle would have dug into the soft earth and gotten stuck.

I had only driven a few more miles when I noticed a cluster of vehicles scattered across the westbound side of the freeway. Approaching slowly, I spotted the bodies of two men and two razorbacks sprawled on the pavement. Then I passed a large Chevy truck, on its side and hit the brakes when I saw movement. Four razorbacks were circling a Mercedes. The largest one was at least three hundred pounds, probably more like four hundred, and the other three were each well over two hundred. They noticed me and stopped circling, the whole group moving to stand between the car and me.

I stared back at them for a few moments, then decided to continue on before they charged. It was doubtful they could damage the Lexus severely enough to disable it, but there was no reason to take the chance. Starting to accelerate,

I had only gone a few yards when I heard a car horn. What the hell?

Stopping, I looked closely at the Mercedes. I couldn't see through the glass because the windows were fogged over. That meant someone was inside! And it might be the *someones* I was searching for. Even if it wasn't, I didn't particularly like the idea of leaving someone to die, trapped by the small herd of razorbacks. Now, how to rescue them?

The sound of the horn had agitated the hogs and they started attacking the car, slamming into its sides with their heavy shoulders. The large one rammed a tusk through the fender and with a powerful jerk of his head tore open a foot long rent in the sheet steel. Fuck me, but these things were strong. And all I had was a rifle with relatively small caliber bullets. Yes, I still had a few grenades, but I couldn't use them anywhere near the vehicle without endangering the occupants.

I pushed the button to lower my window and stuck the rifle through the opening. The razorbacks were only fifty yards away from where I had come to a stop, an easy shot, but I needed to be spot on with my shooting if I wanted to put these things down. Hunching forward, I pulled the rifle stock to my shoulder and looked through the scope.

Transmission

Wishing for a heavier caliber, I aimed for a spot just behind the shoulder of one of the smaller hogs that had come to a stop. Pulling the trigger in burst mode, I sent three rounds into the beast. I was guessing at razorback anatomy, hoping to blow out his heart and lungs with the shot, but I'd never hunted wild hogs and had no idea if this was the best target location for a quick kill.

When the bullets struck, the animal squealed, snapping his head to the side to see what had just attacked him. Not immediately seeing anything he started to snap at one of the other hogs, but his legs wobbled. The wobble almost immediately became a buckle and a second later he fell to the ground and stopped moving. I smiled to myself and targeted the razorback that came over to sniff his body.

Another pull of the trigger, another dead hog. Two down, two to go. But the leader's attention had switched to me and he stood facing my direction. The other razorback was behind him, mostly shielded by his body and the front of the Mercedes. I debated trying a head shot, but he was just so damn big I didn't have a lot of confidence the 5.56 mm bullets would penetrate what had to be a skull as thick as armor plating. He made my decision for me when he charged.

Dirk Patton

Shit! I yanked the rifle back inside the SUV and stomped on the gas. The Lexus surged forward and the razorback changed directions, angling for the driver's side door. Despite his frightening speed, I pulled safely away. Watching in the mirror, I was dismayed to see him stop pursuing and return to the Mercedes. Slowing, I turned the wheel to point the nose of the vehicle to the west and came to a stop. The large hog was stationary on the far side of the sedan, the smaller one still circling. Time to thin the herd a little more.

Switching the rifle to semi, or single shot mode, I targeted the smaller razorback and started putting rounds into him. I was aiming for the same spot that had successfully brought the first two down. My first shot broke his shoulder, the animal stumbling to a stop. I followed up with two more quick shots to the same area and a moment later he slumped the rest of the way to the pavement. Three down, but King Kong was still sheltering behind the car.

I waited patiently for a few minutes, but he wasn't coming into view. Was he smart enough to understand the danger of showing himself, or was he running on instinct? I didn't know, and at the moment didn't care. The day was wearing on and ominous clouds were building to the north and west. I had no idea if

Transmission

that meant more tornados, but I wanted this over with so I could get back to my search.

Removing my foot from the brake, the Lexus idled forward. I steered to the side, trying to gain a vantage point from which I could fire on the beast, but as the big SUV moved, so did he. I stepped on the brake and cursed. He had kept the car between us, moving when I moved. OK, then. What now?

I was only coming up with one idea, and I didn't particularly like it. Get out of the SUV and fight the damn thing on foot. He was faster and stronger, but I was willing to bet I was more agile. I was only a little over half his body weight and should be able to maneuver better than he could. I hoped. Turning the SUV so the passenger side was facing the razorback, I took a deep breath and opened my door.

The passenger window afforded me a clear view of his location and I kept my eyes locked on that point as I stepped out and brought my rifle up. Moving to the front of the Lexus, I stopped, rifle trained on the sedan, ready to adjust depending on which side he came around. I was thirty yards from the Mercedes, and from what I'd seen he could cover that distance in about two seconds. *What the hell are you doing, John?*

We stood like that for close to five minutes, neither of us moving. This didn't bode well. The hogs may be infected, and it certainly appeared the infection was driving them to find and kill humans, but it hadn't taken over their minds the way it had people. This razorback was exhibiting patience and cunning in abundance. By now an infected human would have charged. Well, maybe not the smart females, but that was different. Or was it?

Mentally slapping myself, I dismissed all of these thoughts. The last thing I needed to be doing right now was to get lost in thought and not be ready to react the instant he moved. But he wasn't budging. I could hear him grunting occasionally and he was making the same, odd popping noise the one I'd killed earlier had done. It was going to come down to who was more patient. Me or him.

With little doubt that I could outlast him, I risked a quick glance at the sky. The clouds were still gathering, black on the bottom and the sky actually looked green. I'd never seen that before and didn't know what it meant, but doubted it was a good thing. The weather might force my hand. Push me into action. I sure didn't want to have to fight the razorback in a storm or after dark. The conditions would heavily tip the scales in his favor if I waited too long.

Transmission

I was so focused on the hog that I made a rookie mistake that nearly cost me my life. I didn't maintain awareness of the surrounding environment for other threats. The charging female would have wrapped me up in a tackle if I hadn't heard her feet on the asphalt and immediately moved forward toward the razorback. If I had turned to see what the sound was, she would have taken me to the ground, but by moving forward I was partially protected by the SUV and she was only able to graze my shoulder with her hand.

She screamed as she flashed past, scrabbling for traction to turn and press the attack. At the same time, the razorback squealed and charged around the back of the Mercedes. Knowing I only had time to get one shot off before both of them were on me, I rolled the dice and put a round into the female's leg. The bullet shattered her knee, but she didn't go down. Dashing for the rear of the SUV, I rounded the corner as she screamed, turning to look once I was safely behind the vehicle.

The female was still screaming as she tried to hobble after me, then the razorback arrived. With a blindingly fast movement, he lowered his head when he reached the female, slashing upwards as he slammed into her body. She was lifted into the air and flipped over his back, crashing to the road like a rag doll as he stopped and spun around to finish her off.

For a moment, I was stunned into immobility at the amount of damage the hog had inflicted with that one slash. Both tusks had pierced the female's body at groin level and the upward slash had completely eviscerated her. She was torn open all the way to her neck, blood fountaining into the air from at least two severed arteries.

The razorback ran to the body, stopping and lowering his head to tear open her throat. The shock wore off and I sighted on him, flipping the selector switch to burst. I pulled the trigger and kept pulling it until I had burned through a full magazine. I think I pulled the trigger a couple of more times after the bolt locked open, but I'm not sure. All I'm sure of is I wanted that damn, monstrous beast dead.

When I lowered my rifle and looked, the hog lay on top of the female's head, body twitching as he died. She was motionless, and infected or not, her body had been so thoroughly destroyed by his attack that she had not lived more than a few seconds. I stood looking at them for a few, long moments, then shook myself back into motion. First, I loaded in a fresh magazine, then with rifle ready to go I stepped out from behind the Lexus and started moving toward the Mercedes.

I had only covered a few feet before the back door opened and another beast started running at me. I damn near shot Dog when he first appeared and barely had time to safe my rifle before he slammed into me and knocked me to the ground. He stood on my chest and wouldn't stop licking my face until I finally wrapped him in a bear hug and rolled him to the ground where I scratched his chest and pressed my face against his. I was grinning like an idiot.

When Dog calmed down, a little, I was able to climb to my feet. Rachel had been standing there, watching our reunion. As soon as I stood, she threw herself against me, arms around my neck. Without even a thought, my arms went around her waist and pulled her tight to my body. Our lips met and the kiss quickly became much more than a greeting between two friends. It went on and on, only stopping when we had to come up for air.

We held each other, Rachel leaning back slightly to get my face in focus. She smiled a bright smile and laughed.

"Miss me?" She asked.

14

I could have stood there holding Rachel in my arms for the rest of the afternoon, but there were infected and razorbacks in the area and it was looking more and more like one hell of a storm was brewing. We needed to get somewhere safe, but first things first. Where was Jackson?

The smile at being reunited with me disappeared from Rachel's face and she told me her story in a low, quiet voice. Finished, she took my hand and led me to a ditch on the north side of the freeway where she pointed at a half-submerged truck sitting in the bottom. I asked her to stay at the top and keep watch, heading into the flooded cut in the ground when she nodded. I told Dog to stay with her, wanting his superior senses to help keep an eye out for danger.

Wading through the water, I climbed into the back of the truck, made my way forward and stuck my head into the cab through the broken rear window. I'd known Jackson all of two days, but combat has a way of compressing time and forging bonds. He was my friend, and he was dead. He deserved better. We all did. Reaching out, I pulled his vest and clothing aside and removed one of his dog tags, slipping it into my pocket. A small, gold cross hung from its own chain around his neck and I gently placed it atop his clothing.

Saying goodbye, I made my way back to where Rachel was standing with her rifle up and ready. I had noticed the heavy equipment earlier and now walked over to the backhoe. Climbing into the cab, I was pleased to find the keys dangling from the ignition. Pleased and surprised, but I wasn't going to complain when luck finally came my way.

Starting the big vehicle, I played with the different levers for a few minutes until I got a feel for how the machine operated. I wouldn't be doing the precision excavating that was required for most construction jobs, so I wasn't worried about practicing for what I had to do. Driving the machine to the side of the ditch, I scooped up a big bucketful of dirt, pivoted the arm and dumped it on top of the truck. I kept at it until the hole was filled in and Jackson was buried. It was the best I could do for a fallen brother. Leaving the backhoe where it was, I turned off the engine and climbed down.

"OK, we need to get the hell out of here," I said. "But first, I have something in my pack for you."

Dirk Patton

Rachel followed me to the Lexus, a curious expression on her face. Dog was ranging around the area after having thoroughly checked out each of the dead razorbacks. Pulling out my pack, I retrieved one of the syringes I'd filled with vaccine when I turned the box I'd received from Irina in for study. I had brought two doses, but unfortunately only needed one.

I gave Rachel an abbreviated version of what it was, but after her experience with the girls' parents, and then Jackson, she didn't require any convincing. Turning, she unfastened her pants and lowered them to expose her ass. Tearing open an alcohol swab, I cleaned a small area and stuck the needle in. She twitched slightly, looking over her shoulder at me.

"That was a little bit of revenge for all those antibiotic shots, wasn't it?" She asked with a grin.

"No. That wasn't. This is," I said, pushing the plunger.

Rachel looked confused for a second, then her eyes opened wide.

"Holy shit! That hurts! Bad!" She said, reaching back and rubbing the spot where I'd injected her.

Transmission

She rubbed hard for a few seconds, pulled her pants back up and kept rubbing. Dog trotted up and sat on my foot as I closed my pack and tossed it into the SUV. Rachel walked in a tight circle, rubbing her ass and shooting me an occasional look that said somehow this was my fault. I grinned, opened the back door and waved Dog inside the Lexus.

A few minutes later we were all inside the vehicle, driving west. Rachel was still grumbling, wriggling around in her seat as the painful vaccine spread through her muscles. Dog seemed delighted for things to be back to normal, taking a seat on the back floor and resting his chin on the leather upholstered console between the two front seats. I had to agree with him. It felt good to have the three of us back together.

I pushed our speed up, wanting to get farther west before the storm struck. Even though it was still afternoon, and the sun was shining brightly somewhere, it was gloomy under the oppressive overcast. Rachel finally settled down, reached across the console and took my hand in hers.

"Thank you for finding me," she said, giving my hand a squeeze.

"Try not to get lost again. OK?" I said, squeezing back.

Dirk Patton

She smiled and relaxed back into her seat. I tried not to let myself think about the change in our relationship that had just happened. I hadn't planned it, and in fact was surprised at myself. But, it had happened. And it felt good. Until I thought about Katie. Suddenly, I felt like shit. Like I was betraying my wife.

There was only a very remote chance she was still alive. I was finally ready to acknowledge the facts and not keep going on hope and fantasy. If she was alive, somewhere without the vaccine, she could have already turned. And if she hadn't turned yet, she would within a very few days according to GRU Captain Irina Vostov.

I wanted to share my thoughts with Rachel, but I realized that if I did, she might wind up feeling like a consolation prize. Nothing could be further from the truth. I'd still feel the same way about Rachel if Katie were sitting at Tinker waiting for me. I just wouldn't have acted on my feelings. But that wasn't something I thought I could articulate without hurting her. Damn it.

"You alright?" Rachel asked, reclined in the leather seat, head turned in my direction.

"Honestly, right now I'm about as alright as I'm probably ever going to be," I answered,

Transmission

smiling. Giving up unrealistic hope and moving on is a freeing experience.

15

Colonel Crawford broke the secure video link to Hawaii, Admiral Packard's image blinking out a second later. They'd had a lot to discuss and the call had lasted a long time. Captain Blanchard, who had stayed quiet and out of view of the camera, stepped up and shut down the computer that was used for video calls. Air Force Brigadier General Triplett, commander of Tinker Air Force Base, sat across the table from Crawford. He was a good administrator and did a good job of running the base, but he wasn't a tactician or a warrior. Fortunately, he readily acknowledged that fact and had no problem deferring to the Admiral and Colonel on strategic matters.

Their first topic had been the immediate commencement of mass production of the vaccine. Crawford had urged they begin producing it as quickly as possible and the Admiral had agreed. General Triplett already had Air Force personnel on the way to the University to oversee the production ramp up and ensure there was vaccine being manufactured around the clock. He would take on managing the distribution of the completed product and the prioritization of inoculations.

Transmission

They had moved on to several other topics, including airlifting some needed supplies from stores on the mainland to Hawaii. A couple of hours into the conference, the Admiral had muted the microphone on his end and they had seen an aide step into the camera frame. Packard's unruly eyebrows had shot up, then he'd unmuted and told Crawford that a Russian GRU officer was calling on a secure US military circuit, demanding to speak with Major John Chase.

The Colonel was as surprised as Packard, suggesting the caller be joined to their conference so both of them could hear why the Russians wanted to speak with Major Chase. The Admiral agreed, glancing off to the side at an aide. A moment later there was a dual tone beep indicating a voice caller had joined the video conference.

"This is Admiral Packard, United States Navy. To whom am I speaking?"

"Admiral, my name is Captain Irina Vostov. I am with the GRU of the Russian Federation. It is urgent that I speak with Major John Chase of your Army on a most serious matter."

Packard looked out of the screen at the Colonel and nodded for him to speak.

"Captain, this is Colonel Crawford. I'm Major Chase's commanding officer. We're on a secure line. What is this matter?"

There was a long pause and Crawford was about to ask if she was still on the line when she spoke again.

"If you are truly his commanding officer, you will know what I gave him and what he gave me."

Crawford hesitated. If this were really the GRU Captain the Major had briefed him about, then it would hurt nothing to reveal what he knew. But how could he be sure? What if this was an attempt by the Russians to catch the real Captain Vostov?

"If you're really Captain Vostov, you can tell me the specific injuries one of Major Chase's team suffered while opening the loading bay doors during exfiltration from Los Alamos."

It was the only event he could come up with that had a specific answer but wasn't important enough for anyone that wasn't there to have all the details.

"That would be Technical Sergeant Scott. He fell and broke his right arm, below the elbow. He also suffered a head injury and lost consciousness. How is he, by the way?"

Transmission

She hadn't hesitated for a second. Certainly hadn't had to look through notes to come up with the correct answer. Crawford looked up and nodded at the Admiral, letting him know the correct answer had been given.

"Thank you, Captain," the Colonel said. "Scott is recovering nicely. So, are you calling about the vaccine or the three special packages the Major gave you?"

"The packages, Colonel. They were on board an Antonov cargo plane bound for Moscow. Two hours ago you shot that plane down as it took off from Kirtland Air Force Base. I want to know why you are going back on the deal I made with Major Chase." Her voice had a hard edge to it as she spoke.

"Captain, I assure you I did not shoot down any Russian plane two hours ago," Crawford said, then Admiral Packard interjected before Irina could respond.

"Captain, Admiral Packard. That plane was shot down on my standing orders. As I'm sure you can understand, things move slowly within the chain of command and they're moving even slower after the attacks on my country. Updated orders had not yet reached the team that fired on your plane. No one has violated the agreement you made with the Major."

Dirk Patton

There was silence on the line as Irina thought about what she'd just been told.

"I accept your explanation, Admiral." She finally said after nearly a minute. "But we now have a problem. There is a madman in the Kremlin, and my comrades and I no longer have any way to stop him. If he is not stopped, the vaccine will only delay the inevitable for America. He is determined to destroy your country to the last man."

"Please stand by, Captain." Packard pushed a button that placed Irina on hold, isolating her from the call.

"What do you think, Jack?" He asked Colonel Crawford. Use of the Colonel's first name told him the Admiral wanted the pure, unvarnished truth.

"I think we have three specials in our possession. If we can trust this woman, whom I'm still not one hundred percent sure about, those three bombs won't do us any good. Sure, we can deliver one to each of the three Air Force bases they've captured, but what will that really gain us? A few dead Russians? They'll fly replacements in within twenty-four hours.

"My opinion is that we don't have a better option than making a leap of faith and supplying her with whatever she asks for. I've been doing some research today and her uncle is Fleet Admiral Shevchenko. He's about as moderate as a Russian gets, and personally, I'd much rather see him in control than this asshole Barinov who's been butt fucking us for the past month. Sir."

Packard smiled and nodded.

"Succinctly put, Colonel. OK, I'm bringing her back on." He motioned to his aide. "Captain Vostov?"

"Admiral, I am still here."

"Captain, we are prepared to provide you with whatever equipment and support you require, but I need to check with my superiors first," Packard said.

"That is not acceptable, Admiral! I made a deal with Major Chase and the inefficiency of your military is the only reason we are even having this conversation. I have honored our deal and I expect you to do the same. I happen to know you do not have any superiors to check with. Do not forget. I'm GRU. I know you are the highest ranking survivor, and that your President and Congress are all dead. Do not play games with me!"

Irina's voice was hard and loud. The woman was obviously under a lot of stress.

Dirk Patton

"Captain, there are things you don't know. I will recommend we supply you with what you need, but I will not hand over special packages without proper approval. Major Chase should not have done so either, and under any other circumstances, he'd be facing trial and quite possibly execution."

She was quiet for a long time before speaking again.

"Apologies for my tone, Admiral. It has been a long day."

"Captain, besides the special packages, do you need anything else?" Crawford interjected.

"No, Colonel. We have everything else well in hand."

"Very good. Assuming Admiral Packard receives approval, how would you like to go about collecting the items from us?" He asked.

"2200 hours tomorrow, I will be in El Paso, Texas. It is far enough outside of our CAP that you can come in without being detected, but close enough that my pilot can deviate from his patrol without drawing scrutiny."

"Are you sure?" Crawford asked. "Between El Paso and Juarez, there are about three million infected people wandering around."

Transmission

"The location will be secure. I will call back in precisely sixteen hours for the Admiral's answer and with the rendezvous coordinates. You will have Major Chase available for me to speak with. If I do not hear his voice, no coordinates. Also, he must be the one to deliver the devices. He is the only one I trust to not start shooting simply because his orders did not get updated."

Crawford glanced at the screen, Admiral Packard looking like he'd just sucked on a particularly sour lemon.

"That may be difficult, Captain. He is currently out of radio contact, searching for some missing personnel," the Colonel said.

"Colonel – I have studied the United States Army for most of my adult life. I know how resourceful you are, how swiftly you can move when you must. Even allowing for what has happened to your country. Find him and have him standing by for my call tomorrow. Dosvedanya."

The dual tone beep sounded again, only in reverse order, letting them know she had disconnected.

16

We had only been driving for about half an hour when I spotted black smoke in the distance, directly to our front. Rachel had fallen asleep, my hand firmly grasped in hers. Dog was stretched out on the plush leather seat in the rear. He was snoring like a sawmill going full bore, lying on his back with legs extended straight out. He looked comfortable and I wished I could join him.

My hands ached from the wounds of being nailed to a cross in Tennessee. My chest still hurt where I'd been shot in Georgia, and I was bone tired. My only sleep in the past few days, a couple of naps on the hard decks of aircraft. That was fine when I was twenty-one. Kind of sucked now that I'm not a kid anymore.

When it became apparent the smoke was coming from something burning either on or immediately adjacent to the Interstate, I woke Rachel. She sat up, rubbing her eyes and looking where I pointed ahead. Something with a lot of petroleum in it was burning. I could tell that much from the density and color of the smoke. I lowered our speed and now, at the limit of my vision, I could see bright, orange flames on the shoulder of the road. Slowing further, I kept approaching, reaching down to make sure my rifle was ready to go.

A quarter of a mile from the fire I brought us to a stop. A vehicle lay on its side on the right shoulder, completely engulfed in flames. I knew it hadn't been burning just a few hours ago. We had already passed the Black Hawk I had abandoned, which meant I'd flown over this stretch of the freeway. There definitely hadn't been a fire then, or we would have checked it out.

Nothing was moving, and I decided to transition to the eastbound lanes to give the furiously burning vehicle a wide berth. The Lexus navigated the soft soil in the median without much difficulty, then back on pavement I drove a sedate twenty miles an hour as we pulled abreast of the wreck.

"That's the Bronco I told you about," Rachel said, staring out her window at the fire.

I thought so too. The shape was right, and there were a couple of small areas not yet blackened where I could see what looked like orange paint.

"There's nothing else around. What do you think happened?" She asked.

"Maybe a blowout at speed," I mused. "Or some kind of mechanical failure that caused them to lose control. Or maybe one or both of them turned while they were driving."

Rachel looked at me, the horror of the thought clear on her face. I shrugged my shoulders to say it was all just speculation. Maybe it was something as simple as vehicle failure. It didn't really matter, and once we were clear of the heat from the fire I drove back across the median and sped up to eighty. The Lexus did a good job of smoothing out the road and was well insulated and quiet. Within a few minutes, Dog started snoring again, Rachel's eyes closing shortly after that.

We had moved beyond the path of the previous day's storms, and as Little Rock drew closer, the terrain changed from flat to rolling and I started seeing more trees. There was also a pall of smoke hanging over the area, held down by the heavy cloud cover. I had seen what was being burned to generate all that pollution and knew I didn't want to smell it. Playing with the SUV's controls, I got the air conditioning set to recirculate the interior air rather than bring in fresh. I've smelled burning human flesh before, never mind where, and I wasn't eager to experience it again.

Passing a couple of large truck stops that were dark and abandoned, I slowed when I spied walking figures a few hundred yards ahead.

Transmission

They were on the roadway and appeared to be moving towards the city. Braking to a stop, I raised my rifle and used the scope to look at them. I made a mental note to get my hands on a pair of binoculars. Now that I was west of the Mississippi, the country really opened up. There was a lot of flat terrain without trees, unlike east of the river, and I wanted to take full advantage of being able to see threats at a much greater distance.

Through the scope, I could tell these were infected and there were too many to count. Certainly not a massive herd like we'd fought in Murfreesboro, or seen during our escape from Tennessee, but still more than I was willing to encounter in our luxury, soccer mom machine. The Lexus was comfortable as hell on pavement, had a decent four-wheel drive system for tame off-roading, but it was far from the tank-like protection I wanted before driving into a herd of these damn things.

I messed with the navigation system as Rachel continued to sleep. Dog had wakened when I'd stopped and shoved his head against my arm looking for attention. Giving him a quick neck scratch, I focused back on the map display. A couple of tweaks and I spotted us, discovering we were eighteen miles from Little Rock. Hoping we were close enough, I fished an earpiece out of my collar and inserted it in my left ear, powering up my radio.

I made four calls on four different military frequencies, but didn't get anything in response. I hadn't really expected to reach anyone, but it had been worth a try. Leaving the radio on, I worked with the navigation screen, looking for a bypass route that would get me to Little Rock Air Force Base. There were two options. Continue ahead into the city and turn north on a smaller highway, or backtrack a few miles and take a series of small farm roads. Another look ahead at the small herd and it was an easy decision.

Getting us turned around, I headed east again for a few miles, watching the nav screen and getting off the Interstate onto an unmarked road that ran due north. Following it for a couple of miles, I made a turn to the west and hit the brakes. Some piece of giant farm equipment completely blocked the road. It sat on massive tires and was so long each end extended well off the pavement into the muddy fields on either side. There was a large, glass-enclosed cab that sat a good twelve feet above ground level.

I had no idea what it was, but had a good idea why it had been parked there. It was a quick and easy, yet highly effective roadblock. I didn't think even heavy military vehicles would be able to move it. Rachel had woken when I stopped this time, sitting up and looking around.

"Where are we? Why did we leave the Interstate?" She asked, grimacing and reaching down to rub her hip where the vaccine had gone in.

I spent a few minutes bringing her current as I looked around the area. To either side of the road were muddy fields. They looked like they had been harvested and prepared for planting, but that's as far as the farmer had gotten. They also looked like they were nothing more than deep, soft mud. Finished filling Rachel in on our situation, I decided to step out and check the ground. From the driver's seat, it looked like the type of mud that would suck the Lexus in all the way to its axles and not let go.

Telling Rachel to stay in the vehicle, I carefully scanned in every direction. Seeing nothing to concern me, I opened my door and stepped down onto the road, rifle up and ready the moment my feet touched. Dog scrambled across the center console, onto the driver's seat and jumped down to go with me. His nose immediately went up and tested the air, a low growl emanating from his chest a moment later. I hadn't seen anything when I'd scanned the area, but wasn't about to ignore Dog. If he smelled something, it was there.

Dirk Patton

The wind was out of the southeast, behind me. Whatever he was scenting had to be in that direction, so I turned and put my eye to the rifle scope as I scanned. I missed them on the first pass, black hair blending well with the color of the mud, but caught the movement when they ran onto the road. Two razorbacks. They looked younger, probably no more than a hundred and fifty pounds each, but were still big enough to ruin my afternoon.

They were several hundred yards away and I had enough time to check the fields. One step off the shoulder and I knew there was no way the Lexus could make it. My boot sank six inches deep into the thick mud, making a wet, sucking sound when I pulled my foot out to step back on the gravel at the edge of the pavement. The big SUV would sink to its frame in this quagmire. I had no doubt of that.

Another check of the razorbacks found them about three hundred yards out and still closing fast. I gave Dog three seconds to finish peeing on a small bush, then whistled him into the vehicle. He left muddy footprints on my seat, but I didn't care. Back inside, I got us moving, careful not to drive off the shoulder as I turned the SUV around. Rachel had seen me peering through the scope at the hogs and knew what was coming.

Transmission

By the time we were heading back towards the Interstate, the razorbacks were inside seventy-five yards and showing no sign of slowing. I started to accelerate towards them, then remembered the behavior of the infected humans that would run directly into a vehicle without a thought for their own safety. If the hogs did that, and I had any amount of speed, it could seriously damage the Lexus.

This was a cushy, suburban vehicle designed for trips to the country club, the mall or anywhere you wanted to take along six other people in comfort. It wasn't armored and didn't have a heavy push bar like the truck I'd used to get us out of Atlanta. The razorbacks were probably no more than a hundred and fifty pounds, but combine that with their speed and they could do a lot of damage just by running into us.

I hit the brakes and brought us to a stop when they were forty yards away. Sitting, I watched them charge and they weren't slowing or deviating.

"Put it in park!" Rachel suddenly shouted, making me jump.

I started to turn my head to look at her, but she shouted again and I moved the lever that controlled the transmission. Moments later, the lead hog impacted the front bumper hard enough to rock the heavy vehicle. The hood was too tall for me to see what the impact did to him or the Lexus. A moment later the second one arrived, grazing the front fender with his shoulder and causing a horrible scraping sound as his tusk was dragged along the side of the SUV.

I shifted into drive, accelerating, and we bounced over the razorback that had run directly into our front bumper. Maybe he had been dead, or perhaps only stunned, but one of the tires crushed his head into pulp as we drove.

"What was with shifting into park?" I asked, gaining speed and watching in the mirror as the second hog began pursuing.

"Air bags," Rachel answered. "I was in a McDonald's drive through a couple of years ago and the car ahead backed into me hard enough to cause my air bags to inflate. When I took it in for repairs, the guy in the body shop told me that air bags are disabled if the transmission is in park, even if the motor's running. Said he always shifts into park in drive through lines. I didn't know if that hog was big or heavy enough to cause them to pop, but figured why take the chance."

I nodded, glad she had yelled a warning. Suddenly, the Lexus didn't feel so comfortable. It felt vulnerable. As soon as I could find one, I'd move us to a truck, or preferably a military vehicle. Even though we were only about thirty miles from Little Rock Air Force Base, I had learned the hard way just how difficult it can be to cross even five miles. Modern life has spoiled us. A hundred and fifty years ago, thirty miles was a two-day journey at best. Now, millions of people commuted farther than that just to go to work each morning. Well, did. Morning commutes were a thing of the past. And thirty miles was once again an adventure in survival.

17

I stopped when we reached the Interstate, taking my time to review the navigation screen before proceeding. The idea of trying to bull our way through herds of infected really concerned me. I was also worried about where they were coming from. Were more people starting to turn, or had these been stumbling around the countryside and just now were starting to converge on the city? If these were freshly turned, we might be too late in trying to get the vaccine manufactured and distributed.

"What are we doing?" Rachel asked.

"I'm trying to figure that out. I'm concerned about trying to push on into Little Rock to get to the highway that will take us to the air base. If there're more people turning, it could be as bad as some of what we went through in Nashville and Memphis." I answered, checking the mirrors to make sure there wasn't something sneaking up on us. Couldn't just worry about people anymore.

"Besides swine and birds, are there other animals that humans share viral infections with?" I asked.

Transmission

"Swine, birds, and primates are the big three we commonly hear about, heard about, but almost any mammal has the potential. Think about anthrax – cattle. And that's just one example I can think of right off the top of my head. There are whole fields of study dealing with Zoonosis, the transmission of diseases between humans and animals, and I got maybe a tenth of one percent of it in medical school. I do know that we also have to worry about insects, potentially. Think of all the diseases that mosquitos and fleas transmit. Diseases that won't jump from an animal to a human through casual contact, but the bite of an insect transmits it quite effectively."

"What about dogs?" I asked, getting a wet nose shoved against my arm when he thought I was talking to him.

"Anything's possible," Rachel answered slowly, turning in her seat and reaching out to rub Dog's furry head. "There are several viral infections that can be passed between humans and dogs. You just don't hear about them because most people in America keep their pets and themselves clean and vaccinated. But yes, it's possible."

"Sorry I asked," I said, looking at Dog and starting to worry. He'd killed countless infected by tearing out their throats. That meant lots of infected blood in his mouth. There was no way he wasn't exposed. "I've got another syringe of vaccine I brought for Jackson. Should we give it to Dog?"

Rachel looked out the window, thinking, then shook her head.

"I don't think so. The little bit I know about viruses and vaccines – well, I think it would be as dangerous to use a vaccine on him that was developed for humans as not vaccinating him at all. In fact, many human vaccines are human immune system specific and would kill a dog."

"So what the hell do we do about the infection going the other way, to animals? Any way to stop it?" I asked.

"Maybe, with a concerted effort by a top tier research team with unlimited funds and manpower. In the world we're in? It's going to spread throughout whatever animal can host it until equilibrium is reached."

"What do you mean? Equilibrium?" I asked.

"Until the infection rate is one hundred percent, or so close as to not matter, and the population of infected stabilizes. Some of the population will die. Some will survive. Some will

Transmission

be naturally immune. All of that will have to work itself out and man no longer can do much of anything to affect the outcome." She said, turning in her seat and looking out the rear window. "Whatever we're doing, we'd better do it soon. We need to find shelter. Looks like another round of storms is coming."

Turning and looking, I did a double take when I saw a green sky. How the hell does that happen? But, Rachel was right. We needed to get somewhere safe. I had been delaying making a decision because I was tired. Tired of running and fighting. I needed about twelve hours of sleep and a hot meal. But I didn't see that happening anytime in the near future. Oh well, time to move forward.

Stepping on the gas, I once again headed west on I-40. Soon we caught up with the small herd that was moving in the same direction. They were spread out across the roadway, but looked thinner on the eastbound side. Slowing, I drove across the grassy median and up onto the pavement, driving against oncoming traffic. But there wasn't any traffic, only infected bodies turning at our approach.

I slowed to less than twenty miles an hour, hoping the impact of multiple bodies wouldn't disable the Lexus or cause the air bags to deploy. Steering, I tried to contact as many of them as I could with the corners of the bumper. The bumper was tall enough to strike most of the infected just below their hips, and the ones that were hit by the corners were sent spinning away into the crowd, knocking others off their feet.

There were a few infected in the herd that looked like they had been wandering around for some time, but many of them were clean and wearing clothing and shoes that were in good repair. Freshly turned. A couple of the males even still had rifles strapped to their bodies. Thank God they were no longer intelligent enough to know how to use them.

"You seeing the ones that look new?" Rachel asked, holding her rifle tightly as she stared out the windows at the herd.

"Yep. Not good news," I said, turning the wheel to avoid a particularly large concentration of bodies.

The herd had appeared small when we approached from the rear, but as we kept pushing forward it became obvious that there were more infected than I had anticipated. They were spread out more than I had become accustomed to, and as a result I had misjudged their numbers. I was starting to get more than a little concerned. I had expected to be through

Transmission

and on clear pavement by now, not encountering a denser concentration as we progressed.

Their numbers seemed to quickly increase as they responded to the sound of the straining engine. The herd started collapsing in on us from all sides, females leaping onto the running boards and pounding on the side windows. I couldn't see the far edge of the herd and decided this had been a bad idea. It was time to get us out of there before we got swamped and immobilized. If that happened, it would only be a matter of time before they were able to smash their way inside the vehicle and spoil our evening.

Spinning the wheel, I gunned the engine, less concerned about the air bags than I was with getting us clear of the herd as quickly as possible. Rachel was staying quiet, but Dog was whining and growling, moving from side to side to snarl at females that were hanging on to the Lexus with their faces pressed to the glass. I pushed harder on the accelerator, shoving bodies aside and under the tires.

The engine strained to keep moving us through the crush of infected and we were slowly losing speed and momentum. Fists pounded on the body and glass of the SUV, the sound nearly deafening. I kept my foot on the gas, worrying about being brought to a stop the way the herd in

Los Alamos had stopped the MRAP. Fortunately, before that could happen the crush began to thin, the constant thump of the bumper striking bodies easing as we gained speed.

We quickly reached the rear edge of the herd, which was now becoming the leading edge as they turned to pursue. In the mirrors, I could see the solid mass of males stumbling along in our wake, dozens of females racing ahead of the main body to give chase. Five females still clung to the exterior of the Lexus, and as our speed passed fifty I started swerving as hard as I felt I could without risking a rollover of the top-heavy vehicle. This succeeded in dislodging two of them, but the remaining three clung as tightly as barnacles.

Pushing our speed to sixty, I warned Rachel to brace herself, checked to make sure Dog was seated, then stood on the brakes. The vehicle's nose dipped dramatically and the brake pedal vibrated under my foot as the ABS system kicked in. First one, then the other two females went flying, all of them tumbling down the asphalt to our front. As soon as the third one lost her grip, I took my foot off the brake and floored the accelerator. I ran over one, smashed one aside and completely missed the third as we roared towards the approaching storm.

Transmission

"You're getting good at that," Rachel commented.

"Too damn much practice," I answered with a smile.

We quickly left the infected behind, but were heading the wrong direction. The Lexus' headlights came on automatically as we lost more light to the setting sun and heavy clouds. The entire horizon was dark, the overcast swollen with rain. Lightning continually flashed, lighting the clouds from within. With a couple of miles between the herd and us, I pulled to a stop to take another look at the navigation system.

There weren't a lot of roads in the area. A few small tracks cut through the agriculture that dominated the landscape, but they were primarily for the use of farmers and didn't go anywhere. That was it. West of Little Rock it appeared to change dramatically, but between the city and the river, farmers had taken full advantage of the rich soil of the floodplain.

The only route that might help us move on west was to backtrack twenty miles and take state highway 70 that ran south for a few miles before turning and feeding into downtown Little Rock. With a sigh, I selected this route on the screen and accelerated to the east.

18

We made good time, quickly reaching the turnoff for the smaller state highway and getting off the Interstate. It was almost completely dark by the time we turned back to the west and I lowered our speed so anything or anyone on the pavement wouldn't surprise me. The world around us was dark, no lights to be seen in any direction. Behind us, the lightning continually lit the clouds and the night sky, but the storm didn't seem to be drawing any closer. Ahead, there was a faint glow that I suspected was the lights of Little Rock reflecting off the bottom of the cloud cover.

As we continued to approach the city, it became apparent the light we were seeing was from fires. We were too far away to tell what was burning, but this definitely wasn't the steady glow of electric bulbs. Wrecked and abandoned vehicles were also becoming more frequent and I had to slow further to navigate around them. I was starting to get a really bad feeling.

Just a few hours ago, flying into Little Rock Air Force Base before continuing on east in the Black Hawk, I had been comforted to note how normal everything on the ground looked. Well, other than the mass funeral pyres, but the citizens had done a good job of keeping the roads

Transmission

clear and mopping up any infected that were stalking around. Maybe all these wrecks had been here and I had failed to notice them, but I didn't think so.

A couple of months ago I would have never believed an American city could fall apart in a matter of hours, but I now knew better. If a significant percentage of the population turned, that was all it took to start an incredibly rapid descent into chaos. And once that descent was started, there wasn't anything that could stop it.

We kept pushing forward, reaching the edge of the city and beginning to see infected. They were roaming around individually and in small groups. And they all looked clean, which meant freshly turned. A few were on the road and I avoided them when possible, but had to run down a few to continue our progress forward.

"You should tie me up in the back seat," Rachel suddenly said.

"What?" I wasn't sure I had heard her right.

"Tie me up," she said. "Vaccinations aren't instant. It takes time for the body to respond to the vaccine and produce enough antibodies to create immunity. You just gave me that shot a few hours ago. If I turn, here, inside the vehicle while you're driving... well, I'm just saying it's probably better if you restrain me somehow."

"Are you serious?" I asked, taking my eyes off the road to look at Rachel.

All I could see was her dark outline in the passenger seat, long hair obscuring much of her face.

"I'm very serious," she said in a subdued voice. "The only thing that would be worse than turning would be killing you or Dog after I did."

Hearing his name, Dog sat up and stuck his head between us, chin on the center console. Rachel placed her hand on top of his head and gently rubbed his ears. He let out a contented sigh and closed his eyes.

"No," I said. "I'm not tying you up just because you *might* turn. Hell, I might turn too. I got the vaccine less than twenty-four hours ago."

"Yeah, but you'd be slow and stupid," Rachel shot back.

It's not often that I don't have some sort of comeback, even if it's a simple "kiss my ass," but she came out of left field with that one. It was quiet in the Lexus for a couple of heartbeats, then Rachel started laughing. She laughed long and loud, probably picturing me stumbling around like a moron. Her mirth was contagious and I began chuckling, but couldn't work myself up to the level of amusement she was at.

Our laughter died out instantly when an infected male stumbled into our path. He suddenly appeared from the shelter of an overturned sedan, probably drawn by the sound of our approaching vehicle. I had enough time to hit the brakes, but was still moving at speed when the right front fender of the Lexus struck him. With a loud bang, his body was twisted around and slammed into the passenger door before tumbling to the pavement.

Chastising myself for getting distracted, I dropped our speed further and kept my eyes glued to the road. We were moving into a more built up area, the state highway becoming a four-lane street with businesses along either side. More and more infected stumbled around parking lots and the frequency of crashed vehicles was increasing. Ahead, I could see a large fire, and as we approached I could make out a box truck entangled with a city bus. Both were burning furiously and completely blocked the road.

The infected in the area had noticed us and were all zeroing in on our noise and movement. Several females sprinted at us from the parking lot of a large shopping center. The power was still on. The area lit by street lights, but the flames from the burning vehicles lent a surreal quality to the scene.

Glancing at the navigation screen, I took the first right, turning onto a smaller street. As I made the turn, the power blinked out, plunging everything into inky darkness. Behind, I could see the glow of the fire, and more flames ahead lit the sky. Without the SUV's headlights, it would have been too dark to see on the street. More infected suddenly began appearing at the edge of the lights, males slamming into the vehicle, females screaming and pacing us.

The road swept to the left and as I started into the curve, I stepped on the brakes and brought us to a stop. A block to our front, the street was straddled by two large apartment complexes that pushed right up to the pavement. Both were burning furiously. It was too dangerous to try and drive between them. The heat would be tremendous. This was confirmed for me as a truck parked on the street in front of the building on the right suddenly exploded in a massive ball of flame.

The females that had been chasing us caught up and pounded on the outside of the vehicle, males soon shambling into the gaps between them. I shifted into reverse and got us moving, running over a couple of males, dragging more to the ground as I turned the wheel. Retracing our path, I checked the navigation and made a turn before we reached the main road we had followed into town.

This one was even narrower, lined with small houses and the occasional block of apartments. Cars were parked along both sides of the street and there would have barely been room to meet oncoming traffic. Males repeatedly stepped out from between parked cars as we approached and I held our speed to under twenty so the Lexus didn't take too much damage from the impacts.

The terrain climbed for several miles, then we crested and started down into what had to be a valley. I couldn't see a river below us in the dark, but I knew there was a fairly large one that ran through Little Rock. The houses grew in size dramatically when we topped out and nearly all of them had large decks that must have afforded fabulous views of the valley as well as the entire city spread out in front of us. As I drove, the image of Bill Clinton, relaxing on one of these decks with a cigar and an intern popped into my head.

The city was dark with the exception of numerous fires. There had to be at least three dozen separate locations that were burning, and some of them looked to be quite large and still growing. The downslope was gentle in places, severe in others as the road dropped like it had been terraced. It wasn't long before the SUV's headlights reflected off a vehicle that completely blocked our path. I immediately slammed on the brakes and brought us to a stop.

"Ambush?" Rachel asked quietly.

"Maybe," I said. "Or maybe it's a real accident. Either way, I haven't seen a side road for over two miles."

In the mirror, I could see females approaching. They were still over a hundred yards away, but coming fast. Males were moving amongst the parked cars, struggling to bump their way through and reach us. If it had been an ambush, I didn't think it was still manned. There were too many infected in the area for someone to be sitting and waiting for unsuspecting travelers.

"We're going to try it," I said, stepping on the accelerator.

Approaching the wreck, I got a better look and it was obvious it hadn't been staged. A Chevy sedan appeared to have been traveling in the same direction we were when it crashed into a parked car. The front of the Chevy was crumpled and tangled into the side of the vehicle

Transmission

it had hit. Maybe the driver had tried to avoid an infected, or maybe the poor soul had turned.

The other thing that was obvious as we approached was that I wouldn't be able to push the abandoned car out of the way with the Lexus. The Chevy would just twist around and wedge even tighter. Looking around, I hoped there was a way to drive across the front lawn of one of the houses and bypass the wreck, but they were built on a terrace. Each lot was flat, the upslope side of it cut into the hill and a block retaining wall holding back the neighboring land. This explained the road alternating between steep and flat and there was no way to drive from one lot onto another. Each retaining wall was close to eight feet high, way too much of a drop for the Lexus to survive.

Out of options, I shifted into reverse and focused on the large screen in the middle of the dash. It had been displaying a moving map with our location highlighted, but when I went into reverse it changed to the image from the rearview camera. The quality was surprisingly good. Good enough to see the pack of females bearing down on us.

Hitting the accelerator, I shot backwards and spun the wheel, reversing into a driveway. A couple of males were bulled aside, suddenly growing large on the screen before being sent flying by the rear bumper. Shifting back to drive, I roared out of the driveway as the females arrived. Blasting through the pack, I was fairly certain I killed or disabled at least half of them, but the remaining ones immediately turned around and continued their pursuit.

We quickly outdistanced them and soon found ourselves back in the area where we had first turned off the main road. The bus and truck were still burning away and the flames had spread to an adjacent two-story office building. It was only feet from the building next to it and it wouldn't take long for the fire to jump and spread more destruction.

We were out of options. Little Rock, or at least this part of it, was becoming impassable. Not only did we have to worry about being trapped by infected, fire was a very real concern. The more the fire spread, the hotter it burned. Eventually, the air would become superheated and, when that happened, anything combustible would burst into flames. This place had less than half an hour at the most before it was nothing more than a large, flaming cauldron. Resigning myself to finding another route, I turned back to the east on the main road and accelerated away from the dying city.

19

Lee Roach and Synthia drove through the dark streets of Oklahoma City. They were in the pickup Roach had found abandoned in Arkansas. He had borrowed a heat gun from the motor pool and used it to melt the adhesive lettering off the vehicle's doors, then unbolted the orange light bar from the roof. There wasn't anything to be done with the spotlights that wouldn't leave large holes in the truck's sheet metal, so he'd left them where they were. The truck was now just another anonymous Ford F-150, and Oklahoma was full of Ford trucks.

The truck was the extended cab version, giving him an extra couple of feet of room behind the front bench seat. In this space, a woman lay unconscious from the drugs Synthia had slipped into her drink while pretending to be another refugee just looking for a friendly ear. The woman's hands were cuffed behind her back.

Their destination was a small, abandoned motel on the far side of the city that Roach had identified from reports shared by the Oklahoma City Police. The handcuffs on the woman were convenient, but would also lend a degree of credibility to the story Roach had created in the event they were discovered driving around. He would say the woman had deserted from the Air

Force and he was just transporting her back to the base. He had gone so far as to dummy up a file on the woman with a photo he had taken as part of the processing of arriving refugees for which he was responsible.

It was a pretty thin cover, and he was certain it would never have held up in a pre-attack world. Now, the chances of even being questioned by a roving police officer were so slim as to be nearly negligible. If by some strange chance he was pulled over, his Air Force law enforcement ID should quickly send the cop on his way. But, he was prepared for the worst with a pistol in his lap that he had taken from the Tinker evidence locker. He had no qualms about shooting a cop, and he had a weapon that couldn't be traced back to him.

Synthia sat next to him in the middle of the seat, her shoulder touching his. On the passenger seat rested a large purse, full of the restraints and other toys they anticipated needing for their evening's adventure. Playing the part of an Air Force officer's wife, Synthia had removed all the piercings that her clothing didn't cover. She had also dyed her hair to a single shade of black and had started using heavy makeup to cover the majority of her tattoos.

Roach glanced at her, not exactly sure what he was feeling. He didn't know what

Transmission

fondness for another human felt like. Certainly had never felt love. All he knew was lust and the need to act on his desires. Synthia looked back at him, her eyes glowing in anticipation of what lay ahead. She smiled and placed her hand in his lap, working his zipper down and reaching inside his trousers. A moment later, she firmly grasped his stiffening cock and squeezed hard. He groaned with pleasure, slowing to maintain control of the truck as she alternated between roughly stroking him and gripping him as tightly as she could.

They arrived at the motel in a few minutes, Synthia withdrawing her hand when Roach turned down a side street. He circled the property twice, slowly, looking for any sign of habitation. The area appeared to be completely deserted. It was the far northern edge of town and the residents that were still alive had relocated closer to the center of the metropolitan area. They felt there was safety in numbers and they had reacted to persistent rumors that infected were wandering around the edges of the city.

When all appeared safe, Roach pulled into the dark parking lot, hiding the truck behind a tall block fence that screened the office from the road. Zipping his pants, he stepped out with the pistol in hand and surveyed the area. After a couple of minutes of seeing nothing other than dark and quiet buildings, he moved to the glass door that opened into the lobby.

The door was locked, but Roach was prepared with a small tool that was specifically designed for law enforcement to quickly and easily break glass. With a sharp blow, he shattered the safety glass within the door, knocking a small hole in it that he could reach through. Turning the deadbolt, he pushed open the door with both flashlight and pistol up and pointed ahead of him.

The motel lobby was small and dirty, smelling of stale coffee and cigarettes. A forgotten houseplant struggled in a cheap, plastic pot and a large rack of glossy tourist brochures occupied the wall opposite the reception desk. Roach ignored everything, moving behind the desk after a quick consultation of a room map and grabbing a key from a large, shallow drawer. The key was on a ring attached to a large piece of battered red plastic. 113 was painted on the plastic in chipped gold paint. Dropping the key in his pocket, he went back outside.

Turning right, he stopped at the first door he came to and knocked softly. Waiting a few moments, he tried again, equally gentle. He wanted to knock loud enough to get the attention of any occupants in the room, but not loud enough for the sound to carry and attract any infected within hearing distance. After another fifteen seconds, he inserted the key, turned the lock and with his body to the side, pushed the door open.

When there was no immediate shout or charge of an infected, he poked the pistol and flashlight around the door frame and peeked in. The room was small, semi-neatly made up and vacant. The door to the bath was open and he could see it was empty as well. That left only the shower as a hiding place for anyone or anything that might be inside.

Stepping through the door, he quickly moved to the bathroom and checked. All clear. Glancing around with the light, he wrinkled his nose in disgust. The room was supposedly ready for the next guest to check in, but it wasn't a place Roach would have picked if he'd had any other option. The shower walls were covered with ancient, pale green tile. Black mildew grew in almost every grout joint. The tub was chipped and permanently stained with the dirt of a thousand guests.

Moving back to the main part of the room, he saw a particle board dresser with numerous cigarette burns and chunks of laminate missing, a fogged mirror hanging over it on the stained wall. The bed was a king, covered with a thin and threadbare comforter that looked like the same material that had been used to make the muumuus his grandmother had worn. The bed visibly sagged in the middle. To either side was a small nightstand, both bedside lamps and a cheap alarm clock bolted tightly to them. There was no TV in the room, but he had brought his own entertainment.

Three hours later, Roach and Synthia walked out of the room to the waiting truck. They were both exhausted, yet euphoric at the same time. The young woman had been strong, but then to have survived in the world since the attacks she would have to be. Each of them had engaged in sex with their captive, gradually ratcheting up the abuse as they grew more and more excited. Due to her inexperience, Synthia had accidentally cut her too deeply and nicked an artery. She had bled out and died quickly at that point, Roach and Synthia coupling on the bed next to the woman as she shuddered her final breaths.

When they left, they didn't bother to try and dispose of the body. The odds against it being found were astronomical. Even if it was found, who had the time and resources any longer to conduct a homicide investigation? Roach felt very secure, not the least worried about the DNA that both he and Synthia had left on and in the woman's body.

Transmission

They drove carefully on the way back to Tinker. Roach was surprised when they began encountering infected males, but assumed they had wandered in off the plains surrounding the city. He didn't see the females that were chasing the truck, continuing to follow the sound and glowing taillights when they couldn't match the Ford's speed.

Passage through the main gate was simple now that he had a current Tinker Security Forces ID. The guard flashed a light across Roach's badge wallet that contained the card, saluted and waved them through. Driving slowly once on the base, he followed a perimeter road that passed the giant hangar where he processed refugees.

When the road turned, it came near the barrack where many of the refugees were being housed. He slowed when he saw a figure strolling in the grass along the edge of the pavement. Pulling to a stop, he told Synthia to roll her window down and leaned across her to speak.

"Good evening. Mrs. Chase, right? Captain Roach. We met when you first arrived."

His voice was warm and friendly, a broad and welcoming smile on his face.

"Good evening, Captain. How are you?" Katie replied, turning to face the truck but not walking up to the passenger door.

"I'm fine. May I introduce my wife, Tammy? Tammy, this is Mrs. Chase. She made it here all the way from Arizona with a bus load of kids."

Roach was careful to use the name Synthia was going by, masquerading as her dead sister. Katie stepped closer and extended her arm through the window to shake Synthia's hand. Roach kept the smile plastered on his face as he slipped his left hand into his pocket and withdrew a pair of handcuffs. There was no one else around, and finding her out walking this time of night was a stroke of luck he might never have again.

All he had to do was lunge and slap one end of the cuffs onto her wrist and quickly lock the other to the steering wheel. This would give him time to jump out, run around the truck and subdue the trapped woman. He expected her to fight, but stuck halfway in a vehicle window with her wrist cuffed to the wheel, how much of a fight could she put up?

Synthia was reaching to shake her hand and Roach was tensed to make his lunge when sirens began blaring and bright lights on top of

Transmission

poles scattered across the base snapped on. Suddenly it was like daylight and Roach paused. It was just as well for him. When the sirens started, Katie yanked her arm out of the cab, drew her pistol and moved away from the truck, looking all around the area for what was causing the alarm.

Roach knew this was the perimeter alarm, not air raid. Lights wouldn't be coming on for an air raid and there was a different tone to the sirens. There was a problem at the fence. Either it had been breached, or was about to be.

"What's going on?" Katie shouted, pistol held in a two-handed, low ready grip.

"Perimeter alarm," Roach shouted back. "You need to return to your assigned barrack!"

He stepped on the gas and roared away, cursing whatever had triggered the alarm. A golden opportunity to get his hands on the Major's wife and it was just snatched away from him. Once those sirens started and lights snapped on, there was no way he was going to touch her and risk someone seeing him. Pounding the wheel in frustration, he slid to a tire-protesting stop in front of his house and dashed inside. He had the woman's blood on him, not much, but enough that it might be noticed.

Dirk Patton

Taking a thirty-second shower, he jumped out and dressed in a clean uniform without bothering to dry off. Telling Synthia to stay in the house and lock all the doors, he ran to the Humvee parked in the driveway and roared off. He had been briefed on where to report in the event of different alarms, but couldn't remember where he was supposed to be. He was closest to the main gate, so that's where he went.

Before he arrived, he heard first one, then a second machine gun start firing. The Russians? Were they attacking? But that didn't make any sense. They wouldn't commit ground troops without first softening up their target with an aerial bombardment. That meant infected!

Screeching to a halt behind a phalanx of Hummers, all with machine guns pointed towards the gate, Roach hopped out and moved forward for a better look. There were dozens of bodies lying on the asphalt just outside the perimeter fence. Beyond the corpses, hundreds of infected were rushing forward toward the chain link gate.

Transmission

20

We kept driving east until I was reasonably satisfied that we were clear of the worst of the danger presented by the city. A sign ahead said we were five miles from a junction that would take us back to I-40. I had been wondering if anyone had sent a helicopter to look for us since we were now severely overdue, but with the state of affairs in Little Rock, I expected everyone had bigger problems on their plate.

Rachel had played with the navigation while I drove and it was looking like she had found a route that would bypass the chaos behind us. The problem was that it took us way south of where we needed to be in the event the Colonel had dispatched searchers. I suspected he was getting pretty tired of sending out search parties.

The compromise I'd arrived at was to find a place for the three of us to shelter for the night. If by morning we hadn't seen or heard any sign of a SAR flight, we'd take the new route and keep working our way west. Now, the problem was going to be finding a safe place to spend the night. Not that the big Lexus with its cushy leather seats wasn't comfortable, it was, but I really wanted to stretch out. I can, and have, roughed it with the best of them, and sleeping in the SUV could hardly be considered "roughing it." But, it still wouldn't be as good as getting my exhausted body completely horizontal for a few hours.

Rachel and I had discussed my plan and she agreed. I think she would have agreed to any plan that let her get some sleep. From the corner of my eye, I kept seeing her head slowly tilt forward until it suddenly tipped and she'd jerk herself awake. Dog was the only one of us that seemed alert, his head thrust between the two front seats, eyes bright and ears straight up.

We reached the junction and I slowed, reading the small forest of signs that occupied all four corners of the intersection. There were ads for tourist attractions, restaurants, truck stops, a strip club and motels. A motel would be the ticket! It looked like all of them were back along I-40, so I turned north and drove the short distance to the Interstate.

When we reached the junction with the freeway, it looked like every other Interstate exit in the middle of nowhere across America whose sole purpose was to serve weary travelers. There were four gas stations, a large truck stop, three fast food restaurants and two motels. Everything was dark and, as I pulled to a stop to survey the area, I couldn't detect any movement.

Transmission

I gave it ten minutes, sitting there idling and waiting. After the time was up, there still wasn't any movement. No infected males slowly stumbling towards us. No females pounding on the glass. No razorbacks slamming into the vehicle. This was about as good as it was going to get.

"Which one?" I asked Rachel.

"That one."

She pointed at the motel on the far side of the Interstate. It looked the same as the one that was closer to us, but I didn't bother to ask her why. I've been married a long time. You learn to just go with the flow.

Driving into the dark parking lot, I steered the SUV in a semi-circle so the headlights would sweep across the front of the building. The motel was a local enterprise, not affiliated with any national chain, or at least not any chain I was familiar with. It was a one-story building that formed an L, twenty-five rooms bracketing the parking area on two sides. There were four cars sitting in the lot, only one of them with Arkansas plates.

At this point, four cars most likely meant a minimum of four infected. If we were lucky, they had been killed before turning and there weren't any infected to deal with, but I never count on being that lucky. I pulled the Lexus around so it was facing the office, which had a small extension off the back. The manager probably also lived at the motel, explaining the Arkansas license plate.

When I pulled up, the headlights lit the interior through the glass door. Having already seen us, three infected females were pressed tightly against the glass. They were obviously a mother and her daughters, the two girls not even teenagers yet. Rachel caught her breath when she saw them and I muttered a curse.

"Let's try the other one," I said after a long, quiet moment of looking at the small family. I really wasn't in the mood to shoot a couple of little girls, even if they were infected. Rachel nodded and I spun the wheel and took us back over the Interstate.

The other motel was part of a chain, Motel 6 if it matters, and they hadn't left the light on for me. It had a lot more rooms and three stories. All the doors faced the parking area and I repeated my semi-circle with the headlights. Half a dozen doors stood open. An even dozen cars were in the motel's parking lot, all of them with out of state plates. There was a small road that ran behind the back of the building, and I slowly eased us around the corner to see what was back there. Dumpsters and a couple of old, beat-up cars with Arkansas plates.

"What do you think?" Rachel asked, sitting up straighter and looking around.

"I think I'm rethinking the idea. I'm tired and not making good decisions, but if we go into one of those rooms and even a small herd of infected show up, we're trapped. This is block construction and there aren't any windows on the back side. The only way out of a room is through the front door," I said slowly, looking around.

"But would we be easier to find sleeping in this? If we're in one of the rooms, and quiet, they won't know we're there. Just like the house we stayed in back in Atlanta. That big herd just passed us by," Rachel said in a quiet voice.

I sat there thinking about it for a few moments, then decided she had a good point. I made another circle with the Lexus, scanning for anything approaching. Satisfied it was all clear, I put it in reverse and backed up to the only open door on the first floor, getting our vehicle as close to the room as possible.

We stepped out and I led the way, rifle up and ready, Dog by my side. He was quiet and calm, which reassured me, but I still took my time approaching the pitch black room. Dog stayed quiet, and after a couple of moments of listening I clicked on my flashlight.

The room was small but surprisingly clean, and the furnishings were moderately new. And it was empty. Dog trotted ahead of me, stuck his head into the bathroom then came back and sat down in front of me. If that's not confirmation that there's nothing to worry about, I don't know what is. I still checked the bathroom. Just in case Dog was slipping.

My guess was the occupants of the room had left in a hurry. There were so many possible reasons that I didn't bother to even think about them all. They had left their luggage and clothing behind, as well as all their toiletries on the small bathroom counter. I waved Rachel inside and retrieved our packs from the Lexus. By the time I made it back into the room and closed the door, Rachel was already in the bathroom with the door shut.

I heard her test the water, which was still on, then a minute later the toilet flushed and the shower turned on. I stood to go tell her to turn it off, afraid the water flowing through the pipes would make too much noise, but changed direction and quietly stepped outside. I couldn't hear anything, took a quick look around and went back inside, bolting the door and wedging the back of a chair under the knob.

Transmission

Taking the flashlight off my rifle, I set it on one of the nightstands, pointing at the ceiling and turned to its lowest power. It gave us enough light to see, but wouldn't be visible from outside with the heavy curtains pulled tightly closed. I sat on the edge of the bed and slowly unlaced my boots. I had briefly thought about getting in the shower when Rachel was done, but I was too damn tired. I just wanted to sleep. Wanted some relief from all the aches and pains that were the results of injuries over the past month.

A couple of minutes later, I heard the water shut off. A few moments after that, the bathroom door opened and Rachel appeared, completely nude. Water on her skin glistened in the light as she walked into the room, her long hair wet and dark. I caught my breath and stood up to meet her, staring like a teenager the first time he sees a girl without her clothes. Yes, I'd seen Rachel nude before, several times in fact, but it's different when someone is naked because they want you to see them that way.

Rachel moved to me, not stopping until her body was only a few inches from mine. Smiling, she looked me in the eye and placed both her hands flat on my chest. Her eyes were huge, drawing me in so that nothing else in the world mattered. I was having a hard time breathing.

Dirk Patton

"I'm very tired, but I can probably stay awake for a few more minutes. Probably about long enough for you to shower and come crawl under the covers with me."

She went up on her toes, leaned her head in and gave me a soft, lingering kiss on the lips. I think I forgot to breathe for a few minutes.

My head was spinning with emotion and desire. First, I hadn't been breathing, now I was nearly hyperventilating. I was even hearing voices. Rachel was still smiling and starting to step toward the bed when the voice spoke to me again.

"Dog Two Six, Boomer Three. Do you copy?"

The signal was weak, partially cutting in and out, but I finally recognized Captain Martinez' voice and remembered I still had my radio's earpiece stuck in my left ear. Are you fucking kidding me? Now?

"Dog Two Six copies. Good to hear your voice, Boomer Three," I lied, my voice husky and filled with emotion. I looked at Rachel with a sad smile.

She was still smiling, but now there was a sardonic quality to it as she turned and walked into the bathroom. She paused, giving me a long

Transmission

look at her body, then softly closed the door. Dog sat up and nuzzled my hand, got his ears scratched, belched and lay back down.

21

While I told Martinez where to find us, Rachel got dressed in the bathroom. I sat down on the edge of the bed, head still spinning at what might have been, and pulled my boots back on. Lacing them up, I looked at Dog and realized that I had never had him on a helicopter. I would have to keep a close eye and make sure he didn't get frightened and take off. I didn't think he would, but you never know what's going to trigger fear in a dog.

Rachel came out of the bath, walked over to where I sat and pushed in against me, wrapping her arms around my neck and pulling my face against her chest. Tilting her head down, she kissed the top of my head, gave me a squeeze, then sat down on the bed to pull her boots on. Thank God we weren't going to have to talk about it!

It wasn't long before Martinez radioed that she was two minutes out. I asked her to do a check of the area with FLIR before we exited the safety of the room. She sounded like she thought I was off my rocker when I asked her to also pay attention to any animals she spotted, but didn't question why.

Transmission

"Dog Two Six, you've got eight tangos about half a klick east of you on the freeway, and it looks like there're two large dogs at the gas station across the street from your location."

I still didn't hear a helicopter and guessed she was flying the Stealth Hawk we'd liberated from Kirtland.

"Copy, Boomer Three. Those dogs most likely aren't dogs. We've got a razorback problem. Got a door gunner with you?"

There was no reply for a few moments. Then, "Affirmative on door gunner, but we don't know what a razorback is, Dog Two Six."

"Big, dangerous, wild hogs. Trust me, you don't want to meet one. Just do me a favor and light them up so we can get out of here," I replied.

"Copy, sir. One pig roast coming up."

I could hear the grin in her voice. I was probably going to hear more comments about being a big, bad Green Beret and how I was afraid of Miss Piggy. Hell, I used to watch the Muppets. Miss Piggy scared the crap out of Kermit!

Rachel and I had kept preparing while I'd been talking to Martinez. Now we were standing close to the door, boots laced, packs on and rifles ready to go. A few moments later I heard the ripping sound of a minigun. It fired three bursts, then fell silent.

"All clear, Dog Two Six," Martinez called.

"Copy. We're coming out now," I answered and pulled the door open.

I went out first, Dog tight to my right hip. Rachel was learning, and as I moved with my rifle up and to our left, she stayed right behind me with her rifle covering our right flank. We moved out from under the cover over the walkway and along the side of the Lexus. Now I could hear the Stealth Hawk, but it was a low thrum and about ten times quieter than a normal Black Hawk.

Pausing at the driver's door of the SUV, I unlocked it, reached in and put the keys in the ignition then closed the door without relocking it. The vehicle had allowed me to find and save Rachel and Dog, and there still might be other survivors wandering around that were in need of transportation. I didn't need it any longer, so I'd decided to make a deposit into the bank of good karma. Hey, it can't hurt.

"Dog Two Six, do you see a clear area for pick up? Don't want to risk not seeing power lines," Martinez called.

Transmission
"Stand by," I answered, looking around.

A Black Hawk needs a minimum of fifty meters of clear space to safely land. I assumed a Stealth Hawk would have the same basic requirements. The road to our front was wide enough, but a row of utility poles with both power and phone cables ran down the far side. No way was a helicopter coming in there without tangling its rotor in the wires.

There were small buildings and various types of obstacles in every direction I looked except for one. The truck stop, four-hundred-yards down the road. Behind the main building was a massive parking area where truckers could stop and get some sleep. A couple of semi-trucks with trailers were sitting dark and abandoned, but there was enough space for two or three helicopters to set down at the same time.

I directed Martinez to the area and when she acknowledged, turned to head back to the SUV. Why stay on foot, exposed to attack, when we could drive the short distance? I had just started to walk back to the Lexus when Dog growled. I froze in place and pressed my eye to the scope, scanning for what he'd detected. Trotting through the breezeway that broke the building into two sections were five razorbacks. They were closer to the SUV than we were.

Rachel had frozen as well, standing close to me, but not so close that she couldn't effectively use her rifle. Moving very carefully, I placed a hand on Dog's head to quiet him and keep him from charging. The breeze was blowing in my face, so we were downwind from the hogs. Hopefully they wouldn't detect us and would go on about their business.

Removing my hand from Dog's head, I held steady aim on the lead razorback as the small group moved into the parking lot. I didn't like our odds one bit if they spotted us. I'd seen how fast they were and even with two of us, I doubted we could bring down all five before they reached us. Rifle steady on target, I pivoted to maintain my aim. Without warning, the lead hog came to an abrupt stop, the other four bunching up behind him.

They had moved parallel to us and it couldn't be our scent that had alerted them. The wind was still wrong for that. Almost as one, all five razorbacks turned their heads and looked in the direction they had just come from. A heartbeat later, Dog growled again as eight infected females at full sprint appeared in the breezeway the hogs had just come through. They most likely had heard the helicopter and minigun and were charging in looking for something to attack.

Transmission

They saw us and started to change direction, but the razorbacks grunted and engaged. The speed of the hogs was breathtaking. They covered the distance to the females in seconds, slamming into bodies and slashing with their razor sharp tusks. Four females went down immediately. A fifth narrowly dodged her attacker and tried to continue on in our direction before being knocked down and disemboweled. Five infected females killed in a span of only a few seconds.

But there were still three of them. Not caring about the carnage being wrought on their sisters, they screamed and zeroed in on us. I snapped off two quick shots, Rachel firing once, and all three of them dropped dead to the pavement. Unfortunately, the sound from our suppressed rifles was loud enough to alert the razorbacks to our presence.

Ignoring the dead and dying females, they turned towards us and charged. From the corner of my eye, I saw Dog leap forward to meet the attack but didn't have time to try and stop him. Flipping the fire selector to burst mode I started putting rounds into the charging swine. Rachel was still close to my left side and had also changed to burst, the expended brass from her rifle bouncing off my head every time she pulled the trigger.

Dirk Patton

The lead hog stumbled and fell and I shifted aim. He might not be dead yet, but he was hurt badly enough that, for the moment, he wasn't a threat. Another one went down from Rachel's fire, then another that I had targeted tumbled to the asphalt. Two were still charging at full speed, inside forty yards, when Dog met them. I aimed for the one closest to Dog, hoping to slow or disable it, but held off pulling the trigger for fear of hitting the wrong animal.

As Dog began fighting the razorback, I targeted the last hog and pulled the trigger. Rachel was also targeting the same one and six rounds slammed into its head at the same time. Its front legs buckled and it fell, skidding to a stop no more than ten feet from us.

Dog was snarling as he fought, the hog squealing and grunting as it tried to get its tusks into the fight. It kept spinning, swinging its head around and slashing, but Dog was faster, avoiding the tusks that would tear him open. He would dash in and bite the razorback's rear leg, clamping down and twisting, trying to break the limb. Both animals were moving fast, swirling around each other as Dog pressed the attack, then moving away before the hog could touch him.

Transmission

I wanted to fire and end the fight before Dog was wounded or killed, but had no shot without risking hitting him.

"Dog! Come!" I shouted, rifle at the ready.

I didn't expect him to listen and was so surprised when he disengaged from the fight that I almost didn't fire. Almost. I pulled the trigger four times as soon as Dog was clear, all twelve rounds hitting the razorback in the head and neck. He snorted, shook his head and tried to take a step forward but collapsed and died.

Dog trotted over and stood between Rachel and me, facing the dead hogs. I kept my rifle up, and Rachel quickly ran her hands over him, checking for injuries.

"Not a scratch on him," she said, sounding surprised.

"Good. Let's move!" I said, heading for the Lexus.

I kept my rifle up and aimed at the bodies, infected females and razorbacks, circling wide around all of them. We piled into the SUV and roared across the parking lot onto the road to the truck stop where Martinez was waiting. Reaching the Stealth Hawk, I left the keys in the ignition and the doors unlocked when I got out.

Dirk Patton

Rachel climbed in first, moving past the door gunner who was alertly maintaining watch on the area, minigun ready to fire if needed. When Rachel was inside, she turned and called to Dog who bounded forward and leapt into the aircraft like it was the most natural thing in the world to him. I followed a little more slowly than Dog, climbed aboard and slid the side door shut.

With the door closed, Martinez goosed the engines and we shot off the ground. I wasn't prepared and lost my balance, falling onto my ass in the middle of the deck. The gunner handed me a headset and I slipped it on, ignoring Rachel's laughter at my tumble.

"What took you so long, sir? I was about ready to come looking for you to make sure you hadn't gotten lost."

I should have been irritated, but something about Martinez always made me smile when she's being a smart ass.

Transmission

22

The flight back to Tinker was uneventful. I had chatted with Martinez for a few minutes; then exhaustion hit me. Using my pack for a pillow, I had stretched out on the hard deck of the Stealth Hawk. Rachel snuggled in next to me, head pillowed on my shoulder and her arm and leg draped over me. Dog curled up on the other side, his back against my hip so I couldn't move without him knowing it. He didn't need to worry. I was out moments after Rachel wrapped around me and didn't know anything until the door gunner woke me by tossing shells from the minigun at me.

At first, I thought there was something seriously wrong with him, but he explained that he had started to reach out to shake my shoulder and Dog had given him a look and growl that scared the crap out of him. Grinning, I extricated myself from Rachel, rubbed Dog's head and moved up to the cockpit. Martinez was flying solo and I slipped into the empty seat, stifling a groan.

"Where are we?" I asked after slipping on the co-pilot's helmet.

"About five minutes out." I looked forward, the image in the helmet's visor showing a brightly lit area a few miles ahead. "They've got all the security lights on. Infected at the perimeter fence. Air didn't know specifics, just that there was a problem."

I watched the base as we approached. We were still too far away to see details without using the helicopter's image enhancers, but the whole area inside the fence was brightly lit, standing out against the mostly dark city it bordered.

"Make a slow orbit of the base before we land," I said. "I'd like to see what's going on before we drop in."

"Yes, sir."

Martinez was all business now, cutting our speed and contacting Air to let them know what she intended to do. A couple of minutes later, we flew over the main gate at a thousand feet. I fiddled with the imaging controls, zooming slightly on the ground below. Several hundred bodies were piled outside the wire, hundreds more infected climbing over them in their attempt to reach the people inside the base. Several Hummers with machine guns were clustered inside the gate, keeping the small herd at bay. There were also plenty of armed Air Force personnel on the ground, milling around behind and beside the Hummers. For my taste,

Transmission

they didn't appear to be taking this seriously enough.

If the size of the herd of infected suddenly swelled, they might be in real trouble. Obviously, people in Oklahoma City were turning. Why hadn't the Air Force put up a couple of helicopters and hosed down the infected? They could take out the entire herd in less than five minutes with a couple of door mounted miniguns.

Martinez followed the fence line as she made the orbit. There were a couple more places where infected had piled up in their attempt to get through the chain link, and there were only two Humvees at each of these locations keeping them from breaching. A few other vehicles and Airmen on foot patrolled the rest of the perimeter, but this was a lackluster response to the threat. It was either someone that didn't know what they were doing, or that refused to acknowledge the severity of the situation and was putting peoples' lives at risk unnecessarily. Where the hell was Colonel Crawford?

Orbit finished, Martinez brought us down in front of the same hangar we had landed at less than twenty-four hours ago when we'd arrived from Kirtland. Three Hummers waited for us. Two of them were stuffed full of Rangers dressed in full battle rattle, the third driven by Captain

Blanchard. Thanking Martinez for the ride, I collected Dog and Rachel and jumped down to the tarmac when the door gunner opened the side door.

"Welcome back, ma'am."

Blanchard had gotten out of the Hummer and walked over to greet us. He looked beyond us, wondering where Jackson was. Not seeing him, he looked at me and I shook my head. His face fell and he nodded.

"How?" He asked.

"Turned," I said. No further explanation was necessary. "Where's the Colonel? The response to the infected at the gate looks like amateur hour."

"Agreed," he said, turning and escorting us to his vehicle. "The Colonel is in a meeting with the base commander and the Security Forces CO at the moment. I'm sure he'll explain their error to them. I've got three platoons of Rangers ready to go as soon as the meeting is over so we can get the threat neutralized before something bad happens."

I nodded, holding the rear door open for Dog and Rachel before climbing into the front with Captain Blanchard. He started the Hummer and pulled out, the two vehicles full of Rangers staying close behind.

"Captain Martinez said there was an all-out effort to find me and get me back here, but she didn't know why. Care to fill me in?" I said.

"We heard from the Russian woman you made the deal with in Los Alamos," he said, then proceeded to tell me about the call from Irina. When he was finished, we were pulling into the parking lot for the base commander's offices. "I'm sure you've got lots of questions, but if you don't mind holding them for the Colonel, I'd appreciate it."

I nodded, stepping out when he parked. There was a platoon of Rangers forming a defensive perimeter around the large building and the ones that had escorted us from the hangar jumped out and joined them to strengthen the line. Blanchard escorted us into the building, stopping before turning down a hall that led to several large conference rooms.

"Ma'am, I took the liberty of having the Air Force assign temporary housing to the Major. Can I escort you there so you can get some rest?"

"Thank you, Captain, but not a chance in hell. I saw those infected at the fence and I don't want to be off on my own if they break through. From now on, where he goes, I go."

Dirk Patton

Rachel tilted her head in my direction and put her hands on her hips, facing Blanchard down. He started to open his mouth, thought better of saying anything and looked at me. I just shrugged my shoulders and smiled.

"Yes, ma'am," he said, quickly turning and leading us down the hallway.

We reached a conference room and I excused myself, Rachel and Dog continuing into the plushy appointed room. In the latrine, I took care of what I had to do, then stepped to the sink to wash my hands. Looking in the mirror, I was surprised at how haggard I appeared. My eyes were hollow, face and head covered with several days of stubble with grime ground into every wrinkle in my skin. There was also a fair amount of gore from the fighting in Los Alamos that I hadn't taken the time to wash off before going out to search for Rachel.

Unslinging my rifle, I laid it on the counter and turned the water on. Leaning over the sink, I started trying to wash my face, neck and head as best I could. I didn't really care if I sat in a meeting covered in filth and stinking to high heaven. I just wanted to clean up and wake up a little bit. While I was bent over the sink, splashing water on my head, the door to the latrine opened and I heard footsteps on the hard tile floor.

Transmission

Looking up in the mirror, I was mildly surprised to see a nattily dressed man heading for one of the urinals. He was in his mid to late thirties with stylishly cut blonde hair that had been left to hang across his forehead in a sweep. He was wearing jeans, but not the kind of jeans I've ever owned. These were designed by someone with an unpronounceable name and had probably cost more than my first car. His shirt fit him beautifully, having been tailored to show off a narrow waist and broad shoulders. Ignoring him, I continued to wash.

"How's it going, sport?" He had finished at the urinal and slapped me on the back as he spoke.

I resisted the urge to pull his arm out of its socket and beat him to death with it, settling for a grunt as I grabbed a handful of paper towels out of the chrome dispenser. He stepped up to the counter to use another sink and I moved my rifle out of his reach. Meeting his eyes in the mirror, I immediately disliked him even more.

Under his blonde hair, he had big, blue eyes and a deep, even tan on a face that was recently shaved smooth. I could smell a subtle aftershave hanging in the air. He had the chiseled features that should be modeling something in a men's magazine, and the biggest, whitest teeth I'd ever seen in person. He looked like someone I'd seen or known before, but I couldn't remember who. And if there weren't already enough strikes against the guy, he was chewing gum with his lips parted so that there was a perpetual smirk on his face.

"Bet he owns a Porsche," I said silently to myself, trying not to smile but failing miserably. He took my smile as an invitation to talk.

"Did you see that smokin' hot piece of ass that just walked in with the dog?" He asked in a voice intended to draw me into the 'we're both men of the world' fraternity. "That's one tasty looking little biscuit, even if she is dressed like GI Jane. Bet she's hell on wheels once that uniform comes off. Tits and ass like that, and a mouth that's made for…"

He never finished the sentence. Without taking my eyes off the mirror, I reached out with my left hand, grabbed the front of his expensive shirt and yanked him off his feet. Twisting, I slammed his back against the tiled wall and jammed my right forearm across his throat. His eyes were as big as dinner plates as I put my face in his, applying enough pressure with my forearm to prevent him from drawing a breath, but not quite enough to damage his larynx. Before I could say anything the door opened again.

Transmission

"Stand down, Major!" Colonel Crawford said in a loud, commanding voice.

He had stopped halfway through the door when he saw what was happening. I took a deep breath and released the man, taking a step back as he bent forward and coughed, trying to gulp air. When he was able to breathe, he stood up and glared at me, the fury in his eyes almost a palpable force.

"Colonel, I want this man arrested!" He said, massaging his bruised throat with a manicured hand, not taking his eyes off of me.

"That's not going to happen, Mr. Cummings. I'm sure the Major regrets his actions and will apologize."

"I don't want a fucking apology. I want him in irons! Don't make me go over your head, Colonel."

He turned and glared at Crawford. The Colonel frowned and stepped the rest of the way into the latrine, letting the door close softly behind him. He kept going until he was inside the man's personal space, looking down at him.

"Let's get something straight right now," Crawford said in a low, dangerous voice. "I will decide when and if one of my people gets arrested. Not you. And all I saw was the Major helping you to your feet after you slipped on a wet tile. You should be thanking him."

The man was pompous, but he apparently was smart enough to recognize when he wasn't going to win a battle. After a moment, he straightened his shoulders, smoothed the front of his shirt and smiled at the Colonel.

"Of course. You're right, Colonel. My mistake. Thank you for your assistance, Major. Now, please excuse me."

He side stepped to get around Crawford and exited the latrine.

"What the fuck was that about?" Colonel Crawford whirled on me. "Do you know who that was? That was the fucking Chief of Staff for our new president, here to second guess everything we do."

"Sorry, sir," I said.

And I was. Sorry, I'd put Crawford in a bad position, again. I wasn't the least bit sorry I'd body slammed the little prick against the wall. He stood there, staring into my eyes.

"I notice you didn't say you won't do it again."

"No, sir. I guess I didn't say that, did I?"

Transmission

Crawford glared at me for a couple more minutes before sighing and dismissing me.

"Get the fuck out of here so I can take a piss in peace."

"Yes, sir," I said, grabbing my rifle and heading for the door.

"Oh, and Major? Try to not hurt anyone else before I get to the conference room," he said, turning to face a urinal.

"Yes, sir. I'll do my best," I said and left the latrine.

Walking down the hall, I slung my rifle and out of old habit shoved my hand into my pocket to make sure I hadn't lost my keys while in a restroom. But, I didn't carry car keys any longer and all I felt was Jackson's dog tag. Shit. The Colonel didn't know. I came to a stop in the hall, debating returning to the latrine and telling him, but finally opting to wait in the hall. He and Jackson went back a long ways. This was going to suck.

23

Crawford took the news about Jackson pretty much like I expected. Pain and sadness passed across his face before he locked down his emotions. He accepted the dog tag, put it in his pocket, asked a few questions and thanked me for making sure Jackson's body was buried.

In the conference room, the man I'd met in the latrine sat on the far side of the table from Rachel. Dog, who usually crashed out as soon as you sat down, was sitting close to her side and not taking his eyes off the new guy. I ruffled his ears and took the chair next to Rachel. As soon as I sat down, Dog wormed his way under the table and lay down with his chin on my boot and tail on Rachel's. We weren't going anywhere without him knowing.

The man's name was Brent Cummings. As the Colonel had said, he was the Chief of Staff for the new President. I was still trying to wrap my head around that. Sure, the US has had Presidents assassinated before, but there has always been a relatively well-known Vice President to take over. For what I was pretty sure was the first time in the two-hundred-and-fifty-year history of the nation, we had gone deep down the line of succession. In fact, according to Captain Blanchard, we had gone nearly all the

Transmission

way to the end of the list. If Kathleen Clark hadn't been salmon fishing in Alaska...

The meeting was mercifully short. Crawford and Blanchard brought me up to speed on events that had transpired while I was out playing with the wildlife. I did, I thought, an admirable job of keeping my mouth shut when they told me about the shoot down of the Antonov. I didn't do a good job of keeping my mouth shut when I learned that Cummings was coming with me to deliver the SADMs to Irina.

My objections were overruled. It seemed the President wanted him to meet Captain Vostov so he could report back on his impressions of the woman. What a crock of bullshit. Something didn't smell right, but I didn't know what it was. Yet. I smiled to myself when I thought what Irina, or Igor, would do to him if he talked about her the way he had about Rachel. The meeting broke up with a reminder that Irina would be calling us back at 1020 the next morning. We were all told to gather in the same conference room at 1000.

Captain Blanchard had secured a small, vacant house for me. The house was part of Tinker's on base housing and had been occupied by a young Lieutenant and his wife. They had been away on leave at the time of the attacks and had never returned. As a Ranger drove us to the house, it was obvious there were a lot of empty homes on Tinker.

Pulling to a stop in front of the structure, he shut the Humvee's engine off and got out to hold the rear door open for Rachel. Dog jumped out and headed for the closest tree.

"I'll be right outside, if you need anything, sir," the Ranger said.

"Crawford tell you to keep an eye on me?" I asked him with a smile.

"Actually, sir, he said the lady has a tendency to get misplaced, and when that happens, you're a pain in his ass. Sir." He grinned back. "I'm here to make sure she doesn't get misplaced again."

Rachel looked like she didn't know whether to be mad or not. I, on the other hand, found it immensely funny and couldn't help but laugh.

"Thank you, Sergeant," I said, leading Rachel up the narrow walk to the front door and calling Dog off his investigation of a thick hedge at the side of the small yard.

The house smelled musty from being closed up for at least a month, but it was spotlessly clean with nothing out of place. None of the previous occupants' personal belongings had been removed, and it felt a little creepy. Like we were invading their privacy. Rachel walked over to the narrow mantle above a small fireplace and looked at several photos of a young couple, smiling in various poses.

Besides the small living room, there was a cramped kitchen, a tiny dining room, a shoebox bedroom with a full sized bed crammed in, and a bathroom no larger than what you'd find in a cheap motel. But it was clean and there were crisp linens on the bed and fluffy towels hanging in the bath.

Dog jumped onto the bed, but Rachel was having none of it when he immediately smeared mud on the white comforter. She told him to get down, which he did, but not without giving her a hurt look and snorting his displeasure. He settled for curling up on a small rug in front of the closet, his back to us.

"We got interrupted before," Rachel smiled and started undressing.

I smiled back, tossed my rifle on the bed and started to step forward to take her in my arms, stopping when she held a hand out like a traffic cop.

"Shower's that way, big boy," she said, pointing at the bathroom. "You smell like... well, you need a shower. Don't worry. I'm not going anywhere."

Smiling, I stripped off my vest and clothes, the stink from several days in the field reaching my nose. She was right. I smelled. Bad.

The shower was small, but I was able to get clean and shave my head and face. It seemed like it had taken forever by the time I stepped back into the bedroom, and I guess it had. Rachel was sprawled out across the entire bed, sheet and comforter pulled up to her waist. And she was sound asleep. Walking to the side of the bed, I gently rolled her over and slipped under the covers with her. Moments later I was out, too, falling immediately into a deep sleep.

I woke up to sunlight at the window, long hair spilling across a pillow into my face and a warm, naked female body pressed tightly against me. I was spooned against her back and felt myself responding to the firm ass that pressed tightly against my groin. Mind wandering, I thought about how many mornings I'd had like this with Katie and my erection disappeared as quickly as it had started.

Before Rachel woke up and expected me to consummate our relationship, I carefully slipped out of the bed. Grabbing a clean pair of underwear out of my pack, I went into the bathroom and silently closed the door behind me. Leaning on the sink, I looked at myself in the mirror.

More years of marriage than I cared to think about and I'd never cheated on Katie. Not because there hadn't been opportunities, or in a couple of cases outright offers, but because I'd just not wanted to. I had loved Katie from the first moment I'd laid eyes on her, and while I might look at an attractive woman, I'd never really wanted to touch another one. Until now.

I wanted to be with Rachel. Not because she was beautiful, which she was, but because I had genuine feelings for her. Of course, being beautiful didn't hurt, but there are a lot of beautiful women that I don't want to sleep with. Right now this felt like I was betraying Katie. Odds were that my wife was dead, but… Hell, I didn't know what the 'but' was.

A loud knock saved me from having to think about it anymore, and I stepped out of the bathroom. Rachel was sitting up in bed, eyes puffy from sleep and covers held to cover her breasts. Dog was already at alert in the front room. The knock came again and I headed for the front door after grabbing my pistol. No, the infected don't knock, but I no longer lived in a world where I was willing to answer the door without a weapon in my hand.

"Good morning, sir." It was the same Ranger that had driven us the previous evening. "Thought you might want to know the volume of infected at the fence has increased overnight. I'm being pulled back to man the defensive perimeter. I'll leave the Hummer here for you."

"Thank you, Sergeant," I answered. "Head or heart shots."

"Sir?" He had started to leave but turned back when I spoke.

"Head or heart is all that will bring them down quickly. Don't waste your ammo on body shots."

He looked at me a long moment.

"Thank you, sir," he finally said and turned to trot off down the tree lined street.

I closed the door and was surprised to see Rachel standing in the small living room. She had pulled the comforter off the bed and had it wrapped around her, holding it closed in front.

"Sorry, I fell asleep last night," she said, letting the comforter fall to the floor and stepping forward. "Do we have time before the call from the Russian?"

I looked into her eyes, then lowered my gaze to her nude body. I couldn't speak, wrought with desire for her, yet still unable to stop thinking that I was betraying my wife. Finally, I shook my head. Thankfully, we really didn't have time.

24

At 1000, we were sitting in the same conference room. I felt like a million bucks after a good night's sleep. Crawford breezed into the room and took his seat at the head of the table. Blanchard was right on the Colonel's heels and Cummings wasn't far behind. The Captain set about initiating a video call with Admiral Packard as Crawford settled himself and flipped open a leather-bound notebook. Cummings studiously ignored me, said a bright good morning to Rachel, then seated himself as far away from me as he could get. Dog was in his usual spot and kept an eye on the Chief of Staff. Good boy!

"What's the infected situation, sir?" I asked.

"We're holding our own. I have to brief the Admiral in a moment, so hang on if you don't mind."

He didn't take his attention off the file he had started reviewing when he sat down. A few seconds later the screen at the front of the room flared and the Admiral stared out at us. Pleasantries were briefly exchanged, then Crawford began his briefing.

Transmission

"Sir, the population of infected in the greater Oklahoma City area continues to grow. Tinker is currently surrounded and in a defensive posture. The only ingress or egress at this time is by air. Current estimates are twelve-thousand infected at our perimeter fence.

"There is also confirmation that the virus has mutated and jumped species. Major Chase encountered several feral hogs yesterday that were infected. They exhibit the same aggressive behavior, though they don't seem to discriminate between attacking infected or uninfected humans. Additionally, the differing effects of the infection on male versus female do not appear to carry over to other species. We have a researcher evaluating this information as well as looking into the possibility of the virus moving to additional species.

"Vaccine production and distribution has begun and is steadily ramping up. As of 0700 this date, all military personnel at Tinker have been vaccinated, and we are in the process of vaccinating all civilians that are on base before commencing distribution to the general population. The vaccine is rather simple to produce. There is a large veterinary medicine manufacturer located here that has a high capacity lab, and we are utilizing its equipment. We are currently producing approximately ten thousand doses per day."

"That's great news, Colonel!" The Admiral broke in.

"Actually, sir, it's not," Crawford countered. "Best estimates are that there are close to two hundred and fifty thousand survivors currently in Oklahoma City. Based on information from the GRU, and our own observations, we do not have time to manufacture and distribute enough vaccine to protect all of them before they turn. Our best guess is anyone not vaccinated has seven days at the most."

Everyone was quiet, doing the math in their head. In seven days we wouldn't have enough vaccine to inoculate even a third of the local civilian population. By the time the vaccine left the production facility and was administered, we'd be lucky to treat a fifth of the population. That meant we were about to have two hundred thousand infected in our back yard.

"Can you hold out against nearly a quarter of a million infected, Colonel?" The Admiral leaned into the camera.

"We're going to try, sir, but we're working on an evacuation plan. Large transport aircraft are being brought in from the civilian airport as well as other Air Force bases in the region to prepare for that contingency. There are also scouts deployed to find suitable locations that are not already either occupied by the Russians, or overrun with infected.

"Additionally, I've been working with the Air Force and sending out patrols looking for stranded military units. We've located a Marine Expeditionary Unit that went ashore in Corpus Christi when their ship experienced an outbreak. There are about fifteen hundred Marines still alive and combat capable. We've dispatched C-130s to pick them up and bring them here. I've also got a team going to Fort Hood to obtain heavy armor and we're collecting all heavy construction equipment in the area."

The Admiral looked like he wanted to ask another question, but it was 1020. An aide signaled to Packard that there was an incoming call.

"Looks like our Russian ally is right on time," Packard said to make sure we knew Irina was calling in. He nodded to the aide, and a moment later I heard her voice.

"Admiral Packard, have you received approval to provide me with what we discussed?" She asked without preamble.

"Yes, Captain. I have," he answered.

"Good. I assume you have Major Chase on the line."

The Admiral looked at me and nodded.

"Hello, Irina," I said. "How's the leg?"

"Hello, Major. It is nothing. Just a scratch, but thank you for inquiring. I am glad your Colonel was able to locate you. Have you been briefed on the situation?"

"Yes. I'm ready," I said, glancing at the laptop screen Captain Blanchard had open next to me.

He would input the coordinates she provided so we could see on a satellite image exactly where I was supposed to meet her. When I'd first heard El Paso, I'd been surprised. Was it coincidence, or was Irina sending a message?

I had grown up in the El Paso area, well outside the city on a large chunk of desert, commuting a long way into town each day to go to school. I knew the Soviets, and later the Russians, had worked hard to create and maintain files on American SF Operators, and there was no reason to think they didn't have one on me. It's just a bit unnerving when someone you don't know has that much detail on you.

Transmission

Irina read off the coordinates, Blanchard quietly tapping them into his computer. A moment later a red dot started pulsing on the satellite image he was displaying. I had him zoom to confirm I was right about the location I'd instantly recognized.

"Do you know where we are meeting?" She asked.

"I hope you're not playing games, Irina," I said. "This is way too dangerous to be screwing around, trying to mess with someone's head."

"No games, Major. I simply thought it would make you more comfortable to meet somewhere you were familiar with. 2200 local time. Tonight. Will you be there?"

"Yes, Irina. I'll be there," I said, exasperation clear in my voice. There were a couple of beeps, and she was gone.

"Care to enlighten us, Major?" Asked Admiral Packard.

"Her coordinates are right in the middle of what used to be my family's land, sir," I said. "There's an old windmill and stock tank at the point where she wants to meet. She's right. I know the area very well."

"How secure is the area?" Crawford asked.

"It's the middle of nowhere, sir. I suppose there could be the odd infected wandering around, but it's either a long, rough hike or you need a sturdy horse, good four-wheel drive or helicopter to get to the spot. It's actually pretty smart on her part," I said, remembering the place vividly.

25

As soon as he got the coordinates from Irina, Blanchard had begun working with the Navy to re-task a satellite and get a good view of the location. He also tasked the Air Force with assigning a Predator drone to the operation and it was on station over the ranch at thirty-thousand-feet within a couple of hours.

I had left him to it. I could probably draw a map of the area from memory. In high school, this was where my friends and I had gone to drink and have fun with our girlfriends. I remembered the area quite well, even after several decades.

Rachel and I had stepped outside after the meeting broke up and had the first fight of our new relationship when I told her she wasn't coming with me.

"You're going to leave me here so I'm safe? That's absolute bullshit! The only time I've been safe since this whole thing started is when I've been with you!"

She was pissed, standing toe to toe with me, her face thrust into mine.

"Rachel, I..."

"Fuck that!" She cut me off without even knowing what I was going to say. "Every time you go off without me, something bad happens. Every. Single. Fucking. Time. I thought I actually meant something to you, but I guess you just see tits and ass when you look at me!"

"Goddamn it!" Now I was getting angry. "I've got to go meet some Russians in the middle of fucking nowhere. Anything could go wrong. Vostov could be under duress, forced to set this up so they can get their hands on me. Infected could show up. I need to be focused on the mission, not worrying about making sure someone I care about is OK! Distractions like that are what get people killed."

"You are the goddamn dumbest smart person I've ever met!" She said, the anger clear in her voice. "When we're together, everything turns out OK. You leave me behind, who's going to save your ass when you get in trouble? That little shit the President is sending along? And what happens here when the infected break through the fence? You're going to leave me here alone to deal with that shit?"

Tears were running down her face, and I thought she was going to hit me. Before she could get that far, I reached out and tried to circle her into my arms, but she was having none of it.

Transmission

"You can really be an asshole, you know that? If you leave me here alone, don't expect me to be waiting for you when you get back! If you get back."

She wiped tears and started to turn away. I grabbed her before she could take a step, gripping both of her upper arms so she couldn't hit me, pulled her close and kissed her. She struggled, twisting and trying to pull away, and I was prepared to defend against a swift knee to my balls. But, fortunately, I didn't have to. After a moment, she pressed against me and lifted her arms to wrap around my neck, the intensity of the moment becoming passion in a kiss.

We might have stood there kissing for a long time if a Humvee hadn't pulled to a stop next to us with a squeal of brakes. I broke the kiss, but kept my arms around Rachel, looking over to see who had just pulled up. Two Marines climbed out of the vehicle. Looked like some of the MEU that Crawford had made contact with had arrived. When I saw the Eagles on one of them, I stepped away from Rachel, came to attention and saluted the Marine Colonel.

"Jesus H. Christ, sir. I guess the Army is harder up than we thought. Looks like they'll make an officer out of anything with a pulse."

Dirk Patton

I dropped the salute and looked at the man who had spoken, a Master Gunnery Sergeant.

"Praise be, we're saved! When the infected see your ugly face, they're just going to lay down and die!" I retorted.

Neither of us had sounded friendly and Rachel had taken a step back. Dog stood up and growled softly in his chest at the two men. I eyed Master Gunnery Sergeant Matt Zemeck, looking him up and down as he did the same to me. I hadn't seen him in nearly ten years, and other than a few more wrinkles and a couple of new scars, he looked the same as when we'd first met in a foreign country.

His unit had been on a mission to - well, never mind what they were doing. They had bad intel from the CIA, as amazing as that may sound, and had walked into a trap and been captured. Most had been captured. Two of them had been killed.

My unit had been in the area and, much to the chagrin of the Corps, had been sent in to rescue them. The rescue had gone off like clockwork at first, then more bad guys had shown up and Zemeck and I had gotten separated with about two hundred screaming fanatics between our units and us.

Transmission

It had taken a week, but we'd fought our way out of the country, saving each other's lives more times than I could count. Time passes, and I'd lost touch after leaving the Army. He was about the last person I expected to run into in the middle of the apocalypse.

I'm not a hugger of other men. It's fine if other guys want to go around pressing their bodies against each other, but I prefer to feel a female form when I give a hug. Unfortunately, Zemeck didn't agree with me. With a laugh, he stepped forward and wrapped arms the size of my legs around me and lifted me off the ground like I was a child. Did I mention he's one of the largest human beings I've ever met?

I remembered one time he had come across a little British convertible sports car that he just had to have, regardless of the fact that he was probably taller than the car was long. Once he finally shoehorned himself into the driver's seat, he draped his left arm down the outside of the door and his knuckles touched the ground. I think I had hurt his feelings when I couldn't stop laughing, but it was just too damn funny.

Dog didn't like seeing me lifted into the air, standing and growling at Zemeck with the fur along his back standing on end. I reached down and rubbed his head, Zemeck taking a step back.

Dog settled down and I kept rubbing his head to calm him.

"Colonel, I suspect you're here to see Colonel Crawford?" I said, glad to see an old friend, but needing to get on with prepping for my flight to El Paso.

"Yes. I was told he's here in the admin building," the Colonel answered. I glanced at his uniform and read his name. Pointere.

"I'll show you the way," I said, motioning for Rachel and Dog to stay put before turning and leading the two Marines into the building.

"That's not Katie," Zemeck said when we were inside.

"No, it's not," I said, a lump forming in my stomach.

It had been threatening to start building since I had woken up earlier in the morning with Rachel's nude body pressed against mine. I had been focused on other things since, but his question reignited my guilt.

"I don't think Katie survived. I was over my house in an Air Force bird a couple of days ago and there's nothing left of it. Whole damn city is either burned or empty. What about Chris?" I asked, referring to his wife.

Transmission

"You know those goddamn annoying talk shows for women where all they do is gossip about celebrities, scream at each other and bad mouth men?" He asked. I nodded my head.

"She was a huge fan of one of them. For the life of me, I can't remember which one. She was in New York with her friends. They had tickets for a taping of the show. She arrived the evening of the attacks."

He spoke with a steady voice, but I could hear the pain he was dealing with.

"Ahhh, fuck. I'm sorry, man," I said, stopping outside the conference room where Crawford had set up his office.

Blanchard saw me and stepped out, welcoming the two Marines and ushering them through the door. Zemeck clapped a huge paw on top of my shoulder, sharing a look with me, then turned and followed his Colonel into the room.

Rachel and Dog were waiting for me when I came back outside. In the two minutes, I'd been gone, Dog had managed to find a large stick and convince Rachel to throw it for him. When I stepped out the door, he was just picking it up and running back to her, changing direction when he saw me and ramming it into my leg. I wrestled the stick away and threw it as far out into an immaculate, grassy field as I could. He raced after it and I walked over to Rachel, who waited for me with her arms crossed and a storm cloud on her face.

"Alright. You win," I said, folding her into my arms.

She relaxed and wrapped her arms around my waist, burying her face in my chest.

"What changed your mind?" Her voice was muffled by my clothing and vest.

"Just take your victory and don't push it!"

I chuckled, not wanting to let on that I'd wanted her to go along all the time. I'd just been worried that something would happen to her. But the brief conversation with Zemeck had all too clearly reminded me that bad things happen to the people we care about, even when they're somewhere we think is safe.

26

Transmission

It's almost six hundred air miles from Oklahoma City to El Paso. We were more than an hour into the flight and I hadn't been able to fall asleep. Damn, air travel is boring when you're awake for every minute of the trip. I sat in the back of the Stealth Hawk, Martinez once again at the controls. She had a young Lieutenant flying co-pilot, so I couldn't even go up front and trade barbs with her to alleviate the boredom.

Brent Cummings, the President's COS sat in a web sling at the rear of the aircraft. He was trying very hard to not make eye contact with me, alternately feigning sleep or reading from a thick file. After the briefing and conversation with Irina, I had seen him wandering around outside the admin building, satellite phone pressed to his ear. Probably complaining to the new president about the thuggish military. Fuck him. If he wants to see thuggish…

The remaining three SADMs were tightly secured at the back of the space, close to Cummings. Rachel was crashed out on the deck, head pillowed on Dog as they both slept soundly. I sat looking at them, wishing we were on a beach somewhere, drinking margaritas and throwing a Frisbee into the surf for Dog to chase.

Dirk Patton

I was sitting there, enjoying the daydream, picturing Rachel in a tiny little bikini when the co-pilot tapped my shoulder. Looking up, still lost in my fantasy, I didn't understand at first what he wanted. Finally, I got the message and stuck my headphone plug into a jack on the bulkhead.

"What's up, Captain?" I asked, talking to Martinez.

"Tinker on the radio for you, sir. Captain Blanchard."

"Thanks," I said. There were a couple of clicks then I could hear an open circuit. "Dog two six here."

"Major, I'm watching a large herd of infected moving across the desert, and they're on a track to pass very close to your RP." He meant rendezvous point. "Current speed and distance will put the leading edge in your area at about 2230 local."

"How large?" I asked, sitting up straight and paying attention.

"Herd's about four miles long and half a mile wide. Best guess is close to three million."

I was quiet for a long moment.

Transmission

"That's most of El Paso and Juarez, or close enough to not matter. What the hell is going on?" I asked.

"Wish I could tell you, sir. They entered the edge of detection for the Predator about half an hour ago, and we're doing flyovers to try and figure that out. I'm trying to get some satellite images from the past few days to see if I can determine what caused it."

"If you draw a straight line along their track, where are they headed?" I asked.

"Stand by."

I could hear some clattering as he typed away on his laptop. After a few minutes, he came back on the radio.

"Straight line leads them here to Oklahoma City," he said, sounding a little shaken.

That's OK. I felt a little shaken, too. What the hell was going on? What could possibly entice a herd of three million infected to set out on a several hundred-mile journey? I had wondered what was driving the herds that had collapsed in on Tennessee from the north, east and south, but hadn't given it that much thought. Maybe it was time for someone smarter than me to figure this out before millions of hungry mouths showed up looking for the buffet in Oklahoma.

"Anything else I need to know?" I asked.

I was confident Colonel Crawford already knew about the herd and didn't feel it necessary to instruct Blanchard to tell him.

"No, sir. I'll update you in a couple of hours."

He disconnected, and the circuit went quiet. I sat there looking at Rachel and Dog, trying to return to my earlier fantasies, but all I could think about was the infected. Why the hell had they converged on Tennessee like that? And now, why were they marching on the largest remaining concentration of survivors in North America? It was almost like there was an intelligence directing them. But how?

Was it possible the smart females were able to control the others? I didn't see how. Besides, even if they could, how the hell would they know to head for Oklahoma? Ridiculous ideas from a lifetime of watching bad science fiction movies went through my head.

The females were psychic and knew the location of a large concentration of survivors. Some alien being was directing their actions. Several other stupid thoughts floated around my mind, then I fell asleep and dreamt of that sandy beach, but the only bikinis were being worn by a pack of infected females.

Nearly three hours later, the co-pilot shook me awake to tell me Blanchard was on the radio again. I had been dreaming I was treading water half a mile off a beach full of infected, and a shark had just shown up. I was glad to leave that world behind, even though the one I was in wasn't any better.

"The herd hasn't changed direction or speed," he said as soon as I turned my headset on. "You're going to have half an hour at the most once you're on the ground."

"Can you slow them down with the Predator?" I asked, stretching my back and groaning internally as muscles protested.

"We had to pull the Predator out of the area. The Russians spotted it and tried to shoot it down. We were able to evade, but if I send it back in they're going to get curious about why we're so interested in that area of the desert."

"Understood," I answered. "What about the back up we discussed?"

"On the way. There were some mechanical issues due to delayed maintenance. They're a little more than two hours behind you."

"Well, hell, Captain. I don't call that backup. Do you?" I asked, sarcastically.

"No, sir. I don't. But it's the best we can do," he answered, sounding impervious to my tone. He was a Colonel's aide. Of course, he was impervious to sarcasm.

"Sorry, Captain. Just tired of operating without anyone watching my ass. Anything else?"

"We've got what we assume is Captain Vostov's helicopter on satellite, in-transit to the RP. Satellite thermal scans show two pilots and three passengers. They should be arriving right on schedule. Other than that, the Colonel wanted me to pass on his wishes for a safe and successful mission."

"Thank him for me, Captain. And thanks for the update. I'll check in once the transfer is complete," I said, shutting down the connection.

Removing the headset, I stood and stretched. Dog opened his eyes and looked up at me, tail lazily brushing across the steel deck. He didn't get up and Rachel continued to sleep, head pillowed on his belly.

"She's going to smell like a dog," I thought to myself, barely suppressing a snort of laughter.

Transmission

Bending over, I rubbed Dog's neck, his eyes closing when I touched him. Cummings was asleep when I checked on him. He was really asleep this time, held into a small jump seat by a harness, head hanging down and swaying with the motion of the helicopter. For a moment I thought about sneaking over and dipping his hand in warm water so he'd piss his pants, then I told the teenage boy part of my brain to shut up and headed for the cockpit.

"Where are we, Martinez?" I asked, sticking my head between the two seats.

"About forty-five minutes out, sir. Had to swing a little to the southeast to stay out of the Russian's CAP. We flew over Midland – Odessa about fifteen minutes ago," she said, raising her helmet's visor and turning to look at me.

"Any signs of life?" I asked.

"A few pockets of light, including a large refinery and a couple of oil rigs lit up like Christmas trees. Was able to zoom in on a couple of them and they're pumping oil. The refinery looked like it was in operation."

That was great news. Fuel stores would start running out soon, but if there was still an oil field and refinery that were functional, we might just be able to put planes in the air a few months from now when the reserves ran dry.

"Did you call it in?" I asked.

"I called it in to Air, but they didn't sound terribly excited."

"Get me Captain Blanchard on the radio again," I said without hesitation.

Close to a minute later the co-pilot gestured and I grabbed my headset and filled the Captain in on what Martinez had just told me.

"Are you sure you want to do that?" He asked. Before I could answer there was a click and Crawford joined the conversation.

"I was listening in, Major, and I concur we need to secure that oil field and refinery, but we can do that after you drop off the packages," Crawford said.

My backup was a hundred Marines from the MEU on board a flight of four V22 Ospreys. The Osprey is a tilt-rotor aircraft that can takeoff, hover and land like a helicopter. Once it's in the air, the engine nacelles tilt and it transitions into forward flight like a propeller driven plane. Many think it's a big improvement over helicopters. Maybe it is if you like the ability to carry more troops, and carry them twice as fast and five times farther than a helicopter. The Marines love them. I'll still take a Huey or Black Hawk to get my ass into a combat zone.

Transmission

"Sir, the Jarheads are far enough behind me that it won't make any difference if they divert to secure the oil production. And it might make a difference if they get there sooner. We both know how quickly things go to shit when the infected show up in numbers," I said.

Crawford was silent for a moment.

"OK, Major. I'll re-task them. Just watch your ass out there. I'm tired of having to come find you."

"No worries, sir. The only river around here is less than five feet deep."

I cut the connection and grinned to myself.

"With a mouth like that, I see why you weren't an officer before the attacks. Sir," Martinez quipped.

"Not all of us make it on affirmative action, Captain," I shot back.

"Sir, I'll have you know I happen to have a great pair of tits and killer legs. Nothing impresses a promotion board like tits and legs."

She laughed. The co-pilot had turned in his seat and was staring at us like we had just suggested committing treason or something else equally horrifying.

Dirk Patton

"Relax, Lieutenant," Martinez said to him. "The way people are dying, you may be a Colonel by this time next month. Laugh when you can. There may not be a tomorrow."

She was joking, but it was also a sad truth. The fastest way to get promoted in the military has always been in time of war. Officers and senior NCOs get killed, and they need to be replaced. While it could take years during peacetime to get promoted, it can happen very quickly when people start dying. It's not the way I ever wanted to move up in the ranks, but it's part of being in the military. At the end of the day, without officers to make decisions and NCOs to make sure those decisions are carried out, the military would grind to a halt.

"We've got about half an hour, sir. We're approaching the edge of the Russian CAP and I'm going to take us down onto the deck for the rest of the flight. You might want to strap in and make sure everyone else back there is too," Martinez said, serious again.

"Thanks, Jennifer," I said, using her given name for the first time.

It wasn't disrespectful. It was letting her know I trusted her, and she was part of the team. She'd earned it in spades when we were in Los

Alamos. The woman had more guts and grit than most men I've ever known.

In the back, I woke Rachel. She stretched and sat up, Dog gratefully standing and shaking to loosen the knots I'm sure he had to have. From the moment Rachel had laid her head on him, he hadn't moved. Somehow, he knew she needed the rest and was willing to give up his comfort for her.

With Rachel strapped in, I seated myself and pulled a harness over my shoulders and chest. Clicking the locks into place, I looked up at Cummings and thought about waking him, but dismissed the idea. He was strapped in, so if he got a little surprise the first time Martinez made a hard turn at speed, well, that would probably be good for him.

27

Roach sat behind the wheel of a Humvee, parked on the far side of a grassy field from where a large group of children were playing. He wasn't watching the children, however. His attention was fully focused on Katie Chase as she constantly moved around the edge of the playground, ensuring the kids were behaving and not doing anything too risky. She was dressed in a pair of Air Force issue uniform pants and a simple tank top, her long hair up in a ponytail that bounced every time she took a step. He was mesmerized by the ponytail, fantasizing about holding it in his hand and using it to control her head as he violated her body.

He had fought with Synthia earlier and had sought out the Major's wife to distract himself. They had not been able to indulge their needs enough to satisfy Synthia, and she was impatient. Petulant. He had explained to her that they were cut off. Surrounded by infected with no way to go back into town with another woman. She had screamed at him, sulking off and slamming the bedroom door like the child she really was.

The thought of following her into the bedroom and slipping a knife into her heart had gone through his head. He had even started to move in that direction, drawing the blade he wore under his left sleeve. At the bedroom door, he had paused as he reached for the knob. If he killed her, what would he do with the body?

Tinker Air Force Base was large, but it was also crowded with both military personnel and thousands of civilian refugees. Someone was always awake and about, and he didn't think he could move the body without being noticed. He certainly couldn't keep it in the house. Within a day, it would start smelling and only grow worse until a neighbor or passerby noticed. With a sigh, he had re-sheathed the knife, turned and walked out the front door.

Driving around to clear his head, he had stopped to watch several C-130's arrive, a dozen V22 Ospreys coming in right behind them. The Marines he'd heard about were here. Great. Even more eyes around to prevent him from playing his games. Moving on, he had intended to just drive by the barrack where Katie was housed, but when he'd seen her outside with the children, he'd had to stop. Now all he could think about was the feel of her naked body squirming beneath him as he punished her for the Major's sins.

Curiosity had driven him to make some discreet inquiries, and he'd been terrified to learn that Major Chase was also at Tinker. And so were the bitch and the dog. How the hell had they all survived? It didn't matter. What did matter was that if any of them got so much as a glimpse of him, he was certain he was dead. The Major would kill him on sight; of that, there was no doubt. Unless, he had some leverage.

It was then that he recognized he didn't want to share that with Synthia. She might be a kindred spirit, but she was a liability. Roach had survived as long as he had because he hadn't taken chances. He only took women that couldn't be traced back to him, and he had never told anyone before Synthia about what he liked to do. She already knew enough to get him arrested and, in today's world, he suspected a court martial would be swift. As would the punishment. It would be his word against hers, and she had the marks on her body that would sway belief firmly to her side. But how to get rid of her?

While he had been thinking, Katie had decided the children had played long enough. With help from a couple of other women, she began rounding them up and herding them towards the barrack. With a sigh, he watched until the last child went into the building, the Major's wife bringing up the rear. She paused at the door, looking around like she felt his eyes on her back. As she stood there in profile, he imagined her naked. The strong, lithe body made oh so feminine by her thick hair, large breasts, and curved hips. Then she closed the door and he lost the mental picture.

Cursing, he started the Hummer and drove off, his erection pressing painfully against his trousers. Driving, he turned his thoughts back to Synthia. The decision to cut his losses with her was already made, he just had to come up with a way to do it without getting caught. Roach didn't want to die, but more than death he feared capture and the humiliation of the spectacle he would become.

People would call him crazy. A psychopath. A serial killer. They wouldn't understand. Wouldn't be able to comprehend his needs. Besides, he had never taken anyone that was worth anything. All the women had been sluts. His first kill, the cheerleader in high school, had slept with most of the football team. Then there had been the party girls. The ones in the clubs in short dresses that would sleep with anyone they thought had money or drugs. There had been prostitutes, too, and none of them had been what society would call virtuous. He had done society a service.

Smiling, Roach pulled to the side of the road. He was at the extreme eastern edge of the base and had stopped next to the water treatment facility. The plant was huge, covering a couple of acres with giant tanks and a veritable forest of pipes. Catwalks circled the tanks and were woven through the piping. Butting against the perimeter of the air base, he could see several places where the narrow walkways extended above the fence.

Still smiling, he turned the wheel and accelerated back down the road. Excitement coursed through his body and he had to force himself to slow down. The last thing he needed right now was to get caught speeding on base. Sure, he'd probably not get a citation like most other drivers, but he'd wind up standing in front of Lieutenant Colonel Lewis, getting his ass chewed up one side and down the other. He didn't need that kind of attention.

Roach had always been a master at controlling his emotions, but this was getting the best of him. He drove fast. Nearly double the posted limit, but made it to his small house without encountering any Security Forces patrols. Parking on the street in front, he jumped out and dashed inside, heart still beating a mile a minute. Synthia was sitting on the sofa, refusing to look at him when he charged inside.

"Come on," he said. "I've got us a way to get off the base."

Transmission

She looked up and smiled, jumping to her feet a moment later.

"I knew you'd think of something! Now? You have someone?" She cried, rushing forward to wrap her arms around him.

"We'll find someone in town. There's plenty of women, and more arriving every day! Are you ready to go?"

The excitement in his voice was infectious and Synthia ran to the bedroom to get her shoes and a large purse with her *toys* inside.

"Let's go!" She said brightly, dashing back into the front room, yanking the door open and running outside.

Minutes later they were driving along the perimeter road. The prospect of a new victim had made Synthia forget her earlier anger. She was bubbly and effusive as Roach drove, describing what she wanted to do this time. He smiled and nodded, laughing with her, again driving too fast but not caring. Reaching the plant, he turned into the parking lot and shut off the engine.

"What are we doing here?" Synthia asked, looking around.

"It's our way out. All the gates are shut, but we can get over the fence here and slip into town," he said, opening his door and stepping out.

"But what about the infected?" Synthia asked, getting out and following him into the maze of pipes and tanks.

"There aren't any here. You'll see. We just have to climb up some scaffolding and then take an emergency exit over the fence."

Roach reached out and took her hand in his, leading her deeper into the facility. Pausing, he looked around and identified the catwalk he wanted. Still leading, he moved onto the metal stairs. Synthia was talking a steady stream as they climbed and started out on a series of grates that were thirty feet in the air.

The walkway curved around the side of a tank and suddenly they were out of the shelter of the pipes. As they continued along the bend, Roach could look down through the grating and see the twelve-foot chain link perimeter fence directly beneath his feet. Half the catwalk and the handrail extended beyond.

A chorus of screams sounded from below and Synthia jerked to a stop, staring down at a seething mass of infected. There was an equal mix of males and females, the females having seen them and becoming agitated. Their excitement spread through the surrounding infected like wildfire. They began slamming against the barrier, making the wire mesh ring as it impacted the steel posts that supported it.

"You said there weren't any infected," she said, starting to look up at Roach.

Before she could complete the turn to face him, he hit her on the side of the head with a leather sap he had drawn from his pocket. Synthia's eyes rolled up as her knees buckled, her body collapsing to the metal grating.

"I lied," Roach said, slipping the sap back into his pocket and ripping her purse open.

Inside, he found two knives, a pair of pliers and a small butane torch that would normally be used to lite cigars. Synthia didn't smoke cigars. He took the knives and pliers, putting all of the items into his pockets. If by some miracle her body was found and recovered, he didn't want any weapons found on it. Not that the times didn't justify a young lady arming herself with whatever weapon she could find, it was just one of the small details that he paid attention to.

Squatting, he worked his arms under her body and stood with her cradled against him.

Stepping forward, he grunted as he lifted her to clear the handrail, her eyes fluttering open.

"What are you…" She started to say, but the words turned into a brief scream when he dropped her to the waiting mouths below.

Synthia struck one of the males, knocking him to the ground and coming to rest on top of his body. Before she could move, several females fell on her, almost sounding delighted in their screams. She screamed once more, but it was brief, cut off when a female locked her teeth on Synthia's throat. Roach stood staring down, fascinated. And strangely aroused at the orgy of blood that was taking place just beneath his feet.

"Don't have to worry about body disposal anymore," he mumbled to himself, turning to head back to the Humvee, then freezing when he saw he was being watched.

A man was on an adjacent catwalk, dressed in a set of blue coveralls with Tech Sergeant stripes on the sleeves. He stared at Roach with his mouth open in a silent 'O' of shock at what he'd just witnessed. Roach mentally screamed at himself for not having made sure there weren't any maintenance workers on site before killing Synthia.

He didn't move at first, standing as still as the shocked man. Flicking his eyes around, he

Transmission

found the path to get to the other catwalk and started walking forward with his empty hands raised in a calming gesture.

"It's not what it looks like," he shouted to the man. "She was infected. Just starting to turn. I had to get rid of her before she killed someone."

While he was talking, Roach had covered half the distance to the connecting walkway that led to the one the man was standing on.

"I didn't have a choice. She was going to become one of them!"

Roach pointed at the mass of writhing bodies on the other side of the fence and the man automatically turned his head and looked down at the infected. As soon as his attention was diverted, Roach sprinted. He reached the connecting walkway, made the turn at speed by grabbing onto the handrail and charged the man. Drawing one of Synthia's knives he ran with it held low, ready to thrust upwards in a killing strike. The man finally recognized the danger and turned to run.

But he had waited too long and allowed Roach to draw too close. He took three steps when Roach thrust the knife into his lower back. The ten inch, razor sharp blade sliced into his kidney which immobilized the man by instantly throwing his body into severe shock. Roach pushed him down onto his face, pulled the knife out and stabbed two more times to make sure he wasn't able to move or fight back.

Grabbing the man's feet, he dragged the body along the catwalk until he was back at the spot where he had thrown Synthia over. Looking down, he could see what remained of her corpse, shocked at how much had already been consumed by the infected. Working his arms under the man, he avoided the blood as best he could and levered the body up to balance on the handrail. It teetered for a moment before tipping fully over and crashing onto the heads of the infected that were still feeding on Roach's earlier offering.

Transmission

28

Martinez brought us in fast and low. She made a sweeping turn around a couple of hills, flaring at the last moment and landing next to the stock tank I remembered so well. We were thirty minutes early, but needed every last second. Slamming the side door open, I jumped out on the sand. A brand new, fresh from the box, pair of NVGs let me see everything. I took full advantage of them and scanned the area, happy when I didn't detect anything to worry about.

I moved away from the aircraft, which was Rachel's signal to come out and a moment later she and Dog jumped down. She also had a new set of NVGs, and Dog... well, he didn't need any. Cummings waited until she was well away from the Stealth Hawk before following. I didn't like him, and Dog had instantly picked up on that, so Dog didn't like him. Dog would growl at him if he made any sudden moves or got too close to Rachel or me.

He had protested Dog coming along, but I'd told him I'd leave his ass behind before I did Dog's. He'd seen something in my face to convince him to drop the entire subject. Perhaps he was worried about me leaving him stranded in the West Texas desert.

Dirk Patton

On the far side of the flat area, I could see a large, earth colored object that looked like a partially deflated water balloon. In a way it was. It was a fuel bladder that an Air Force tactical team had dropped here several hours ago, flying in and out in a stripped down Pave Hawk. The Stealth Hawk we were flying didn't have the range to get us here and back home to Tinker, and with passengers, we had no room for one of the fuel bladders. In fact, we'd come in on fumes.

The team that had brought the fuel had carried two bladders. One to leave for us, the other to refuel their helo so they could get back. Now, we had to get our aircraft fueled in a hurry. I didn't want it on the ground when the Russians arrived. Looking over my shoulder, I motioned at the cockpit and Martinez and her co-pilot jumped out. I helped them stretch out a hose and connect it to the bladder and the helicopter.

While they handled the fueling process, I unloaded the SADMs, stashing them at the base of the old windmill. The Stealth Hawk finished fueling in twenty minutes. We got it disconnected from the bladder and I helped Martinez disconnect from the aircraft's fueling port.

"Watch your ass, sir," she said. "I won't be far if you need me."

Transmission

"Keep an eye on that herd with FLIR," I said. "If they start heading this way, come get us."

This was already the plan, but I felt better reinforcing it. A couple of minutes later, the helicopter lifted off and I was glad for the NVGs protecting my eyes from the storm of sand and debris that the rotor churned up. Cummings, to whom I hadn't issued any, turned his back and covered his face. He also didn't have a weapon.

He'd thrown a fit when I vetoed his request for a rifle, claiming he knew how to use one. I didn't care if he was the best fucking shot in the world, I didn't trust him with a weapon. He'd gone over my head, complaining to Crawford, but the Colonel had supported my decision and shut him down.

In less than thirty seconds, I could no longer hear the helicopter. I shook my head in amazement at how quiet the damn thing was. Scanning the area again, I was glad to see it was still clear of infected.

"So this is where you used to bring your girlfriends. Not very romantic, is it?"

Rachel had stepped up beside me and was keeping watch on the area to my rear.

"Oh, I don't know. I used to do pretty good here. Something about the spot. Got you here, didn't I?"

She didn't say anything, but a moment later a sharp elbow struck my lower back. Good thing I was wearing a plate carrier vest with ballistic plates.

"Ouch!" Rachel muttered, rubbing her bruised arm. "Why didn't you remind me you were wearing body armor?"

"That would take all the fun out of it," I answered, then our banter ended when we heard the sound of a distant, heavy helicopter rotor.

It wasn't Martinez. The Stealth Hawk didn't make that much or that kind of noise. Had to be our Russian friends. Moving quickly, I put Cummings and Rachel behind the stock tank and told them to keep their heads down until I called. Dog and I settled behind a large pile of boulders at the edge of the area.

The sound of the helicopter kept growing louder and I was finally able to see it with night vision. It was a Russian Hind MI-24, complete with stubby wings and a whole lot of missiles. Basically a flying tank. It was a dated design, but still as deadly as the day it was drawn up by the Soviets.

Transmission

The Russian circled once before coming into a hover and gently setting down where Martinez had landed. The Hind's rotor was significantly larger than the Stealth Hawk's, which meant a lot more sand got blown up into the air. For a moment, that was all I could see, then the rotor slowed and the air began to clear.

My rifle was up and aimed at the helicopter, but unless someone got out, I knew I'd just be wasting bullets if I decided to shoot. The Hind is heavily armored and light weapons like the M4 can't hope to cause any damage. Well, I might be able to chip his paint a little if he really pissed me off, or maybe flatten one of the landing gear tires.

The side door slid open and Irina Vostov jumped down, favoring her injured leg. She was dressed in clothing more fitting for the environment than the skirt and lab coat I'd last seen her in. Despite dressing for the circumstances, she'd revealed her vanity by selecting camo pants that hugged her curves and a skin tight black shirt. Her blonde hair glowed where it spilled across the black fabric. She wasn't armed, but right behind her came Igor and the other Spetsnaz soldier I'd met in Los Alamos. They both had sound suppressed AKMS rifles up and ready, looking around through NVGs.

Dirk Patton

Telling Dog to stay put, I slowly stood, rifle hanging on its sling and my hands out to my side. Igor spotted me instantly and started to swivel his rifle in my direction, but caught himself in time when he recognized me. He pointed me out to Irina and they began walking in my direction. I shoved the NVGs off my face and met them half way across the open space.

"Did we really need to meet all the way out here?" I asked Irina by way of greeting.

"Aren't you happy to see me, Major?" She asked with a smile. "I thought you liked bringing girls to this spot."

She leaned in and kissed me on each cheek. I stared at her for a long minute. Her eyes were twinkling and the corners of her mouth were turned up in a small smile.

"I won't bother to ask how you know that," I said.

"I don't mind telling you," she responded with a laugh. "Those days are over. The days of us spying on each other. Killing each other. Like the KGB Colonel you killed in Afghanistan. That kill brought you to our attention for the first time, and we spared no effort to find out everything about you. You should see your file. It's quite impressive."

Transmission

"I'd love to get a look at it," Rachel said from behind me.

I let out a long, mental sigh. Reminder to self. Leave the girlfriend at home when you're on a mission. If you don't, she'll forget everything you've taught her as soon as she sees you talking to an attractive woman.

I performed the introductions, to a degree. Irina didn't need to know anything about Rachel. Dog had come out when Rachel had walked up behind me and, to my chagrin, he immediately took to Igor. Within minutes of meeting, he was on his back getting his belly scratched, giving me a look that said, "don't you wish you were the one doing this?" Fucking traitor.

Reminding myself about the approaching herd of infected and that time was short, I waved Cummings forward and introduced him to Irina. She held her hand out and he took it, holding it well beyond the amount of time dictated for a professional greeting. Irina pulled hers away and wiped it on her pants. I couldn't tell whether it was a subconscious act, or intentionally sending a message.

"And why is it you are here, Mr. Cummings?" She asked, a frown creasing her forehead.

"I am the Chief of Staff for the President of the United States," he said in a pompous voice. "She has asked me to meet with you to lodge a formal complaint in regards to the unprovoked attacks on the United States by the Russian Federation."

"Excuse me?" She stared at him with her mouth open and I realized I was doing the same. "Do you understand what I'm doing and why I'm here?"

"We understand perfectly," he said, crossing his arms across his chest. "And while the military may support your actions, I'm afraid the President does not. She would like to resolve this diplomatically. In fact, she is in contact with President Barinov and is working out terms that are mutually beneficial to both of our countries."

I didn't believe what I was hearing. It was like one of those dreams where everything is so surreal that you can't move or speak. This douche bag was telling us that the new president was betraying us to the goddamn Russians. Stunned, I looked at Irina who appeared to be as completely mystified.

"What the fuck are you talking about, Cummings?" I growled, anger pulsing through me. Had this idiot and his boss betrayed us?

Transmission

"The President has decided that we're better off to work with the Russians than fight them," he said in a condescending tone. "She's working out the details right now and will be flying to Moscow in a couple of days to meet with President Barinov. I'm here because we knew Admiral Packard and Colonel Crawford would never stop fighting, even with a Presidential order. It's my job to put an end to the United States military involving itself in Russia's internal problems."

I stepped in and grabbed him by the straps of his ballistic vest and pulled his face into mine.

"What did you do?" I asked in a low voice.

He still didn't show fear, only the supreme confidence and arrogance of someone who thinks they know better than anyone else. Uh oh. A man like Cummings wasn't brave by nature. I knew his type, having encountered plenty of them, both during my time in the Army as well as the corporate world.

He was what I called a paper warrior. He played his games behind the scenes, striking deals and betraying people who thought they could trust him. These types of people didn't stand up and exhibit a backbone unless they had an ace in the hole. Unless, they knew someone had their back.

"Civilians are back in control of the American military, and we will not allow the hawkish actions of a few officers to continue. It's time to start acting like civilized people again," he said with a sneer.

I lifted him off his feet and shoved, sending him sprawling onto the dirt.

"Move and I'll kill you!" I said, finally seeing a flicker of fear cross his face.

"Igor," I said, lowering the NVGs over my eyes and turning to look around.

Igor was a well-trained operator and didn't need to have it explained. He dropped his goggles over his eyes and raised his rifle. Before we spotted anything, a shot sounded, and the other Russian soldier was punched off his feet by a bullet that took off most of his head.

Transmission

29

Igor grabbed Irina and I grabbed Rachel. We all ran for cover of the large rocks I had been behind when the Russians had landed. I noted that Cummings was running out into the desert, towards the firing that was directed at us, but didn't have time to do anything about it at the moment. Bullets were spattering off the rocks, and I spun to run backwards and fired a long burst of full auto fire out into the desert. I didn't have a target, but hoped I could make our ambushers keep their heads down long enough to reach safety.

A bullet smashed into my chest, knocking the wind out of me and I stumbled, nearly falling. Igor had already propelled Irina behind the rocks and pulled me to safety as more rounds struck all around us. I reached to where I'd been shot, thankful for the ballistic plate in my vest that had stopped the bullet. It had still hurt like a son of a bitch and if I didn't have a broken rib, I certainly had a bruised one. But I didn't have a hole in me, and I was still alive.

The Russian pilot had started the Hind's engines and the rotor was just starting to spin when I heard the distinctive sound of an RPG being fired.

Dirk Patton

"Down!" I screamed, wrapping one arm around Dog and the other around Rachel a second before the high explosive struck the helicopter's rotor housing.

The explosion was loud and violent, but the helicopter had been designed to withstand this very type of attack. Its hull was dented and burned, but the rotor continued to speed up. Moments later there were two more RPGs fired in series, the first to arrive penetrating the windshield and destroying the cockpit and everything in it. The second one struck the rotor head and sheared it off, sending it spinning away to smash into the windmill, which collapsed under the impact.

Cummings was still running. Fleeing towards the ambushers that I could only assume were Russian troops sent by Barinov to put an end to the coup. Raising my rifle, I hesitated a moment. This was the fucking White House Chief of Staff, which meant I was only a step removed from pointing a weapon at the President. Then I remembered my oath when I'd enlisted in the Army.

Well, I remembered part of it. The part about defending the country against enemies, both foreign and domestic. Fuck it! We had an unelected president plotting with an invading enemy to ambush American forces. I don't know

Transmission

what the original intent was when the whole domestic enemy thing was added to the oath, and I didn't care. As far as I was concerned, betrayal deserved only one response.

But I had spent too long making my decision. More enemy fire started hitting the rocks and I had to duck behind them without putting a bullet in Cumming's well-barbered head.

"What the hell?" Rachel shouted in my ear.

"Son of a bitch betrayed us!" I said. "Him and the President. There's a team of Russians out there sent to take us out and get the SADMs secured so they can't be used."

Irina and Igor were also having a conversation in rapid Russian. She looked worried. He looked pissed off. I was curious. Our attackers had RPGs. The rocks we were behind would provide some protection, but not enough. Why weren't they attacking?

"Why didn't we see them?" Rachel asked, fear making her eyes large. She sat hunched low to the ground, both arms wrapping Dog into a hug.

"They were in place ahead of us," I answered. Irina and Igor had finished their conversation and were watching me, listening. "Night vision only lets us see what we could see in the day. It's not magical. They can still conceal themselves. They're probably also using thermal blankets to hide their body heat from the FLIR in the Stealth Hawk."

Irina nodded her head. "That's what Igor thinks as well."

Before she could say anything else, a male voice speaking Russian shouted out. Irina and Igor tilted their heads to listen. After a few moments, she turned to me and translated.

"It is Colonel Kirov. He is my commanding officer. He knows I am here and orders me to surrender immediately," she said in a quiet voice.

Fear, whether of the man or the situation I couldn't tell, was apparent in her face.

"So he's GRU. How many soldiers will he have with him?" I asked.

Irina consulted with Igor before answering.

"He'll have at least one squad of seven. Possibly two. He likes to do things on a grand scale, so it wouldn't surprise me if he brought two squads when he only needs one."

Transmission

"Spetsnaz, or regular Army?" I asked, shrugging out of my pack and starting to remove the ballistic plates from my vest.

"Spetsnaz. Definitely," she answered. "What are you doing?"

"You're forgetting, Irina. I grew up here. I know this country like the back of my hand. They don't. Would you ask Igor if I can borrow that laser designator he has attached to his rifle?"

I continued to lighten the load on my body so I could move quickly and quietly in the dark.

"You're not doing what I think you're doing," Rachel said, but Martinez' voice in my earpiece distracted me.

"Dog two six," I answered her, glad we were using encrypted radios the Russians couldn't eavesdrop on.

"You must be having a hell of a party down there. The herd has changed direction and is coming straight for you."

Damn it! The RPGs, gunfire, and exploding helicopter had been loud, alerting the herd to our presence.

"How long?" I asked, reaching out and taking the small laser unit from Igor, nodding my thanks.

"You've got fifteen minutes at the most before you have a whole wave of sprinters crashing the party. Ready for extraction?"

"Negative."

I spent half a minute filling her in on what had happened and what I was going to do. Irina spoke softly to Igor, translating what I was doing. With confirmation from Martinez that she was ready, I shared the rest of my plan with Irina and handed her one of the SADM keys. She took it and wished me luck, then turned to Igor to explain in Russian.

"Stay with Irina," I said to Rachel.

She reached out and took my hand and I could tell she wanted to say something. Maybe argue my plan, maybe not. Either way, I didn't give her the chance, turning and crawling towards the rock face to our rear.

As I moved, Irina shouted back to Colonel Kirov. Her job was to keep his attention focused on her. It was apparent that they wanted her alive. I was almost certain they wanted to take her back to Russia for a very public trial and execution. A reminder to anyone else with treasonous thoughts of what happens when you plot to overthrow the government.

Transmission

The rock face I crawled towards looked like a solid, vertical chunk of stone that stuck up out of the sand. It was actually two solid, vertical chunks with a narrow path between them that was well hidden. A thorough and time intensive search of the area would have found it, but I seriously doubted the Russians had gone to that level of effort. I knew it was there because on more than one occasion I'd used it when I was a teenager.

Leading deep between the two massive hunks of sandstone, it twisted, turned and climbed until reaching the highest point for at least ten miles in every direction. That high point was a great place to spread out a horse blanket and "watch the stars" with a girl.

What I didn't remember was just how narrow the damn path was. Guess I'm a little bigger than I was when I was sixteen. Several times, I had to force my way through when the path narrowed, and once I had to remove my vest to squeeze my body between two boulders. Behind me, I could hear Irina shouting in angry Russian, still keeping the Colonel occupied. At least I hoped she was keeping him busy and he hadn't already sent his troops forward to capture or kill my friends.

Dirk Patton

A faint sound from behind caused me to stop and spin, but it was just Dog, nails scraping on a rock.

"What the hell are you doing here?" I asked him in a low voice.

He looked at me and wagged his tail, then came up and bumped my leg with his head.

"OK, let's go," I said after almost telling him to go back and stay with Rachel. Then I heard another sound and I didn't even have to turn my head to know who it was.

"You can't do anything you're told to do, can you?" I asked Rachel as she slipped easily between the boulders that had given me problems.

"We'll discuss the fact that you're not in charge later," she said. "Right now, we'd better get moving. It's already been five minutes."

Shaking my head, I kept going, soon reaching the part where we climbed. A few minutes later we emerged on top of a giant rock. Dropping to my stomach, I motioned Rachel down and crawled to the edge that overlooked the ambush site. With the NVGs back in place, I had a view that would be the envy of an owl. I could clearly see the Colonel that was talking to Irina, and in a large semi-circle around him were

Transmission

twelve soldiers. That meant there were probably two more I couldn't see, and it was those two that worried me.

Sniper team? Or were they advancing on Irina and Igor? I kept looking, spotting Igor just arriving at the debris that was all that remained of the windmill. He was crawling on his belly, using the minimal depressions in the terrain to stay hidden. Irina was still huddled behind the rocks. I could clearly hear her voice, and she was quite animated.

Turning and looking farther out, I scanned again. Where would I be? Three hundred yards away, another group of large boulders sat tumbled together. Taking my time, I checked every horizontal surface, nook and cranny, finally spotting the two-man team. They had a commanding view of the ambush site, the sniper with his rifle trained on the rocks Irina sheltered behind.

Moving slowly, I positioned the laser on the flat rock in front of me and turned it on. A focused beam of light that was invisible to the naked eye shot out and struck the rock a few feet below the sniper's position. It was clearly visible in the NVGs and I took a moment to adjust it until I was illuminating the rock about a foot below the two Russians.

Dirk Patton

"Boomer three, Dog two six," I said softly into the radio.

"Boomer three. Better step it up, sir. Females at your location in five," Martinez answered immediately.

"Copy. Target is painted. Red force is now exposed and oriented southeast to northwest," I said.

"Fox one," Martinez replied a few moments later.

She must have been close because it was only a couple of seconds before the Hellfire missile arrived, homing in on the reflected laser light. The warhead struck the rock a foot below the two men, but it could have hit ten feet away and had the same effect. The detonation killed both men and vaporized their bodies and equipment a fraction of a second after the missile's arrival. It also blew a chunk the size of a truck out of the side of the massive boulder.

I quickly moved the laser to shine on the GRU Colonel's chest, noting that Cummings was standing next to him. Both men were staring at the rocks where the Hellfire had detonated.

"Target two painted," I said quickly.

Transmission

"Fox two," Martinez answered almost instantly.

Kirov knew what was coming and started running. But it was too late. The missile faithfully homed in on the laser and struck the ground a few feet behind him and only a couple of feet to Cumming's left. Both men and a couple of the Spetsnaz were blown into a few million pieces in the blink of an eye.

Martinez had been close, the Stealth Hawk streaking overhead only a few seconds behind the Hellfire. Immediately opening up with a minigun, she began shredding bodies. Three more Russians went down under the withering fire, but these were trained, combat hardened troops. They didn't break and run, nor did they freeze under the attack.

Ground fire erupted as all of the ones still alive targeted the helicopter. I had my rifle up and ready, drilling the grenadier a few moments later when he raised an RPG in the direction of the attacking Stealth Hawk. Martinez looped out of range of their weapons, and I checked on Igor. He was looking in my general direction and waving. He was ready.

"Extraction now!" I called on the radio, turning the laser to reflect off the ground at my feet so Martinez could spot me easily with her night vision.

Circling the area, she approached from behind and brought the big helicopter into a hover behind the protection of the rocks. We ran, Rachel hopping through the open door then turning to grab Dog when I lifted him up. I scrambled aboard and shouted for Martinez to go.

She spun the aircraft and the deck tilted. I started sliding out the door, catching myself at the last moment by grabbing on to a flailing safety tether. Pulling myself back in, I snapped it in place and shouted at Rachel to hold on tight to Dog as I dug a Fast Rope extraction line out of a locker.

Clipping it into place, I kneeled at the open door, ready to push it out as we came into a hover over Igor's position. The minigun fired again and I heard a couple of pings as Russian bullets hit the helicopter. Kicking the line out the door, I watched it uncoil and hit the ground a few feet from Igor's prone body. He fired another burst at the ambushers before jumping up and dashing to the rope.

He got his foot in a loop in record time and Martinez lifted him off the ground and moved to Irina's position. She dropped a little altitude and Irina dashed for the line and Igor's waiting arms. He wrapped her up after getting her foot in a loop and, on my shout, Martinez spun us around and climbed to clear the rocks. Just before we were out of sight, there was another ping followed by a loud explosion from the tail of the Stealth Hawk.

Even over the roar of the engines, rotor and air flowing through the open door, I could hear Martinez start cursing in her native tongue. A moment later the helicopter began vibrating, the shaking rapidly growing worse.

"Oh shit!" Rachel yelled.

I snapped my head around to see what was wrong. She was staring through her NVGs out of the open side door. I looked and the breath caught in my throat. A seething mass of infected was directly beneath us, stretched out for miles. The size of the herd had been described to me, but nothing prepares you for seeing three million infected people, all moving together with the sole intent of killing every living thing in their path.

30

Frantically pulling on a headset, I shouted into the mic the moment it was on my head.

"Martinez, talk to me."

"Tail rotor damage," she answered, strain apparent in her voice. "I'm barely keeping us in the air. We don't have long."

"Get a call out while we're airborne," I said. "The Marines should be getting close to Midland. They can come get us if you can get some space from this herd."

She didn't answer, but I was confident she was on top of things. I also had no doubt that she needed every bit of concentration to keep us in the air. Checking on the infected, I looked back out the door and was dismayed to see we were still flying over the herd. Leaning out, I made sure Igor and Irina were hanging on. They were, and I didn't worry too much about them. Igor seemed very protective of his Captain, and I suspected he would hold on as long as there was an ounce of life in his body.

We cleared the edge of the herd a minute later, but it seemed like we were losing altitude. The shaking was growing worse and a high-pitched roar from the tail section had started up.

Transmission

Leaning back out the door, I looked behind and estimated we were about two miles from the infected. Not nearly far enough with the speed and endurance of the females. They'd run us down within an hour, even with a two-mile head start.

Another few minutes of flying and it felt like the helicopter was going to shake itself to pieces, and us with it. Rachel had squeezed herself into a corner, Dog wrapped in her arms and sitting in her lap. A quick check to verify our Russians were still with us and I spoke to Martinez.

"Did you reach the Marines? I asked.

"Two and a half hours away, best case," she said through clenched teeth.

"How much longer can you keep us in the air?"

"You want to land, we're out of time. Crash, maybe two minutes. If we're lucky," she gasped.

"Put us down," I ordered. "And don't forget our passengers hanging around below us."

We immediately began losing altitude, faster than I liked, but I was sure Martinez was doing everything she could. Our speed came off until we were barely moving as we descended. Realizing what she was doing, I leaned out the door and watched. As we continued down, the end of the line brushed the ground, more of it quickly coming into contact with the desert floor and dragging through the sand.

I could see Igor tighten his big arm around Irina and lift her out of the loop she was standing in. Damn that guy was strong. Timing it just right, he dropped her when they were only a couple of feet in the air. She hit and tumbled across the ground, Igor jumping a moment later and rolling to a stop next to her.

"Clear!" I shouted on the headset and Martinez brought us the rest of the way down.

To say it was a good landing would be kind. But then I've always heard pilots say that any landing you walk away from was a good landing. I guess I can't really argue with that, but we hit hard. Bone jarring, teeth clacking, spine compressing hard. Disconnecting my tether, I grabbed Dog from Rachel and pushed him out the door. Unhooking her, I pushed her too before sticking my head into the cockpit to make sure Martinez and the co-pilot were OK.

They had already shut down the engines and had their doors open, ready to get out. I didn't waste another moment, following Rachel

Transmission

and Dog out the side door. Irina and Igor ran up and I turned as the two pilots joined us.

"How far from the herd?" I asked Martinez.

"Just over four miles. You think they'll follow?"

"Some of them are. I was watching. There's a lot of them going on to the battle site, but the whole edge on this side started peeling off and following when we flew over. We were loud as a washing machine and really got their attention." I checked my watch. "The first females can be here in far less than an hour. We've got to move and hope the Marines don't stop off for a beer."

We spent two minutes gathering supplies and equipment from the helicopter and distributing it so that everyone was equally loaded. Then I squatted down over the backpack that Igor had rescued from the windmill. Pulling the flap open, I checked the serial number and pulled out the correct key. Energizing the unit, I paused.

How long did I set it for? How soon would the leading edge of infected be here? And how many of them? I didn't want it going off too soon and only killing a handful of the fastest females. On the other hand, I didn't want it going off too late with thousands of them already past and hot on our trail. For that matter, I wasn't even sure we had anything to worry about.

By the time the infected arrived we should be at least a couple of miles away. Why was I worrying about them following us when we had enough space between us that they couldn't possibly know where we went?

"Because you plan for the worst and hope for the best, dumb ass," was the answer that went through my head.

Making my decision, I set the yield to max, or one kiloton, and the timer to forty-five minutes. I had also debated what yield to use, racking my brain to remember the training I'd received. A one KT, or one kiloton, nuclear detonation is equivalent in force to one thousand tons of TNT. A ground level blast will create a lethal shockwave out to a radius of five hundred meters. The fireball, which burns at one million degrees Fahrenheit, is deadly up to six-tenths of a mile. Then, there's the initial pulse of radiation as well as secondary fallout.

The initial pulse would be lethal at a radius of half a mile, even though it would take a few agonizing hours to die. Secondary fallout at three and a half miles, but this time there would be several painful days of skin, hair and teeth

Transmission

falling off your body as your organs shut down. Bearing in mind that all of these were *minimums*, and hoping that I was remembering accurately, it was time to haul ass. I wanted to be at least four miles away when the damn thing detonated. Nuke ready to go, I lifted it up and set it inside the Stealth Hawk. Then we ran.

Igor and I may not have spoken the same language, but we were both soldiers and understood the concept of fast movement with a small group. I took point and set the pace, Igor taking rear guard. Dog ran next to me, though to be fair he trotted. I can't move fast enough to make Dog actually run. Rachel tucked in behind us with Irina, Martinez and her co-pilot filling in the middle.

It was my job to make sure we were moving fast enough to reach all of the minimum safe distances when the SADM detonated. It was Igor's job to make sure no one fell behind. He would poke, prod or kick ass as needed. Oh, and we also had to keep our heads on a swivel for any infected. Assuming that the only ones in the area were in the herd would be foolish and potentially suicidal.

I started us off fast. Before the attacks I spent a lot of time in the gym, lifting weights and running on a treadmill. Normally, I'd start out with my first two miles at six miles an hour, then play with the speed after that to break up the monotony. My body was still familiar with that routine and I settled into what I was confident was a six-mile per hour pace. After five minutes I checked over my shoulder. Irina and the co-pilot were already showing signs of distress. Martinez looked as relaxed as always and Rachel gave me a smile.

Turning back to the front, I scanned our surroundings as I ran. Sand, rocks, and cactus were all I saw other than an occasional coyote. Dog either saw or smelled his four-legged cousins, growling as he trotted along at my heels. I was glad he didn't decide it was a good idea to engage the animals. The last thing I needed was to have to go chasing after him.

Fifteen minutes, or a mile and a half into our run, I stopped when there was the sound of a body falling behind me. Irina had tripped and gone down. Not seeing anything other than smooth, hard sand, I imagined she was already at the limit of her endurance. Igor stepped forward and helped her to her feet. I raised the NVGs and looked at her face. She was spent.

I met Igor's eyes and he nodded, shrugging his pack off and handing it to me. My pack was still at the site of the ambush where I'd dropped it to set up Martinez' attack, so I slipped his over my shoulders. Igor stooped, pressed his

Transmission

back against Irina and grabbed her legs before straightening up with her in a piggyback carry. He bounced her a couple of times to make sure he had a solid grip then nodded he was ready to run again.

I was starting to turn back to the front when there was a brilliant flash of light on the horizon behind us. It was the SADM Igor had armed and left at the site of the ambush. Hopefully, several hundred thousand infected had pushed into the area looking for the source of the noise and had just been atomized by the blast. We stood rooted in place, watching for a few moments as the incredibly hot fireball boiled skyward and created a mushroom cloud. Rachel came to stand next to me and took my hand in hers.

"It's getting old watching nukes go off with you," she whispered, eyes glued to the specter in the distance.

I squeezed her hand but didn't know what to say. Settling for putting more distance between the second bomb and us, I got everyone running again. This time, I moderated the pace a bit in deference to Igor's burden and moved Martinez to run with him to make sure there was a sharp set of eyes watching our rear that didn't have a full grown woman as cargo.

Another twenty minutes of running and I brought us to a halt with a raised hand. Ahead, at the limit of the NVGs range, I could see movement. It was too far away for the goggles to resolve what it was, but I didn't expect anything moving in the desert tonight to be friendly.

We were now three miles from the second bomb, and other than secondary radiation we were clear of any danger it presented. There was a breeze blowing, as there always is in west Texas, and it was at our backs. That meant the fallout from the first bomb, as well as the one yet to detonate, was coming towards us. Signaling everyone to take a rest, I moved to the back of the group and whispered to Irina what was going on so she could fill in Igor. We needed to keep opening the distance.

Getting us moving again, I kept us at a walking pace this time. We needed to run, to get farther away from the bombs, but we also needed to maintain some sound discipline so we didn't alert whatever was moving ahead of us in the dark to our presence. Our scent would most likely do that as the breeze was blowing directly across us in that direction.

I was keeping half an eye on my watch as we walked and at the right time stopped and had everyone lie down, cautioning them not to look to our rear until after the detonation. Lying down didn't have anything to do with the direct danger posed by the bomb. When it went off it would light up the entire horizon, drawing the attention of everything for miles around. We were between the movement I'd seen and the bomb, and I didn't want us silhouetted by the fireball when whatever was out there looked in that direction.

30 seconds after I got everyone on the ground, the bomb detonated. This one was much closer than the last one, and I felt and heard the explosion. The flash lit up the desert like noon, and the fireball cast a glow like the fires of hell across the landscape as it climbed into the night sky. The extra light was compensated for and utilized by the NVGs, and I was finally able to clearly see what the movement was. More infected. Thousands of them, perhaps tens of thousands. And when the bomb went off they all turned and started coming in our direction.

31

The approaching infected were maybe a thousand yards in front of us or a little more than half a mile. I wasn't worried about the herd behind at the moment. The closest ones had to have been at least a couple of miles behind when the nuke detonated, most likely more. Unless there were some freakishly fast females that had somehow managed to track us, I didn't think there was any way there could have been any infected make it far enough beyond the disabled helicopter to escape the blast. And with that hellish inferno in front of them, I wasn't worried any longer about being tracked by the slower ones.

But I was worried about the approaching herd. I wanted a better look, wanted to stand up so I could see, but there was still a lot of light from the mushroom cloud behind me. I had no doubt there were females that would see me if I stood up and silhouetted myself like an idiot. I settled for getting up on my hands and knees, hoping my shape would blend into the surrounding terrain, and I'd look like nothing more than a rock.

The herd was still coming directly at us, and it was larger than I had first thought. I was facing directly east, the herd stretched out like a

Transmission

snake in its direction of travel, which had been north, and there were infected across the entire horizon. I couldn't see an end to the mass of bodies either to the north or south. The only good news was that there weren't any females sprinting out ahead. Yet. That was no small amount of good fortune as a sprinting female could cover 500 yards in about a minute. Way faster than we could.

We couldn't go back. Even as I kneeled there in indecision, the wind was pushing fallout from not just one, but two nuclear bombs in our direction. It wasn't a strong breeze, but it would be no more than an hour before this entire area was irradiated. The only positive was the sheer number of infected that would receive a fatal dose of radiation, and that we probably weren't going to die from radiation poisoning. The bad news – we were probably going to get ripped apart and eaten before the fallout arrived.

Two options were all I could come up with. Run north, or run south. Which direction would get us around the end of the herd faster? North would get us closer to the Marines that were coming to get us, so that's the way I decided to go. Scrabbling around in the sand, I gave the rest of my group a fifteen-second dump of what we were doing and why. Nods and frightened expressions answered me.

Getting to my feet, I began running north. I ran in a crouch, bent at the waist, hopefully changing my profile enough that the infected's brains wouldn't identify me as a human. The others followed suit, bunching up tightly behind me. Irina had recovered somewhat while we'd been stopped and ran on her own. This was good, as I didn't think Igor could have carried her very far like this.

We ran for what seemed like hours but was probably closer to ten minutes. Running bent over with your knees flexed is not a natural position, and my legs and lower back had started burning before we had gone a couple of hundred yards. I was also trying to keep my head up to watch for danger to our front as well as constantly looking to my right to check on the approaching infected.

Another ten minutes and we had covered no more than a mile. Looking ahead I still couldn't see an end to the herd and for a moment was pissed that I hadn't been warned about this second threat. I'd been told there was one herd. Had they split apart at some point, or was this a completely different group that no one had seen? Dismissing my questions and anger until there was time to actually worry about anything other than survival, I started looking for a place to hide.

Transmission

I had angled us towards the west, away from the infected, as we ran. My hope had been to buy time before they reached us, enough time to clear the front edge of the throng. But we weren't going to make it. They were within 100 yards of us now, the length of a football field, and it was only dumb luck that had kept us from being spotted.

50 yards ahead I could see a shallow, dry wash cutting across the desert floor. The two or three times a year it rained, the wash would fill with a raging torrent of muddy water, but I knew it would be dry at the moment. Glancing behind, I was glad to see everyone staying close. Irina was still running on her own, but Igor had moved next to her and had a firm grip on her upper arm as he helped her keep moving without standing up straight.

As we approached the wash, I got a better look at it. It was only about five feet deep, the edges having been cut to a near vertical angle by rushing water. Maybe twenty feet wide, it wound across the terrain, following the lowest ground which was where the water drained. Would there be infected in the wash? Only one way to find out.

Putting on as much speed as I could, I dashed ahead, Dog at my side. I slowed enough when I reached the edge of the drop off to make sure I wasn't about to jump onto anything that would end my night, then leapt when all was clear. My boots came down in deep, soft sand that had been deposited by eons of rain storms, Dog jumping down next to me and sinking in nearly to his belly.

As the rest of my group made the small drop into the wash I started looking for shelter. I'd been in a lot of these washes as a kid, using them to stalk the coyotes I liked to hunt. I remembered those days well and knew that every time the wash made a sharp bend the water would carve out the wall on the outside curve. Most of the time there was rock that couldn't be carved out, but occasionally there was a soft spot, and a nice, deep cave would form.

Feeling the pressure of the approaching herd, I looked in both directions, seeing two sharp bends, but neither of them had the shelter I was looking for. Making a decision that was solely based on not wanting to move closer to the infected, I headed southwest in the wash. Dog was growling almost constantly now, and I realized he smelled the herd. Had the wind shifted, or were there infected ahead of us? At the moment, all I had time to worry about was getting someplace where we could hide.

Transmission

Movement in the wash was just as difficult as I remembered. With every step my boots sank several inches into the loose sand. With every change in body position the sand under my boots shifted. It was like trying to walk on the dry sand on a beach. Moving around a gentle curve, we came to a sharp bend, and there was what I was looking for. A deep undercut in the outside wall of the wash.

The opening was only about three feet tall, another two to three feet of hard-packed sand and rock above it. Rushing to the opening, I peered inside, thankful for the NVGs. These undercuts make great dens for wild animals, and nothing would have surprised me. Rattlesnake. Coyote. Bobcat. Javelina. Mercifully, there weren't any occupants. Just a smooth, sandy floor stretching to the back of the small space where the ceiling tapered down to meet the ground.

Moving out of the way, I waved the group inside. Rachel was the first one in, and I told Dog to go with her. He stood his ground staring at me, not wanting to hide when he knew there was a fight coming. I gave him a quick hug, then shoved him through the opening just ahead of Martinez and her co-pilot. I really needed to learn his name. Next came Irina, panting with sweat dripping from her face. Once she was in it was obvious there wasn't room for both Igor and me. Not hesitating I motioned him inside.

He shook his big head, but we were running out of time. I shook mine and pointed into the cave emphatically, eyes locked on his. After a moment, he nodded and dropped to his knees and scrambled inside. It took him a moment to get all the way in and twist around to face the opening with his rifle across his knees. I kicked sand up in front of the entrance, then ripped a creosote bush out of the ground and stuck it in the loose earth. The entrance was completely concealed.

Taking another few seconds I raked the ground at the cave mouth with my foot, erasing the tracks leading inside. No, I didn't think the infected could follow tracks, but there was no reason to chance it. Basic camouflage completed, I moved to the center of the wash and used my rifle's stock to begin digging. The sand was deep and soft, and it moved easily. That was good because I could hear the approaching herd.

The scrape of feet on the desert floor. The low, guttural snarls from the males. The frequent sound of a body falling as a male tripped on something. I happened to glance up and 20 yards away a pair of males bumped their way around the closest bend in the wash. While I was looking up, three more fell over the edge, landing with dull thuds on the sand. Within moments, they were getting back to their feet and resuming their march in my direction.

The hole wasn't even three feet deep, but I was out of time. I had scraped it out in the shape of a shallow grave and threw myself into it, hoping I wasn't tempting fate. Wiggling around, I got on my back and pulled as much sand over my body as I could before having to go absolutely still and silent. I lay on my back, rifle on the front of my body. The Kukri was in my left hand and Ka-Bar fighting knife in my right.

The males approached, dragging their feet through the loose sand, constantly stumbling in the difficult footing. I watched the first one approach, dragging his shoulder on the far wall as he moved. It seemed to take forever, but he passed me without pausing. The second one followed in his footsteps. Number three was also using the wall as a guide but was on the same side as the cave. I was watching him approach when the sound of a pair of feet landing in the wash drew my attention.

A female had jumped down from the edge and was stalking along with her head lifted and slightly tilted to the side. From ten yards away I could hear her sniffing the air, and she was moving directly for the cave. The male had continued, rubbing the sandy wall as he moved.

When he reached the cave he tripped over the bush I had stuck into the ground, falling face first to the ground right next to me. I gripped my weapons tighter and held my breath.

It seemed to take him forever, but he finally pushed off the ground and slowly clambered back to his feet. He started moving away from me, and I silently exhaled, then drew and held another breath as the female approached. She was moving stealthily, her actions and body language reminding me of a cat stalking its prey.

The male kept moving, and I shifted my eyes to check for the other two I'd seen fall into the wash. They had stopped a short distance from me and stood in the dark, swaying back and forth. Something had to have alerted them, and I suspected they were listening and smelling for any prey in the immediate area. The female kept moving closer, finally coming to a stop directly between the mouth of the cave and me. I could see her looking around and hear her sampling the air. She knew we were close.

Suddenly she snapped her head to the side and looked directly at the bush hiding my group. I had heard nothing, but perhaps someone had made the faintest of sounds that had alerted her to their presence. She turned to fully face the wall of the wash, with her back to

Transmission

me and reached out to touch the bush. As her fingers started to wrap around a branch, I moved.

One of the things that I'd been taught most of my life, first in football, then later in the Army, is that when it's time to go, you GO. Fast. Hard. Explosive. And that's what I did, coming out of the hole and shedding sand like some kind of subterranean monster. At least that's what I was going for. Truthfully, I was probably a tad bit slower than I used to be, but I was still fast.

As I came up, I released the Kukri, leaving it lying on the sand and reached out with my free hand. Grabbing a fistful of the female's hair, I pulled with all my strength. Her head wrenched back as she started to fall backwards onto me. Before she could scream, I stabbed into the side of her throat with the Ka-Bar, slashing out and severing her trachea and both carotids.

Letting the momentum take us, I fell back into the hole and pulled her on top of me where she thrashed and twitched. I scooped the Kukri out of the sand, so I had a weapon in each hand again. Blood fountained out of her neck and rained back down on both of us. Soon I was soaked, but she spasmed one final time and lay still. When her heart stopped the twin geysers of blood stopped, then the smell of her voided bowels and bladder hit me.

Dirk Patton

My kill had been quiet, and I was sure it hadn't drawn attention from the passing herd, but the two males that had been hanging back listening had heard us and were stumbling forward in the sand. I lay perfectly still in my shallow hole with the dead female on top of me. Blood covered my face and had run down and pooled in one of my ears, but I didn't dare move or make a sound as the males approached.

I wasn't worried about being able to defend myself against them. I had two blades, a pistol, and a rifle. What I was worried about was having to defend myself, and in the process draw the attention of the whole herd, which would come flooding into the wash and overwhelm all of us in seconds. The males came to a stop next to the dead female, sniffing the air as they stood swaying.

32

Roach was in a near panic as he drove away from the water treatment plant. His heart was racing, hands were shaking, and a cold, greasy sweat covered his face. He hadn't planned. Hadn't prepared. Had killed too close to home and had gotten sloppy. He'd been seen.

He'd taken care of the witness, but what would he have done if the man had been armed and willing to fight? What if there had been two men there working? Slamming his palm on the Humvee's steering wheel he screamed in frustration at his own weakness. Weakness that had led him to get rid of Synthia without thinking it through first.

Yes, she was a liability. She had known things that could send him to the gallows, but had he really needed to kill her? Yes. He had. He had needed to correct his mistake of bringing her along. She had seemed like a good partner at first. Mature beyond her years. Then the immaturity of the teenager had revealed itself when she didn't get what she wanted when she wanted it. Why had he been so stupid?

Roach suddenly slammed on the brakes, bringing the Hummer to a shuddering stop in the middle of the road. What would he tell people?

Dirk Patton

Not that he and Synthia socialized, but people knew about her. How would he explain her disappearance? There was no logical way off the base, so he couldn't say she left after an argument. If she left him, she'd still be somewhere on the base.

He sat there, staring out the windshield. Trying to solve the problem of what lie to tell that would be accepted without question. The more he thought, the more angry and frustrated he became as he realized there wasn't any lying his way out of this. If someone looked closely enough at him and Synthia, and couldn't find her, there would be questions asked he couldn't answer. Sure, they couldn't prove anything, but...

A sudden rapping on the window next to his face startled him. A young female Airman stood there wearing a Security Forces badge on her Air Force uniform. Then Roach noticed the idling Hummer sitting behind him with Security Forces stenciled across the base of the windshield. Shit, he'd been sitting in the road and drawn the attention of a cop. He popped the door open, rather than rolling the window down, and stepped out onto the pavement.

"Are you OK, sir?" The Airman asked, taking a step back. "Are you hurt?"

Transmission

"Hurt?" Roach was confused, looking down at his body where her eyes were focused.

He was covered in his second victim's blood. He had thought he was being careful to stay clean, but he hadn't been careful enough. Looking up, he met the young woman's eyes and saw only concern, not suspicion. Glancing to his left, he confirmed she was riding alone before turning back to face her.

"No, I'm fine." He said in a pleasant voice, shuffling a step closer to her. "I was just over at the..." Roach lunged.

The woman was young, barely 19, and had only become an Air Force cop a couple of months before the attacks. She wasn't experienced. Wasn't hardened by the job and most definitely wasn't prepared for Roach's lunge. As he had started shuffling forward, he had reached into his pocket looking for a weapon. The first thing his fingers had found was the pair of pliers he'd taken out of Synthia's purse.

Now he wrapped his hand around them and punched the side of the woman's head with all his strength. She didn't even have time to scream before the strike and was knocked unconscious, collapsing to the pavement. Returning the pliers to his pocket, Roach scooped her up and placed her on the rear floor of his Humvee. Looking around, he spied a small parking lot adjacent to the base chapel and hopped into her vehicle and drove it into the lot where he parked it behind the building, so it was hidden from the road.

Running back to his Hummer he jumped in, took a deep, calming breath and started driving again. Slowly. He couldn't afford any more attention from the Security Forces right now. He knew how lucky he was that it had been a young, inexperienced woman that had come across him. A cop that had been doing the job for a few years would have had their weapon out and ready as soon as they saw the blood on his clothing.

Quickly reaching the house he had shared with Synthia, he pulled into the driveway and shut down the engine. Taking a minute to look around he was thankful to not see any neighbors. Getting out of the Hummer he slowly walked to the front door, still looking around, and opened it. Walking back to the vehicle, he did a final scan, still seeing nothing. If anyone on the street was home, they were occupied with something indoors.

Grabbing the young woman, he lifted her and quickly carried her into the house, kicking the door shut behind him with his foot. He went straight to the small bedroom where he dropped her on the bed. Removing her weapon, he also used her handcuffs to secure her to the headboard, then walked back out to the living room and locked the front door. Stepping to the window he checked the street again, but still saw no one moving.

Excitement mounting, he returned to the bedroom and stripped the woman naked. He had to unlock the cuff on her wrist for a moment to get her vest and uniform blouse off, relocking both hands over her head with the cuff chain looped around a bolt he'd secured in the headboard for when he tied up Synthia. The woman was still unconscious, so he gagged her then tied each foot to a bedpost with strips of a sheet.

Looking her over, he frowned when he saw the tattoo on her right hip. It was large and multi-colored, and he couldn't tell what it was supposed to be or what it represented. But it was distracting, and he decided to do something, so he wasn't bothered by it when they began playing. In the small bathroom, he began looking for something to cover the tattoo, glancing up into the mirror and seeing the blood on himself. He took a few minutes to clean up, changed clothes, then grabbed the pancake makeup Synthia had used to cover her ink and set to work. A few minutes later he stepped back to survey the results. It wasn't a perfect job. He could still faintly see the tattoo, but it was good enough.

Roach liked his women conscious and aware of what was happening to them. That was the excitement for him. The fear in their eyes. The terror as they realized what he was about to do to them. The resignation when they finally accepted their fate. The final moment when the light in their eyes blinked out, which if his timing was good was at the same moment as his release into their body.

Hoping she would wake soon, Roach moved back into the kitchen and set about preparing a meal. He had already killed twice today, and was about to indulge in the pleasure of a third, and he was ravenous. Laughing to himself as he worked, he soon had a large steak and baked potato ready and took the plate into the bedroom to watch the woman while he ate. Sitting on a small chair, he balanced the plate on his lap and cut into the steak.

Roach sat and ate the entire meal without taking his eyes off the woman's face. Several times he had drifted into fantasy, and the face morphed into Katie Chase. The thought of her made him think of the Major, which soured his mood and dampened his excitement. Why was he spending time on this whore when it could be the beautiful redhead tied to his bed? He'd made another mistake.

Standing he walked to the kitchen and washed the cooking pan, plate and utensils he'd used. Putting them neatly in their place, he walked back to the bedroom and looked at the woman who was just starting to show signs of regaining consciousness. Yes, he'd made another mistake taking this one, and he needed to correct that error. Retrieving a thin-bladed dagger from a dresser drawer, he stepped to the side of the bed, placed his hand on the woman's chest to make sure he had the right spot, and plunged the blade directly into her heart.

She died instantly, and there was very little blood. Roach knew that once the heart stopped, bodies didn't bleed, despite what Hollywood liked to portray. Dead bodies might seep blood, but it didn't come flooding out of them in great gushes unless an expert was draining the corpse with the right equipment. Wiping the dagger clean, he returned it to its place and from a different drawer pulled out a sheet of painters plastic.

In only a few minutes he had un-cuffed the body, placed all of the woman's clothing and equipment on top of it, and had worked an edge of the plastic under her hips. Moving quickly, he wrapped her up like a mummy, using duct tape to secure the bundle tightly. Corpse ready, he stepped into the bath to check himself in the mirror. No blood this time.

Leaving the body lying on the bed, he walked into the small, untended backyard. The previous occupant of the house had left some cheap garden tools leaning against the back fence, and Roach made use of a shovel to dig a grave. The Oklahoma soil was dark, rich and soft. Easy digging for the first four feet, then he hit rock. Deciding four feet was good enough, he went back into the house and got the wrapped body.

Some men like Roach will stop to say a prayer over their victims. Some will thank the victim for their sacrifice. Others will even cry for the dead. Roach was none of these. Walking up to the hole he'd dug he unceremoniously dropped the woman's corpse into the ground, and without a second's pause began shoveling dirt in on top of it.

He worked for close to an hour. Filling the hole, then stamping on it with his boots to compress the dirt. He repeated the process several times, finally finishing with a pile of dirt that was smaller than the space the body occupied in the ground. There was also a rake resting against the fence, and he quickly spread the dirt across the entire surface of the yard, ending at the narrow concrete pad that served as a back porch. Looking over the area, he was satisfied it would pass a casual inspection. Leaving the rake against the back of the house, he headed inside for a shower and to figure out how he would take Katie.

33

The males stood there for what seemed like forever, but couldn't have really been more than a couple of minutes. Try lying perfectly still and silent with a corpse on top of you and blood pooling in your ear. One minute feels like an hour. Eventually, they started moving away, but I couldn't relax. More males were falling into the wash as they moved across the desert.

There was now a nearly constant parade of infected moving through the wash, and I hoped everyone in the cave would stay absolutely quiet. Of all of them, I was the most worried about Irina. When I'd first met her in Los Alamos, she had not seemed to be used to seeing or dealing with the infected. I was concerned she would panic and make a sound that would draw the attention of the passing bodies.

I was lying there, concealed by the dead female, worrying about the group compromising their position when a male stepped off the edge of the wash directly above me and crashed down on top of the corpse that was on top of me. Shit, that hurt, and the son of a bitch wasn't in any hurry to get up.

Transmission

He finally started moving, reaching down to push himself up. His hand pressed on my left arm, and he paused for a moment. Then he actually squeezed my arm. What the hell? I'm not a goddamn roll of Charmin! What was he doing? Could he tell by feel that I wasn't dead and wasn't another infected?

His squeeze became a grip that tightened enough to hurt and a gurgling snarl burbled up out of his throat. Somehow he knew that he had his hand on an un-infected arm. Or perhaps he wasn't sure, but would just react to anything that felt like a meal. He started pulling, trying to drag me towards him, his snarling growing louder.

It was time to do something before his agitation drew the attention of other infected. Working my right arm through the sand and out from under the corpse, I stabbed with the Ka-Bar at where I thought his head was. I felt the tip of the blade penetrate flesh, then skitter across bone without hitting anything vital. His only response was to grip my arm even tighter and crawl fully on top of the female.

She was lying across my body at a slight angle, shoulder at my chin, and in his squirming, he wound up with his face directly over mine. For once I wasn't thankful for the night vision that let me clearly see. He had apparently turned some time ago. His lips and most of his nose were missing; exposing teeth and cartilage that made him look like something out of a macabre nightmare. My stab with the blade had torn a long gash in his cheek and left a flap of skin hanging down, blood from the wound dripping onto my face and beginning to cover the NVG's lenses.

Pinned under the weight of the two bodies, all I could do was stab with the knife again. This time, I could partially see my target, and aimed for his ear. The razor sharp steel met some resistance, but I put every ounce of force I could into the strike, and it pushed through, the hilt coming to a stop against the side of his head as the blade sliced into his brain. He went limp, and I cursed as more blood dripped out of the new head wound and completely covered the NVGs. Now I had two corpses on top of me and was blind as a bat.

I had some limited movement with my right arm, but other than that I was stuck. I couldn't reach my head to remove the goggles, but maybe that was best. There was still an occasional drop of blood splattering onto them from the dead male, and they were all that was protecting my eyes. Sure, I'd had the vaccine against the V Plague, but there were any number of other nasty viruses that could be transmitted by body fluids.

Transmission

Forcing myself not to think about HIV or Ebola or Hepatitis, I concentrated on listening to the feet of the infected moving in and near the wash. It was easy to tell the males from the females. The males constantly dragged one or both feet, routinely stumbling on the uneven footing. The females sounded just like a normal, uninfected person. Their steps were quick and steady. And what the hell was that sound?

At first, I thought I was just imaging it, or it had something to do with over 350 pounds of corpses piled on top of me. But soon I realized it was coming from each of the infected. It was a low pitched humming. Not constant. They would stop making the sound to snarl and gurgle, and several times I heard one stop humming to sniff the air. Why were they doing that, and why hadn't I noticed it before?

With nothing but time to think, I realized that I'd never been close to them with my ears as my primary source of sensory input. Maybe they'd been doing it all along. I didn't know and didn't know if it meant a damn thing. It just seemed odd. I kept listening and noticed something else. All of them were humming almost exactly the same note. I'm not a musician and couldn't begin to guess what that note was nor what key it was in, but it struck me as very odd that all of them would choose the same note.

I suspected the probability of that was less than I had the patience or ability to calculate.

The volume of infected moving across the desert continued to increase until it sounded like I was submerged in a sea of them. Males were constantly bumping into and tripping over the bodies on top of me. Fortunately, I was covered well enough that they didn't notice me. The occasional female walked by, but they were rare. I assumed they were avoiding the wash that was mostly full of the uncoordinated males.

Then as quickly as the volume had grown, it began diminishing. This made sense. The herd had been traveling in a direction 90 degrees opposite their current movement and had spread out into a long, relatively thin line. When they made a left turn to head for the location of the nuclear detonation, there was only the narrow width of the mass to pass by, even though the length most likely stretched for miles to the north and south.

Close to 15 minutes later, I listened as the last footsteps within range of my ears slowly shuffled away to the west. I lay there, breathing as shallowly as I could, listening. Five minutes went by and I still hadn't heard anything, so I decided it was as good a time as any to move.

Transmission

First, I had to get the corpses off of me. I tried pushing up, but nearly half an hour of dead weight resting on me had caused one of my arms and both legs to fall asleep. I was reaching for the male's body with my free arm when I heard a bush rustling. Was it Igor, moving a branch to peer out? My NVGs were covered with congealed blood, and I couldn't see a damn thing. Soon the bush rattled again, and I heard the faint scrape of someone or something moving through the sand on the floor of the wash.

"Viyebnutsa." I recognized the big Russian's voice but didn't understand what he'd said. At the moment, I didn't care, as I felt the weight on my chest lessen when he hauled the male off of me. A moment later he lifted the female, and I was able to take the first deep breath I'd had since killing her.

Ripping the NVGs off my head I looked up at his smiling face, his hand extended to help me to my feet. I gratefully accepted the assistance, nodding my thanks to Igor and raising my rifle to scan the area. Nothing moving other than the people crawling out of the cave.

"That was horrible!" Irina said softly when she stood up between Igor and me.

"It could have been worse," I said.

"No. I don't mean the infected. That damn dog of yours has gas. Bad gas. I thought I was going to be sick." She said, waving a hand in front of her face to emphasize her point.

I watched Martinez reach fresh air and take a big breath; then Dog came running out, happy to be back in the open. He looked around, ran down the wash with his nose to the ground until he found the right spot and squatted.

"What the hell did you feed him when I wasn't looking?" Rachel asked in an accusatory tone when she got to her feet. "I was almost wishing the infected would find us just so we could get out of there."

I tried not to laugh. I really did. But I couldn't help myself. The teenage boy part of my brain still finds fart jokes hilarious, and the thought of all of them jammed underground with Dog ripping one after another for half an hour just about put me back on the ground.

When I regained a degree of composure, I looked up to see Irina walking away, shaking her head. Igor was scanning with his rifle, but I could see a huge grin on his face. He could smile. He'd been right at the entrance and able to get fresh air. Rachel stood staring at me, hands on her hips. Dog had finished his urgent business and was back by my side looking at Rachel with his version of an innocent expression. I glanced down at him, up at the look on Rachel's face and had to turn away before I lost it again.

"OK, we need to get moving," I said, trying to be serious again.

At the edge of the wash, I started walking until I found a spot where the bank had collapsed and a couple of small boulders were half covered in sand. Cleaning my NVGs with some water from a canteen, I pulled them on and stuck my head above the lip of the wash. The good news was there weren't any infected in the immediate area, immediate being defined as within 50 yards of us. The bad news was that even though the bulk of the herd had passed us, there were still what appeared to be several hundred stragglers coming towards us.

But they were moving slower than the majority of the herd, and while I was concerned about them, I wasn't too worried about being able to fight our way through. Climbing out of the wash I turned and helped Dog scramble up, Igor pushing from below, then helped Irina. Everyone else climbed up without much effort, and as soon as we were all clear of the wash that had saved our lives, I started us running to the northeast.

34

We ran for another 20 minutes. There were a lot of males moving slowly across the desert, and rather than try to dodge around them I opted for putting them down. I shot the first half dozen we encountered, then decided it might not be a bad idea to conserve my ammo. Switching to the Kukri, I slashed and stabbed as I ran past them.

The two bombs were now far enough behind us that I was cautiously optimistic any fallout would drop to the ground behind us. It helped that the wind had shifted and was now blowing directly in my face, then I started worrying that it would carry our scent to the herd. Males weren't a concern. As long as we could keep moving, they couldn't catch us. But the females were another story. I called a halt and turned to look back to the west.

Other than males we had passed that had turned to pursue, I didn't see any movement, but that didn't comfort me. Night vision is not designed or intended to help you see long distances. It amplifies the available light to a level useful to the human eye. Typically, don't expect it to benefit you at any range greater than 100 yards unless you're looking at a large object or there's a decent amount of moonlight to help

Transmission

out. A useful reminder is that if you couldn't see something at noon, you won't see it with night vision.

Glad there wasn't a whole scrimmage line of females about to pounce on us, I turned back to the front and started running again. Dog was at my side, where he'd been the whole run, and he suddenly came to a stop. I pulled up a couple of steps past him, raising my fist to tell the group behind me to freeze in place. The fur along Dog's back was standing straight up as he lifted his nose and tested the breeze.

Turning my head back to the front, I made a slow scan of the area, seeing nothing other than a few males at least 75 yards away. He wouldn't have stopped for them. We'd been running by males for a while, and they hadn't interested him as he knew I would take care of them. Something else had caught his attention, and he didn't like what he smelled.

A shout from behind snapped my head around, and I froze for half a second when I didn't understand what I was seeing. The Stealth Hawk co-pilot was frantically trying to walk backwards. It looked like his right foot was caught by something on the desert floor. He yelled again and fell backwards as a male that had an iron grip on his ankle emerged from the sand and started crawling up his body. Igor was closer and stepped forward to kill the infected, tripping and falling on his face when another buried male grabbed his foot.

"They're under the sand!" I yelled to the group, dashing in to help.

I reached the male attacking the co-pilot first, hearing Martinez start cursing in Spanish as I shot the infected in the head. Spinning to help Igor, I moved on when I saw the dead infected and a bloody knife in his hand. Two of them had come up on either side of Martinez, and she had already killed one of them when I looked in her direction. The second one fell quickly when she stabbed into his eye with her dagger.

For the moment, no more infected were reaching up from under the ground to pull us down. Dog still stood where he'd stopped, looking to our front and growling. I made another scan of the area and didn't see anything, but then I wouldn't if there were more that had buried themselves. Why the hell did they do that? I could understand females being that smart, but males? Another thing to think about when I had time.

Dog hadn't detected the handful that we had just killed. That bothered me a little. But he was detecting something that had him spooked, and that bothered me a lot. I didn't know if we were facing a much larger concentration of infected, or if there was some new threat ahead that I couldn't see.

"That's new," Rachel spoke quietly. She had moved up to stand next to me and look at Dog. "What do you think's ahead that's got him upset? More razorbacks?"

"Not in this part of the state. Too dry. I don't know; he didn't even twitch at these." I said, gesturing at the bodies lying on the ground behind us. "Maybe there's a whole bunch of them buried in the sand, and this is just the outer edge. Or maybe there are females ahead. I'm trying to remember if he's ever reacted differently to males or females. I don't think so."

Rachel thought about that for a moment. "Not that I can remember, but maybe. Maybe we weren't paying close enough attention to notice. What are we going to do?"

I looked at my watch. The Marines were still an hour out. Ideally, I'd have liked to find a defensible position to set up in and wait for them, but there weren't any close. We had moved into an area that I didn't know. Maybe there were some hills or rocks ahead that we could use. Maybe not. All I was certain of was that there was something ahead that wasn't to the liking of a bad ass, 100-pound German Shepherd.

That final thought convinced me we needed to change direction. Looking around, I still didn't see any females in pursuit. That was good. We'd turn and go due north unless Dog warned of something in that direction as well. Calling him, I started walking that way. He fell in beside me, Rachel moving to walk on my left. As we continued on, Dog kept looking to his right and growling, but no matter how many times I checked I couldn't see anything.

We walked for about half a mile, Dog still growling at what I was starting to think were phantoms when Rachel touched my arm and pointed off to our left. Several large rocks sat on the flat desert, looking like some giant had been playing with them and just tossed them there when he was done. There was a little light from the moon to help the NVGs, and I guessed they were about 300 yards away.

As we were looking at the rocks, Dog came to a stop again. Looking in our direction of travel, he growled loud and deep, then took a step back. Since I'd know Dog, I'd never seen him take a step back from anything. Looking to our front I had my rifle up, scanning, but still couldn't see what had him worried. I couldn't imagine him responding to infected like this. He hadn't been afraid to meet a razorback head on. What the hell could actually scare him?

Deciding discretion was the better part of valor, which means if Dog was scared I was smart enough to pay attention, I motioned to my left and got the group moving towards the rocks. Signing for Igor to take point, I held my ground with Dog and Rachel at my side. When they had moved a dozen yards I sent Rachel after them, Dog and I following.

I had hoped that as we moved in the new direction whatever was concerning Dog would lessen, but as he walked he kept looking over his shoulder and growling. Were we being pursued? Not by anything I could see, and I was looking as hard as I could. Part of me hoped I'd spot the threat, another part was perfectly happy to stay ignorant of whatever could spook Dog.

We'd covered about half the distance to the rocks when Dog came to a stop and turned to face behind us. His legs were spread; head below shoulder level with teeth showing as he growled. My rifle was up, scanning for anything, but for as far as my NVGs could see there was nothing moving. I flashed back to one of my favorite, campy monster movies, Tremors, and almost laughed at myself for thinking there were monsters tunneling through the sand to come eat us.

Dirk Patton

Then my NVGs started having problems. I reached up and slapped them, but the distortion across the horizon didn't go away. Powering them off and on, I wasn't happy to see the problem was still there. The sky was slightly lighter than the ground, and whatever was wrong with them made the night sky along the horizon ripple and shimmer.

"What the hell is that?" Rachel asked. She had stopped and come back to join Dog and me when we'd stopped.

"You see it too?" I asked, suddenly very concerned. It wasn't the NVGs malfunctioning. "I thought my goggles were damaged."

"If you're talking about what looks like the sky warping, yes I see it. What the hell is it?" Rachel sounded frightened. I didn't blame her.

"I got no idea, but I think we'd better get to those rocks as fast as we can," I said, grabbing Rachel's arm and sprinting after the group. Dog fell in beside us, and soon we caught the rest of the group. I urged them to a sprint, and no one bothered to question why. They just ran.

We reached the first rock in what had to be record time. Rachel and I were spooked and had run like the minions of hell were at our heels. That had gotten everyone else running as hard as they could. There were actually quite a few large

Transmission

rocks, some as short as a couple of feet, others soaring thirty or more feet into the air. I glanced over my shoulder and still saw the odd distortion. And it looked like it was getting closer.

I clambered up onto the smallest rock, careful not to slip and fall onto the small stones that littered the ground at its base. The rock I stood on was butted up against one of the very tall ones, and as I peered around its curve, I could just make out a narrow gap between it and two other very large monoliths. Another glance at whatever was approaching and my mind was made up.

I called Dog, and he leapt onto the rock, paws slipping until I reached out and grabbed him by the scruff of his neck and hauled him the rest of the way up. Pointing where I wanted him to go, I turned back to help Irina as he jumped down into the gap. It took almost a minute to get everyone over the smaller rock and into the gap, Igor and I backing in behind them with our rifles to our shoulders. I checked on the group and was glad to see Rachel and Martinez with rifles aimed up at the top of the opening to defend against anything attacking from above.

"What fuck?" Igor mumbled in my ear in his guttural Russian accent.

Dirk Patton

I shrugged my shoulders. I didn't have a clue what the hell it was and trying to explain to him that I was deferring to Dog's warning would be about impossible unless I called on Irina to translate. Right now we didn't need the distraction. We needed to be focused on defending against whatever was coming.

Standing very still, I listened, expecting to hear running feet and snarls any moment. I had about convinced myself that the distortion I'd seen was a dust cloud thrown up by the running feet of thousands of females. If that was the case, and they saw us hide in the rocks, we were screwed. There was no way we could hold off that many. They'd just keep attacking and piling into the opening until we ran out of ammo, then the feast would begin.

Rachel came up behind me and placed her hand on my shoulder. I turned my head, and she leaned in and kissed me on the cheek as if saying goodbye. The kiss lingered a moment; then she went back to stand next to Martinez and resume her watch of the tops of the rocks. OK, so I wasn't the only one having grim thoughts.

The first indication of their approach was a low thrum coupled with a leathery scraping sound. At first, it was just at the threshold of hearing but quickly grew louder. Dog was growling steadily, and I heard Irina call him. A moment later he went quiet, and I glanced back to see her on her knees with her arms circled around his neck and face buried in his fur.

The noise steadily increased, never to a level one could say was loud, but certainly of sufficient volume to draw your attention. A few seconds later the sky above us, even with the NVGs, went dark as it was blotted out. What the hell? I stared through my goggles, but couldn't tell what was over our heads. I started to reach for the flashlight mounted on my rifle, but Igor's big hand covered mine before I could turn it on.

I looked at him, and he shook his head, mouthing something in Russian that I didn't stand a chance in hell of understanding. Regardless, I had been about to make a foolish mistake and was glad he had stopped me. Looking back up, I could see that the cloud had lowered. I was able to tell that it was made of what had to be tens of thousands of bodies, suddenly realizing it must be birds. Then some of the bodies broke away momentarily and flew around the top edges of the rocks. Bats.

Millions of small bats. This whole area of the country is riddled with small caves and massive caverns, and it's about impossible to find one that isn't hosting at least a few thousand bats. But this many together at once? I'd never seen nor heard of that. Had the virus jumped to them too?

Bats navigate and hunt using echolocation. They produce a very high pitched sound, above the range of human hearing but within range for a dog, that bounces off of all the objects around them and lets them paint a mental picture of their surroundings. Hopefully, we just appeared to be some smaller rocks to them. Thankfully, Igor had stopped me from turning on my flashlight. Bats may not have great vision, but they would certainly have seen the light.

It was a very long five minutes before the last of them passed over us, the sound slowly fading as they flew farther and farther away. When I could no longer hear them, I eased out a breath. Everyone else was looking around, a mix of frightened and shocked expressions on their faces.

35

"What in the hell was that?" Rachel asked once it seemed safe to talk.

"Can bats catch a virus that started in humans?" I asked her, stretching out to get a view of the horizon.

"Of course, they can. They're actually worse disease carriers than rodents. You don't think..."

"I don't know, but that was one shit load of bats. First the razorbacks, now these. What's next?" I asked.

"What are razorbacks?" Irina asked.

"400-pound, bad tempered wild hogs with sharp tusks," I said, turning my attention to Irina. "Was there any testing for this when the Chinese engineered the bug? Did you fucking people realize you were going to kill the whole goddamn planet?"

Irina met my stare for a few moments, then looked around the group. All eyes were on her, and she eventually dropped her gaze to the sand at her feet.

"I don't know." She said in a subdued voice. "What do you want me to say? I've already told you who started this and why. Don't forget why we're out here in the first place. I'm trying to stop this before it gets worse."

"Gets worse?" I turned to face her fully. "What the hell are you not telling me?"

Irina had lifted her face and looked me in the eye again. I could see the wheels turning as she tried to think of the right thing to say, so I interrupted. "We're in this together, Irina. I accept that you're trying to help, but you need to stop keeping things from me." I wanted the unvarnished truth this time.

"We're controlling the infected." She finally said with a sigh. I was stunned. Wasn't sure I'd heard her right. Controlling them?

"What?" I blurted out.

"How?" Rachel interjected. "How are you controlling them?"

"I'm not, but the SVR is. The nerve agent and virus send them into a rage but left to their own devices they will remain solitary or in some cases, form small hunting packs. There's a way to control them. Make them form into what you call herds, and become an unstoppable weapon. That's why Tennessee was converged on like it was. The decision was made to take out one of your main refugee aid centers." Irina's voice grew stronger as she became more confident that we weren't going to flip out and blame her. Not that I didn't have that impulse, but I knew she didn't have anything to do with this and was trying to help us.

"The herds are being controlled and directed?" I prodded her.

She nodded. "From satellites. The Chinese discovered that certain harmonic frequencies can excite and attract the infected from great distances. Our engineers developed a way to transmit high energy pulses from a satellite that when they strike any dense object, like stone or steel, that object will then vibrate at the right frequency to emit the sound that attracts them. I don't understand it, but what I know is it's not a sound humans can consciously hear, but more like something we can feel. The infected are hyper-sensitive to the transmission and are drawn like moths to a flame."

Son of a bitch, the humming I'd heard! It wasn't just some random effect of the virus. It was their response to the inaudible sound waves they were feeling. And this herd had been on its way to Oklahoma City before I'd distracted them with a couple of nukes.

Dirk Patton

"But they can be distracted and diverted, right?" I asked, wanting to make sure I was piecing this together correctly.

"Yes. Loud noises, food, and bright lights can distract them. Quite a few different ways, but then when the distraction is over, they return to chasing the sound from the satellite."

"Don't you think it would have been a good idea to tell me this in Los Alamos?" I asked, trying to keep how upset I really was out of my voice.

"If you hadn't shot down the plane carrying the bombs, President Barinov would be dead by now. My uncle would be in power, and the transmissions would have been shut off. No, I didn't think it was important for you to know at the time." She was starting to get angry, but I didn't really give a shit. She should have told me. I understand 'need to know' as well as anyone, and if there was ever a case of me needing to know, this was it.

Her comment also reminded me that her co-conspirators had been betrayed. Our new president had royally screwed the pooch. I suspected Irina's uncle had already been stood up against a wall and shot for treason, along with everyone even remotely associated or related to him. The only reason Irina was still alive was the

Transmission

Russians wanted to use her to get their hands on the remaining nukes so they could be taken off the playing field. Well, they'd succeeded at that.

"Irina," I'd just had a bad thought. "Do infected animals respond to the harmonics the same way infected humans do?"

She looked back at me, understanding dawning on her face. "I don't know. I'm not supposed to know about the control of the humans. If my uncle hadn't briefed me, I wouldn't know any of this."

"Do you know which satellites the SVR is using?" We still had some Navy ships, and the Navy had missiles specifically designed to shoot down orbiting satellites. If we knew which ones to target.

"No, and I don't think my uncle did either." She answered.

Shit. There were way too many Russian satellites in orbit to start trying to shoot all of them down. Besides, their military was still intact. As soon as a Navy ship started firing off missiles to knock down their satellites, the Russians would pull out all the stops to sink the ship. A suicide mission is one thing if you know that in exchange you'll achieve your goal. But to die for nothing was a waste of lives and critical military assets. Not that it was my decision to make, but that would be Admiral Packard's thinking. And he'd be one hundred percent right.

Right now we needed to get the hell out of Texas and back to Tinker so I could brief Crawford and the Admiral on all the recent developments. Neither would be happy to find out we couldn't trust President Clark.

"Passossee mayee yaitsa!" I heard Igor say. I wasn't positive on the translation but was pretty sure he'd just said, "suck my balls".

He was leaned out over the smaller rock, looking to the east with his night vision. I moved over next to him, lowering my goggles and facing the direction he pointed. A moment later I muttered my own version of his curse. At least one hundred females were charging across the desert. And they were coming our way.

Transmission

36

We didn't have much time. Less than a minute before the leading edge of the females would arrive. I didn't think they knew we were there. Didn't see how they could know. We'd run and hidden from the bats well before the infected should have been able to see us. The wind wasn't blowing across us and towards them, so they couldn't have scented us. Then what the hell had them excited enough to be sprinting across the desert?

I didn't know and didn't have time to keep worrying about it. There were two ways into the narrow gap we were sheltering in. Over the rock that Igor and I were leaning on to look at the females, or 50 feet in the other direction there was a very narrow opening between two massive rocks that were both well over 20 feet tall. The gap was so narrow that perhaps the women in my group could have squeezed through, as well as Dog, but Igor was as big as me, and there was no way we could shrink our chests and shoulders. But the approaching threat was female, and they'd be able to squeeze through if they tried.

We were in a very defensible position, surrounded by rocks that soared vertically for at least 20 feet. Without specialized gear, no one was going to climb them. Moving quickly, I got Igor, Martinez and the co-pilot positioned to defend the narrow gap. I'd finally learned the co-pilot's name was Evans. As they got themselves ready, Rachel and I prepared to defend our end. Irina didn't have a rifle, but held Igor's pistol in her hand, ready to help. Dog stood between Rachel and me, hackles up, ready for a fight.

"You ready?" I asked Rachel, watching the front runners close to within 100 yards.

"As I'll ever be." She said. The words didn't sound confident, but her voice was rock steady.

"Between us, we've got a little over 600 rounds. Make every shot count. If I yell that I'm out of ammo, clear some space because I'm going to be swinging some very sharp blades." I said, putting my back against the rock opposite where Rachel stood.

I met her eyes and she nodded, then gave me a brief smile. I checked on Irina, and she was obviously frightened but was ready to join the fight if we needed her. I had told her to stay back and only use the pistol to defend herself in the event a female made it past me, Rachel and Dog. About the only way that would happen would be if all three of us had fallen to the onslaught, but I decided not to dwell on that thought.

Transmission

Turning back to the opening, I watched as the first few females raced past. What the hell? They weren't after us, so where were they going? I knew from past experience that this wasn't herd movement. They didn't run like this unless prey was in sight, or they were reasonably sure there was prey in the area.

The bulk of the group wasn't far behind the leaders, and soon there was a solid wall of females running past, but just as quickly they had all moved on with only dust hanging in the air to mark their passage. I exchanged looks with Rachel, gave it a few seconds and moved forward to stick my head over the rock.

There were no more females coming, and the ones that had just run past had curved around the rocks we were hiding in, and I couldn't see them. Where were they going in such a hurry? As I thought about it, I started to get an idea. Could there be more survivors out here in the desert? There was no reason why that wasn't possible and was about the only thing that could explain the females' behavior.

Checking back to the east, I still didn't see any danger. Making up my mind, I clambered onto the rock that guarded our refuge, but still couldn't see the females that had run past. I was turning to ask Irina to go get Igor when I heard gunfire start from the west. With confirmation of my idea, I called to Rachel to send Dog over the rock then get Igor.

Jumping to the ground, I ran around the curve of the rock formation and far ahead I could see the group of females attacking some people who were huddled between two vehicles as they fired pistols and rifles at the infected. I almost hesitated to jump into the fight but knew I couldn't leave these people to be killed when I could help.

I kept running, a few moments later Dog catching up and running at my side. OK, trotting. But I was running. Not as fast as the females, it took me nearly two minutes to get close enough to start helping the people that were surrounded by the screaming mob. Watching as I ran, I saw one of them go down when a female charged in, leapt into the back of a pickup and slithered out of the bed into the midst of the survivors. Before they realized there was danger amongst them, she had wrapped her arms around a stocky man from behind and sank her teeth into his neck.

When he started thrashing and screaming, the rest of them turned and froze for a moment before going to his aid. The momentary lull in their firing allowed several more females to charge in and attack, taking more survivors to the ground. At this rate, they wouldn't last long enough for me to save any of them.

Transmission

100 yards out, I flopped to the ground, shoved my NVGs off my face, sighted through the rifle scope and began picking off targets. My rifle was suppressed, and I was too far away for the females to hear it, so for the moment, I was relatively safe. Every time I pulled the trigger a female fell. Dog had gone to his belly next to me, and I saw him look behind us out of the corner of my eye, but he didn't growl. A few seconds later Igor and Rachel ran up and lay down on either side of me.

They started firing, bringing down more females, and soon we had made a noticeable dent in the group of infected. Bodies were everywhere on the ground surrounding the survivor's position, and we kept firing. The rest of the group arrived, and I paused long enough to tell them to hold their fire. The only sound suppressed rifles were mine, Rachel's and Igor's. We didn't need the others in the fight badly enough to compromise our position by firing an unsuppressed weapon.

Dog looked around again, this time with a growl, then leapt to his feet and disappeared behind me. I snapped around in time to see him take a female to the ground, but there were at least a dozen more he couldn't stop, and they were inside 30 yards.

"To the rear!" I shouted a warning and got off two shots.

Igor reacted instantly, most likely not understanding my words, but no doubt having seen Dog run to our rear and me turn and fire. My two shots both missed as I'd just snapped them off without aiming. Well, miss isn't entirely accurate. They struck a female, but in the torso. I missed her head and her heart. Igor shot one perfectly between the eyes, the heavier Russian bullet destroying her face and head. Rachel was slower to react and never got a shot off.

As the females approached, I realized without even thinking about it that they were too close and coming too fast for us to be able to stop them with our rifles. Dropping mine, I leapt to my feet and whipped out the Kukri and Ka-Bar fighting knife. Igor stood up next to me with a straight bladed Russian bayonet in his hand, and we automatically stepped away from each other so we'd have room to fight.

The closest female was inside 10 yards when an unsuppressed rifle fired from my left. Damn it! We had these ready to jump on us, and someone had let their nerves get the best of them and alerted the others that we were here.

Transmission

"Rachel, watch my back!" I shouted as I stepped into a leaping infected and stabbed with my knife.

The blade missed her heart, but I used it to leverage her body and severed her spine at the base of her skull with the Kukri. Spinning away from the falling body, I met the next one and kept stabbing, cutting and slashing as I moved through the group. Dog was on to his third and Igor was piling up bodies around his feet. Martinez had also brought her dagger to the party and was stopping any of the infected from reaching Irina or Evans.

I had learned to fight with edged weapons from a grizzled former East German, who had defected to the United States in the early 80s. He had won Olympic gold in Montreal in 1976 for his country with the epee. Lesson one, day one had been keeping your feet moving and never give your opponent a stationary target. Igor, on the other hand, followed the standard Soviet doctrine of stand your ground and overpower everything that comes at you. We were both good. Martinez was in a class by herself.

Despite having come into the fight late, she had protected two of her teammates and already put down more of the infected than Igor and I combined. I didn't know why this woman was being wasted in the cockpit of a helicopter. She needed to be on the ground!

"Need some help here!" Rachel shouted. I finished another female with a thrust to the heart and looked over my shoulder as she fell.

The earlier unsuppressed shot had drawn the attention of the females that were attacking the group of survivors. A large knot of them had broken off and sprinted towards us. Rachel had been shooting them as fast as she could, and there were several bodies littering the path the group was following, but they were getting close, and she knew she couldn't keep up.

One of the rules of combat is that you don't take your attention off your attacker. That's a rule that I know well and honestly, can't remember a time I've ever violated it. Until now. Because it was Rachel that called out. Concern for her safety overrode years of training and combat experience without so much as a thought. And I paid for it in spades when a female slammed into me and sent me sprawling in the dirt.

Both weapons flew out of my hands when I hit, and the wind was knocked out of me. I guess I was fortunate that my head came down on soft sand and not a rock, but as the female drove her knees into my stomach and lunged for my throat with her jaws, I didn't feel very lucky. I got my hands up and on her shoulders an instant before she would have torn me open. I tried to push her off, but she was already adjusting and locking her legs around my waist.

Female infected are strong as hell, and the big ones are really strong. This was a big one. As I struggled with her, I had no doubt that pound for pound she was stronger than me. Guessing her at around 180 pounds, I was having trouble keeping her snapping teeth at a safe distance.

Irina, seeing the trouble I was in, dashed over to help. She came up behind the female and raised Igor's pistol for a headshot. When I saw what she was doing, I shouted for her to stop, but she either didn't hear me or didn't think I was talking to her. Seeing what was coming, and not wanting to get shot by a bullet that punched all the way through the female's head, I twisted sideways a fraction of a second before Irina fired.

At the same time, I saw her finger tighten on the trigger and heard the shot. Immediately I felt something strike my temple, and everything went dark. The female on top of me stopped trying to bite me, and I pushed her off my body, feeling a wave of nausea rising before I blacked out.

37

When I woke up, my head felt like a field artillery unit had set up shop right behind my eyes and was determined to fire off every single shell in their possession. I was lying on my back and started to sit up, but a strong hand pushed on my chest and kept me horizontal. A weak, red lensed flashlight came on, and I was relieved to see Igor's ugly mug looking down at me. Rachel leaned in, gave me a smile, brushed my cheek with the back of her hand and the light turned off.

"How are you feeling?" She asked from the darkness.

"Like shit," I said. "How do I look?"

"Worse." She quipped. "Just lay still for a bit. At the moment we're OK. Martinez just talked to the Marines on the radio, and they're a little less than half an hour away."

"The infected?" I asked.

"All dead. We finished off the females without you." I heard a snuffling and a second later a wet nose rubbed across my face. Dog gave me a thorough sniffing before lying down with his muzzle inches from the side of my face.

Transmission

"He hasn't left your side," Rachel said. I slowly raised a hand and rubbed Dog's head, then let it fall. That had been all the energy I had.

"What happened?" I asked.

"Irina shot you." I heard Martinez' voice. Shot? A surge of adrenaline hit and I tried to sit up again, this time, Igor helping instead of stopping me.

"What the…" That was as far as I got before the dizziness and nausea struck like a Mack truck. I fought it as long as I could, but finally gave up and pitched to the side and threw up. I hadn't eaten in a while, so it was a little bit of water, then the dry heaves. My body didn't care that there wasn't anything in my stomach to purge, it was determined to try.

When the worst of it passed, I straightened back up, and Rachel placed a cool hand on my forehead. My head pounded bad enough that it felt like it was going to split open, but I'd experienced the worst of the sickness. Other than a splitting headache I seemed to feel OK. At least I was moving and talking.

"What the hell happened?" I asked, again, checking myself over for bullet holes and happily not finding any.

"A female was on top of you and Irina shot it in the head trying to help you. The bullet went through the infected's head and creased your temple. Knocked you out. You've got a nice, deep crease along the side of your head. An inch to the side and you wouldn't be here." Rachel said. That bullet had really rung my bell. I couldn't remember anything that Rachel was telling me.

I reached up to my pounding skull, and my fingers touched a thick gauze pad taped to the right side of my face. Now that I knew where the worst injury was, I could feel the burning pain from the furrow the bullet had carved in my flesh. I looked up when Irina knelt down in front of me.

"I'm so sorry," She said. "I thought I'd killed you." Even in the weak moonlight I could see a large swelling around her left eye.

"What happened to you?" I asked. She glanced around, not answering at first.

"I might have hit her." Rachel finally spoke up. She didn't sound one bit sorry.

I looked at Rachel, then back at Irina. The whole side of Irina's face was swollen, and the skin was already changing color. It looked black in the night, but I'd had a few of those bruises and knew it would be an angry shade of purple in the light. Neither woman said anything else, and I met Igor's eyes. He shrugged his shoulders and turned away with a grin on his face.

"Sorry, I missed that," I mumbled to myself, raising a canteen and taking a cautious sip of water. The water was tepid, but I could feel coolness all the way to my stomach as I swallowed.

"Want some aspirin?" Rachel asked, digging through the med kit in her pack then holding out a small, clear plastic bottle. I took it, popped the lid and dumped several into my hand. Washing them down with some more water, I hoped my stomach wouldn't rebel when the pills started dissolving.

"What happened to the people the infected were attacking?" I was starting to think a little clearer, suddenly remembering why we had left the safety of the rocks to fight the females.

"All dead," Martinez answered. "They ran out of ammo before all the females were put down. And, don't know if it matters, but they were part of a drug cartel from Juarez. I recognized their tattoos."

I thought about that for a couple of moments. On reflection, it didn't really surprise me that cartel soldiers had survived this long.

They would have been heavily armed and had access to fortified locations in which to hide. There was no doubt they knew how to shoot. But what the hell were they doing out here in the middle of the desert?

"Movement to the south." This was Evans, the co-pilot, who had been keeping an eye out with a pair of NVGs. My pair, I realized when I reached up, and they weren't on my head.

Irina said something to Igor, and he rose up on his knees and looked. He adjusted something that I assumed was a magnification setting on his Russian-made goggles and grunted a reply that Irina translated.

"Four vehicles approaching." Irina translated. "About a kilometer away."

"We need to move. Now." I said, climbing to my feet and bringing my rifle around to check on it. As soon as I stood up the pounding in my head increased tenfold and my knees nearly buckled. I stood there a moment, swaying slightly, and Rachel quickly got up and steadied me.

"Have you checked the vehicles?" I asked, referring to the ones that belonged to the dead drug runners.

Transmission

"Out of fuel. Probably why they were stopped here." Martinez answered.

"OK. Let's get back to the rocks before those vehicles arrive. If they've got night vision, they'll probably see us, but at least we'll be fairly secure until the Marines show up." I said.

I started to run towards the rocks, but only made it a couple of steps before my head reminded me that I wasn't one hundred percent. Or even fifty percent for that matter. I stumbled and would have gone down if Martinez hadn't grabbed my arm. Nodding my thanks, I settled for a fast walk but was apparently still weaving around as Rachel stepped beside me and circled her arm through mine.

"You've most likely got one hell of a concussion." She said.

"Most likely." I agreed. "I'll try not to let any more bullets bounce off my skull."

"No worries there. You're head's so thick, I don't think they could do anything except bounce off. But just in case, try to avoid that. Now that I've got you, I don't want to lose you." Rachel squeezed my arm, and I tried to put on some more speed.

"They've seen us," Evans said a couple of minutes later. "The lead truck just changed directions and is coming directly at us." I looked at the rocks ahead and guessed we were still about two minutes away from the shelter they afforded.

"How far are they?" I asked, pushing myself into a trot.

"Maybe a minute." He answered. Shit. We weren't going to make it before they arrived. Not without me able to run.

"Martinez, get everyone in the rocks. Now. Run." I ordered, trying to push myself faster and nearly falling.

"We're not leaving you behind." She said without turning around.

"That's an order, Captain!" I said as firmly as I could.

Martinez looked over her shoulder at me and then shook her head. "Sorry, sir. But under the UCMJ, an officer that has sustained an injury or wound to the head and is deemed to be mentally impaired as the result of said wound cannot issue a lawful order."

"Goddamn it, Martinez…" I started to say, but Rachel leaned her head towards my ear and told me to shut up.

Transmission

Well, if they weren't going to listen, then I had to make sure they were safe. Pushing myself into a run I almost collapsed. The pounding in my head returned, a pulse of pain coordinated with each time one of my feet hit the ground. The desert in front of me was undulating, the horizon warping as I struggled forward. I would surely have fallen flat on my face if not for Rachel's assistance.

I could hear the sound of the engines behind us now, and Igor moved in on the opposite side of me from Rachel and grabbed that arm. Together, they propelled me along at a speed greater than I could achieve at the moment. Dog ran a few yards in front of me, and I just focused on following his bushy tail.

My world had compressed to a dark tunnel. Peripheral vision was gone, and all I could see was Dog's ass as he led the way. The sound of the approaching vehicles was replaced with a roar that reminded me of the ocean, and my stomach was threatening to spasm and force the water and aspirin back up. I was only vaguely aware of the sound of gunfire from our rear, almost like when you're dreaming and something is happening that you're aware of but not involved in.

But, I guess I was involved because Igor released my arm, turned and fired a long burst from his rifle. I was aware that Martinez was also firing to our rear, and I thought I should stop and do the same, but the thought didn't translate to action. I kept running with only Rachel's support. We were moving slower, but I managed to stay on my feet, and following Dog I somehow managed to maintain a straight line. I think.

Before I knew it, we were at the shorter rock that guarded the entrance to the gap, and Rachel scrambled on top of it. I stood looking at her for a moment, then realized she was yelling at me to get Dog. Stooping over, I leaned a shoulder on the rock to keep from falling down, wrapped my arms around Dog's body and lifted until Rachel could grab his front shoulders and pull him up with her.

I climbed onto the rock, feeling like I was moving through molasses, then Rachel was dragging me, and we wound up tumbling off the backside of the boulder and collapsing on the sand. Moving out of the way, I pulled Dog to me as first Irina, then Martinez and finally Igor joined us. Igor immediately rested his rifle across the top of the boulder and began firing at the newly arrived vehicles.

"Where's Evans?" Rachel asked. Irina turned and shook her head. She didn't need to say anything else to get the message across.

38

The firing subsided quickly, and mercifully my headache began to recede. Slowly I was starting to think again, and I was able to stand without help. Martinez and Igor stayed crouched behind the cover of the rock, rifles aimed out at the desert. There wasn't room for me to squeeze in. Besides, they didn't need my help. It sounded like some of the trucks were driving away, most likely intending to circle the area and see if there was a way to attack us from the rear.

"Talk to me, Martinez," I said, glad to hear my voice sounding strong and clear.

"Five vehicles. Four pickups and one Suburban. Each truck has three men in the cab with multiples in the back. Hard to get a count with them driving around us in circles. No idea on the SUV, but it's probably their jefe." She said, using the Spanish word for the man in charge.

"Cartel?" I asked.

"That's my guess. All heavily armed. Looks like AKs, pistols, and machetes. There's a pintle mounted in one of the trucks, but so far no sign of a weapon for the mount. Thank God!"

"OK, we need to get that rear opening covered again. Rachel, take Irina and Igor with you and make sure we don't get surprised from that side. I'll stay here with Martinez. We need to hold these guys off until the Jarheads decide to show up for the party." I was feeling better, and it must have showed as everyone jumped into motion without any arguments or second guessing.

I sent Dog with Rachel, trusting him to keep her safe, but also calling out to her to keep an eye on him. These weren't infected we were fighting, and I didn't want Dog taking a bullet because he wasn't behind some kind of cover.

"Good to see you feeling better," Martinez said when I joined her at the boulder.

"Who says I'm feeling better?" I asked sarcastically. "And the next time I tell you to leave me behind…"

"I'll disobey that order, too. Sir," She interrupted, unapologetically. "Would you leave me behind?"

"No. But that's different." I said, watching two of the trucks pull up next to the Suburban and stop.

"Why? Because I'm a woman?" She challenged.

Transmission

Jesus Christ! Sometimes, I really just can't win. I had several things on the tip of my tongue to say but bit all of them back.

"Just fucking with you, sir," Martinez said with a small laugh, letting me off the hook. "I know why you wouldn't. I was in Los Alamos with you. Remember?"

I smiled, thought about calling her a bitch, but settled for resting the dot in my scope on the face of the man driving one of the pickups. If these guys were cartel, they were just the thugs that were recruited locally. The Mexican drug cartels like to hire and use trained soldiers whenever they can. And with the money they have, finding former SF operators from just about any country on the planet isn't a problem.

It made sense that none of those guys would have stuck around when the world fell apart. Money was now less valuable than toilet paper, quite literally, and they had taken off to find their families or to reach what they thought would be a safe area. All that were left were the locals whose loyalty was based on blood or community ties.

Two of the trucks were unaccounted for, but I figured out where they were a moment later when I heard automatic weapons fire from the far end of the gap. They'd found the opening and a big, pissed off Russian guarding it. The guys to my front heard the firing as well and started to move, but I pulled the trigger and sent a bullet through the head of the man I'd sighted on.

The rest of them started scrambling behind the vehicles, several of them ripping off long bursts from their AKs in our general direction. This was un-aimed firing intended to keep our heads down while they sought cover. Knowing that gives you the advantage of not feeling the need to throw yourself onto the ground, and I shifted aim to one of the men who wasn't as well hidden as he thought and pulled the trigger. And missed. Fired a second time. And missed.

The concussion was apparently affecting me more than I realized. These guys were less than 100 yards away, and I know I can damn near shoot the wings off a fly at that distance. Especially when I'm shooting from a static position with my rifle firmly resting on a stable object.

Martinez had fired twice, and there were two bodies lying on the sand to confirm her accuracy. Taking my face away from the scope, I rubbed both eyes, then sat back and poured some water over my head. Other than feeling good it didn't do anything to reduce the halo in my vision.

"You OK?" Martinez asked when she noticed what I was doing, then had to duck when bullets began smashing into the rocks around us.

"I'm fine," I said. "Just don't depend on me for any down range kills for a while."

The firing from our front quickly dwindled to nothing. That was out of character for cartel types. They liked to use bullets the same way they liked to spend money. The more, the better. Either they were running low on ammo, or they were up to something. Poking my rifle through an opening no more than six inches tall I used the night vision scope on the rifle to see what they were up to. I would have preferred my goggles, but they were still on Evan's head, and he was lying dead somewhere out in no mans land.

"Hola, amigos!" A thick, Mexican voice shouted out in Spanish. I tried to spot the man talking, expecting it would be jefe, but whoever he was he was smart enough not to reveal himself.

"We are all in trouble here, don't you think? Let's put our guns down and talk like men." The speaker switched to thickly accented English. Martinez glanced over at me, and I shook my head. Put my gun down, my ass. Charlton Heston said it best. "From my cold, dead hands." Personally, I would have added a few descriptive expletives to the end of that, but he was a classier guy than I am.

"ETA on the Marines?" I asked Martinez. She made a call on the radio in a low voice that I couldn't hear.

"Ten minutes. They're pushing beyond the safe speed limits for their aircraft." She said.

"Brief them on our situation, and I want this fucker targeted as well as his buddies at the other end. Tell them these guys killed one of ours and I want them erased from the fucking planet." I growled.

Normally I don't get pissed off in combat. It is what it is, and while emotions are something that can't be avoided, anger is one that all too often leads to bad decisions. But every now and then it's OK to get mad. Get really pissed off and unleash some hell on earth. We didn't start the fight with these guys. In fact, we started out trying to help some of them, and the new arrivals didn't even try to find out what was going on when they showed up. Just came in guns blazing and killed Evans, and damn near the rest of us. Now it was about to be our turn to return the favor.

Transmission

Martinez said something into the radio, turned to me and told me the frequency the Marines were on. "Keep this prick occupied while I talk to them," I said, adjusting my radio. "What's their call sign?"

"Thor five five." She said, turning and yelling towards the parked trucks in Spanish.

"Thor five five, Dog two six," I said when I had the unit on the right channel. Thor? Really? I had a sneaky feeling I knew who was going to answer.

"Hear you've pissed off the locals, Dog two six." Zemeck chuckled in my ear.

"You know me," I answered. "What's taking you so fucking long? Stop off for a beer in Amarillo?"

"Negative. Pussy in Abilene. Your sister was in town." He responded without missing a beat. And you wonder why Soldiers and Marines shouldn't drink in the same bar.

"Hope she left you with a smile on your face, Thor. Got some locals down here that think it's OK to shoot a young Air Force LT. I need you guys to come in hot." I said.

"The lady already briefed us. On you in five minutes. We facing anything real?" He was asking if the bad guys had anything that could bring down an Osprey.

"Not that I've seen. Just small arms, Thor."

"Copy. Get ready to duck. Thor five five out."

Martinez was carrying on an animated conversation in Spanish. I recognized a few words and could tell she wasn't exactly exchanging pleasantries with the man. I was keeping a close eye on my watch when I wasn't trying to spot a target through my rifle's scope. The conversation sounded like it was growing more heated and reached a point where Martinez stuck her rifle over the top of the rock and loosed a long burst of automatic fire in the direction of the vehicles.

"What the hell?" I asked when she retreated from their return fire.

"You said keep them occupied. That's what I'm doing." She said calmly, an innocent expression on her face. I couldn't help but laugh. The more time I spent around her, the more thankful I was that she was on my side.

I checked my watch again. Two minutes left. Peering back through my scope, I saw movement along the desert floor. Someone was

Transmission

crawling across the sand at an angle that would reach the rocks a couple of dozen feet to our right. An area that we couldn't see. I kept scanning and saw more movement as another man worked his way to our left.

The desert isn't perfectly flat, undulating with small hillocks and crisscrossed with shallow channels carved by water as it rushed to the larger washes. All of that meant there wasn't much of these guys exposed as they moved. My head was still pounding as I watched them through the scope, but I happily noticed that the halo in my vision was gone.

Telling Martinez to take the guy on the left, I sighted in and started tracking the one on the right. He was a large lump moving across the dark terrain, a large belly holding too much of his body up off the ground. I held on him until I liked the sight picture, then pulled the trigger and put a bullet through his ass, which was sticking up higher than the rest of him. He screamed and rolled, twisting to reach the part of his anatomy that had been shot. His change of position exposed his head, and I drilled a round through it.

Martinez fired her first shot as I fired my second. I shifted to look at her guy, glad to see he was no longer moving. "Nice shot," I said, then turned my head when the sound of approaching aircraft reached my ears.

"Marines are here," Martinez commented dryly. "Really sucks to have to be rescued by them. You know we'll never hear the end of it."

I grinned as an Osprey suddenly appeared right over us, rotors tilting up to put the big aircraft into a hover. The wind they created was fierce, whipping up the sand and small rocks. I had to squint to see, but when they opened fire on the three vehicles and the men hiding behind them, I forgot about everything else. A belly-mounted minigun hosed down the target, and I could hear the ripping sound of a second one behind me.

The pilot slipped to the side as the minigun continued to pump slugs into the three vehicles. It only took a few moments of concentrated fire before first one, then in quick succession, the other two exploded. The fireball was huge, lighting up the night and casting stark shadows among the rocks.

Minigun falling silent, the Osprey moved a safe distance from the burning vehicle and touched down in a maelstrom of sand and debris. The back ramp was already on its way down, and a second after landing a squad of heavily armed Marines boiled out of the aircraft with Master

Transmission

Gunnery Sergeant Zemeck leading them. A second set of explosions from the rear told me the rest of our attackers had been neutralized.

The Marines quickly spread out to form a defensive perimeter and Zemeck, and two others walked over to check the area and make sure there weren't any of the cartel members left alive. I sent Martinez to retrieve the rest of our group and clambered on top of the rock I'd been using for cover. I made sure to leave my rifle slung, not wanting an over eager Marine to mistake me for a bad guy.

Zemeck saw me and waved. I waved back, hopped down and strode over to meet him. He was standing a dozen yards from the burning vehicles when I walked up next to him.

"Guess that just about makes us even." He said.

"Not even close," I answered with a shake of my pounding head. "What the hell did you do other than come along for the ride? I think it's your pilot I need to buy a beer for. Typical jarhead. Let someone else do the work and take all the credit."

"You trying to stop bullets with your head again?" He asked, clicking on a small flashlight and shining it on my bandages.

Dirk Patton

"Not trying, unfortunately," I said.

"You need a medic?"

"I'm good. It's not a hangnail so your medic probably wouldn't have any experience treating it." I grinned.

"How 'bout I leave your sorry ass out here, and you can find your own ride home." He shot back.

"That might beat being stuck inside that sardine can with a bunch of Marines for the next few hours." I mused.

A Lance Corporal that had accompanied Zemeck stood staring at us. I saw his eyes flick to my oak leaf, then to Zemeck. He was probably wondering what the hell his Master Gunny was thinking to be talking to an officer the way he was.

"Lance Corporal, you got any body bags in that Osprey?" I asked him.

"Yes, sir." He answered. "Why?" He probably thought I was going to make another smart ass comment.

"We've got a fallen man we need to bring back with us," I said. He nodded and ran off towards the idling aircraft.

Transmission

Zemeck and I walked over to where Evans lay. He was face down, sprawled out as he'd been shot in the back while he was running with us for cover. I kneeled and retrieved my NVGs, then gently rolled him onto his back and straightened his arms along his sides while we waited for the body bag.

The rest of my group started walking up, and three of the Marines raised their rifles when they saw Igor and recognized his uniform. I gestured to Zemeck, and he got them calmed down, and their rifles lowered. After making the introductions, Martinez and I gently placed Evan's body into the bag and zipped it up. She grabbed the feet, and I took the head, and we carried him into the waiting Osprey.

39

Roach was worried. The maintenance Sergeant and the Security Forces Airman he'd killed and buried in his back yard were drawing a lot of attention. At first, there had been a lot of concern that they had turned, that maybe the vaccine wasn't effective, and this had dramatically raised the profile of, and the search for, the missing people. Her vehicle, equipped with a GPS locator, had been found quickly where Roach had hidden it behind the base chapel. Now there was an effort to pull and review the archived footage from all the cameras around the base chapel and the water treatment plant.

Unsure if there was a camera focused on the areas where he'd attacked the two people, Roach had retraced his path from that day and been dismayed to see one on the front of the chapel that was pointed directly at where he'd taken the Security Forces Airman. But it was a long way off and didn't appear to have a long lens on it. Its focal point was most certainly the parking lot in front of the building, but if it captured him in its frame would they be able to enhance the image and make an identification? There were also numerous cameras in and around the water facility that he could see from

Transmission

the road. He didn't dare try to gain access to the plant to see how many more there were for fear of drawing unwanted attention.

He had approached the Major that had vetted him when he first arrived at Tinker, with an offer of assistance on the investigation. The Major was leading the investigation, but rejected Roach's offer, telling him to stick with his assignment of overseeing the refugees. With infected ringing the base there weren't any new ones coming in, and Roach's duties had shifted to babysitting the large civilian population that had sought shelter at the Air Force base.

Concern was quickly becoming panic for Roach as the investigation moved forward. He hadn't been careful, acting on impulse in getting rid of Synthia. His lack of planning and preparation had started a domino effect, resulting in the death of the maintenance worker at the water treatment plant and the young Security Forces Airman. How had he been so careless?

Sitting in his small living room, Roach considered taking his rifle and going into the Security Forces offices and killing the Major and anyone else in the building. He thought about how he would do it, how it would feel to pull the trigger and see these people cut down. With a smile, he decided that was the right course of action, then thought better of it and began mumbling to himself as he thought. It would only delay the inevitable. And there would be more cameras that would capture him in the act.

He had to leave the base. That was the only answer. If he stayed here, a Security Forces tactical team would be knocking his door down and dragging him away at any time. He couldn't let that happen. He'd rather die than go through the humiliation of capture and a court martial. He had to escape. But how? And to where?

Roach got up and started pacing, still mumbling to himself as he weighed his options. Driving off the base wouldn't work. There were too many infected at the fence, and the base was on a hard lockdown. That left flying. But how the hell would he coerce and maintain control of a pilot? And if he could, where would he go that was safe?

Walking into the tiny kitchen, Roach poured a finger of whiskey into a cheap glass. He downed it in one gulp, coughing as it burned his throat. Out of frustration, he threw the glass against the wall where it shattered into a hundred glittering pieces. When the glass broke, his mind suddenly cleared and he was able to think without the distraction of panic. The first step was to find a safe location.

Transmission

Back in the living room, Roach pulled out his Air Force issue laptop and booted it up. After dealing with numerous login protocols, he was online and knew exactly which sites to check. A few clicks later and he was reviewing the reports of the numerous scouting parties that were being sent out daily. The scouts were tasked with locating resources, primarily food and medicine that the base needed to continue operating.

As a side benefit, they were also searching and cataloging large buildings that could be fortified and used to house civilians if necessary. It was these that Roach began eagerly reviewing. He rejected many of the structures that were listed. Hospitals and schools had too many windows and too many doors for him to even hope to successfully barricade against the infected. A sports arena caught his eye, but he dismissed it after reading the scout team leader's comment that infected would have to be cleared out before the location could be occupied.

Then, two-thirds of the way down the page, he found the perfect place. It was large, coming in at nearly four-hundred-and-fifty thousand estimated square feet that was all on a single level. There were no windows and very few entrances, and the team had secured all of the doors on their departure, noting how to access the building from a rooftop helipad. It was already cleared of infected. There were several kitchens, and though it was noted there was lots of fresh food that was rotting and would need cleaned out, there was also an estimated two tons of canned and non-perishable food in storage.

Roach changed programs and pulled up a map of Oklahoma. It was about an hour away by helicopter, and there weren't any major cities close. That meant there shouldn't be a large population of infected in the area. Clicking back to the report, Roach noted the coordinates of the building on a notepad and sat back to think about how he would get there.

His neighbor! The man was a pilot, assigned to a transport wing, and flew Globemasters. But Roach knew he was also rated for rotor wing or helicopter. Controlling the man wouldn't be hard. He was a newlywed with a pretty young wife. He would do whatever he was told to do to save her. Accessing another system, Roach was pleased to find the pilot was currently on a flight that was in-bound to Tinker from Fort Hood in Texas. He'd be on the ground in less than 90 minutes.

Roach moved to a window that looked at his neighbor's house. Standing there, he stared and continued to flesh out the plan in his head. Half an hour later, he felt he was ready. The plan was more rushed than he would have liked, but

Transmission

he knew there was a clock ticking down the last moments of his freedom if he remained on the base. Part of him was surprised that about a hundred Security Forces hadn't already broken his door down and taken him into custody. That is if he made it into custody and wasn't shot for "resisting arrest".

In the bedroom, he made his preparations and quickly changed into a fresh uniform. A 9 mm pistol was part of his uniform, the daggers concealed in his clothing weren't. He set a short barreled H&K automatic rifle on the bed, not wanting to have it with him for the first part of his plan. Checking himself in the mirror he was satisfied with what he saw and walked out the front door, marching smartly to his neighbor's house and ringing the bell.

The houses were small, and it didn't take long for the woman to answer the door. She was young and pretty, but chunkier than Roach liked his women. He pasted a smile on his face when she started to open the door and held it as she looked at him through the screen.

"Hi," he said, brightly. "Vanessa, right? I'm Captain Roach from next door." He turned slightly and pointed at his house.

"Hi." She said a curious look on her face. She hadn't met Roach but knew her husband had spoken with their new neighbor a few times. She'd seen him and his wife coming and going, sometimes at odd hours.

"I'm really sorry to bother you, but I'm hoping you can help. My wife, Tammy, is having a bit of a rough time. I don't know if you knew we barely escaped from Nashville, and she's having some issues and could really use another woman to talk to. I was hoping..." Roach let the last sentence trail off, depending on her to be eager to jump at the chance to help another woman.

Vanessa pushed the screen door open and stepped into the doorway. "Oh, the poor thing. Of course, I'd be happy to talk to her. Military wives have to stick together. Bring her around and we'll have a good talk."

Roach made a pretense of hesitating as if embarrassed before speaking again. "See, that's the thing. She's locked herself in the bathroom and won't come out, and I have to report for duty. I'm sure you know how that is. I don't really want to leave without knowing she's OK, but my CO won't be very understanding if I'm late."

"Oh," Vanessa said. "Of course. Let me turn the stove off and I'll be right there."

Transmission

"Thank you!" Roach called as she turned and hustled into the kitchen.

"No problem." She said over her shoulder.

A few moments later she pushed out through the screen, pulled the door closed behind her and walked with Roach the short distance to his house. When he opened the front door, he leaned in and shouted for Synthia, calling her Tammy, telling her they had a guest. Feigning disappointment, he shook his head and stepped back to usher Vanessa through in front of him.

Stepping into the living room, she glanced around at the furnishings. There was no need to orient herself to the layout as the two houses were identical copies of each other, and several hundred more than had been built by an Air Force contractor to a single set of unimaginative but functional floor plans. Roach followed her in, softly closing the door after him.

"Bathroom?" Vanessa asked, confirming that was where Synthia (Tammy) was. Roach nodded and reached into his pocket.

Vanessa turned and started to walk to the short hall, still unaware of the peril she was in. Roach stepped behind her, drew a lead filled, leather sap from his pocket and hit her across the back of the head. One thing he was skilled at was disabling his victims without causing serious injury, and he struck with just the right amount of force to knock Vanessa to the floor, unconscious, but otherwise unharmed.

Returning the sap to his pocket, Roach picked her up and carried her to the bedroom. He put her in the kitchen chair he had positioned ahead of time. It was sitting directly in front of a dark blue blanket that covered the window. Quickly restraining the woman, he also gagged her so she couldn't scream and possibly be heard by a passerby.

Next, he opened the closet and pulled out the rest of the items he needed. A wide, leather belt that Synthia had purchased at the Base Exchange went around the woman's body, just below her breasts. Roach attached a large analog clock to the belt and on either side of it a bundle of six road flares, heavily taped to disguise them. Finally, he attached several wires that ran from the back of the clock and disappeared into each bundle of flares.

Stepping back, he eyed his work and smiled in satisfaction. Raising a small digital camera he had been using to record images of all the refugees, he took several pictures of Vanessa from different angles. After reviewing them on the small camera screen, he deleted them, turned on a couple of lights in the room and shot several more. When he reviewed these, he was happy with the results.

The images showed Vanessa tied to a chair, gag in her mouth, a bomb strapped to her body. The red hand on the clock face, which indicated the time the alarm was set to sound, was set for seven hours from now. Roach was confident that anyone that wasn't EOD – Explosive Ordinance Disposal – rated would look at the photo and completely believe it.

40

It was two hours later when Air Force Captain Robert Tillman walked through his front door. He paused, hand on the knob when he saw Roach sitting on his living room sofa. Roach had his pistol resting on his right leg, hand lying on top of it. He didn't want to shoot the pilot, couldn't shoot the pilot, but he didn't know how the man would react.

"Close the door and sit down, Captain," Roach said, nodding at a lone armchair a few feet across from him.

"Vanessa?" Tillman shouted out, leaning slightly to the side to see into the kitchen.

"She's not here, but she's safe. For the moment." Roach said. "And every moment you waste by not doing what I tell you is bringing her closer to dying."

Tillman was in shock, still rooted in place with the door knob gripped tightly in his hand.

"Pick up that camera and turn it on. You'll be interested in the pictures on it." Roach had left the camera on a small table that sat adjacent to the front door.

Transmission

Looking down and seeing the camera, Tillman closed the door and picked it up. Turning it on, his face went ashen when he saw the image come up on the screen. He looked up at Roach, his face slack with shock, and Roach knew he had him. The man had no fight in him. Just fear of losing his bride.

"Why are you doing this? What do you want?" He stammered, seeming to have trouble breathing.

"Why isn't important. As far as what I want, well, nothing much." Roach said as if making casual conversation. "I simply need you to fly me somewhere in a helicopter. When we get there, I tell you where Vanessa is and how to deactivate the bomb. Look closely at that picture. See the red hand on the clock? That's when the bomb goes off. You've got just under five hours left. Where I want to go is about an hour by air. Plenty of time for you to make the round trip. When you drop me off, I tell you where she is."

Captain Tillman couldn't do anything other than stare at the picture.

"Look at me, Captain," Roach said, waiting until the man raised his eyes. "You have no choice in this. Do what I'm asking and she lives, and you'll be back together in time for dinner.

Disobey me, try to warn anyone, do anything I don't like and she dies."

Roach pulled out a small radio transmitter that was used by Security Forces to call for backup in an emergency. He was counting on it not being recognized by anyone that hadn't used one before.

"This is a remote detonator. I can kill her from a hundred miles away." He lied but was masterfully convincing. "Do you understand what you have to do?"

"I understand," Tillman said in a voice that was nearly inaudible.

"I didn't hear you." Roach prompted.

"I understand, but if you've hurt one hair on her head..." He never finished the sentence. Roach had anticipated some resistance and as soon as Tillman said "but" he leapt to his feet, jammed the muzzle of the pistol into his throat and snatched the camera out of his hand.

"Take a close look, Captain," Roach said, holding the screen up in front of Tillman's eyes. "If you want to be a hero, be a hero by doing what I tell you and saving her. Making empty threats that you have no way to carry out is a waste of time she doesn't have. Do you really want to find out what all those sticks of dynamite will do to her?"

"No. Don't hurt her. I'll do what you're asking." He finally said through clenched teeth.

"Marvelous!" Roach cried with a smile, thoroughly enjoying himself.

For a moment, he almost believed the lie that Vanessa was still alive, but he had killed her with a quick dagger thrust to the heart minutes after he'd taken her photo with the fake bomb. Moving away from the pilot he turned the camera off and pocketed it, but kept the pistol in his hand just in case the man decided to try something stupid.

"Here's what you're going to do," Roach said, moving, so the armchair was between them. "There's a Pave Hawk fueled, armed and ready to go for a scout mission that's scheduled to take off in two hours. It's on the apron in front of hangar 23."

"How do you know that?" Tillman asked, a surprised look on his face.

"I'm Security Forces, Captain. There are not many systems on this base I can't access. Including flight planning and operations. Now, no more questions. Tick tock. Remember?" The man nodded, swallowing nervously.

Dirk Patton

"Here's what's going to happen. You're going to go straight to the flight line. Once you arrive, I want you close to that helicopter. I'm going to create a distraction that will pull security away. As soon as it's clear, you are to board the Pave Hawk and be ready to take off immediately when I arrive.

"If you're not there, I detonate the bomb. If there's anyone with you, I detonate the bomb. If you tell anyone, and they try to interfere in any way, I detonate the bomb. Vanessa's life is in your hands. Do what I'm telling you and a couple of hours from now you'll be back together. Am I perfectly clear?" Roach stared into the man's eyes, looking for any sign of rebellion. He saw anger and fear, but nothing else.

"You're perfectly clear. I'll be there waiting. Where are we going?"

"I have a set of GPS coordinates I'll give you once we're in the air and clear of the base. Now, I've got a couple of things to do and will meet you at the helicopter. Don't forget your wife's life depends on your cooperation. Say nothing." Roach wanted to keep reinforcing the threat. He was a little concerned about overplaying his hand and pushing Tillman to go for help, but he had to make sure the man believed his wife would die if he didn't cooperate.

Transmission

"On your way," Roach ordered, waving his hand towards the door.

Tillman stared at him for a few heartbeats before turning and walking away. Roach stepped to the front window and watched him climb into his car, slam the door and start the engine. As soon as he was out of the driveway and en route to the flight line, Roach holstered his pistol and dashed out the door and across the lawn to his waiting Humvee.

Driving cautiously, he crossed the base, passing the large hangars where the refugees were processed. They were close to the perimeter fence, but there was a road that circled the base running behind them, and this was where he headed. Pulling to a stop on the pavement, Roach took a careful look around the area.

He was screened from the main part of the base by a hangar. He could see at least a mile in either direction, and there was no sign of any patrols. In front of him, hundreds of infected were jammed tight against a 12-foot-tall, reinforced chain link fence that was topped with dual coils of razor wire. There weren't enough of them to have started piling up and spilling over the fence, but there were enough to cause a hell of a panic.

Dirk Patton

Getting out of the Humvee, he unwrapped a stout chain from brackets welded to the front bumper. The chain was long with hooks on each end and was there to aid in the recovery of a vehicle that got stuck off road. Roach had a different use for it in mind.

Dragging the chain behind him, he trotted 20 feet to the closest steel post that supported the fence. The infected grew more agitated every step he took towards them, the females starting to scream when he reached the fence. Careful to avoid the fingers that were being thrust through the mesh, he threaded the chain around the post and slipped the hook on its end through one of the links.

Running back to the Hummer he glanced over his shoulder, surprised at how fast the crowd of infected was growing in response to the screams from the females. Picking up the free end of the chain, he hooked it into a D-ring that was welded to the vehicle's frame and stuck out through an opening in the rear bumper. A quick tug and he was satisfied it was secure and climbed in behind the wheel.

Lifting the H&K off the passenger seat, he worked the sling over his head and got it into a comfortable position. A glance in the mirror and then he floored the throttle. Roaring forward, the Humvee gained momentum as the chain paid

Transmission

out behind it, then after 30-feet, it snapped taut. The heavy Hummer jerked hard when it hit the end of the chain, the reinforced steel post resisting, but it hadn't been designed to withstand the force Roach was able to put on it.

With a screech of tortured metal, the post started to bend at the first instant of tension. A moment later it was torn loose from the concrete piling it was mounted to. The chain link mesh that was attached to the post began to deform, but it had already been stretched tight when the fence was installed. It gave a couple of inches, then began tearing with a sound, not unlike fabric being ripped in half. A couple of seconds later a 30-foot wide gap opened up in the fence line and infected began pouring through onto Tinker Air Force Base.

Roach drove a hundred yards as fast as he could, dragging the fence section behind him. Screeching to a stop, he jumped out and quickly unhooked the chain from the back bumper, hopped back in and roared away, female infected in hot pursuit.

"If that doesn't pull security off the flight line, I don't know what will." Roach thought to himself as he drove, a broad smile breaking out across his face. He followed the perimeter road for a quarter of a mile then turned to cut across the base. He had one more stop to make before going to the helicopter.

Transmission

41

I had never been in one of the Marine's Ospreys before and was surprised how roomy it was. And fast, compared to a Black Hawk. But then that was the whole idea. It didn't replace helicopters. It provided a different advantage. But the one disadvantage was not having a side door I could slide open to get some fresh air.

I've spent a lot of my adult life in the company of fellow soldiers in the field. When you're fighting, running, hiding, all the things warriors do, you sweat. And there's not a nice, hot shower waiting around every turn. So that sweat ripens and ripens and ripens. And God help you if anyone you're with gets one of the MREs with Chili and Beans or Southwest Chicken and Black Beans. Then you've got a constant stream of farts to mix with the body odor.

Well, these Marines had been in the field for a while. And it seemed like all of them had eaten something with beans recently. The inside of the Osprey was just foul. Eye watering foul. Wrap a towel around your face and breathe through your mouth foul. But I was in no position to criticize. I was a bit ripe myself, and I'm not too proud to admit my farts can peel paint.

Dirk Patton

Martinez and Igor seemed immune, as I expected, but Rachel and Irina looked like they were ready to throw up. They were seated as far apart as they could get, neither apparently having forgiven the other. Dog lay sleeping at Rachel's feet, unaffected by any smell so tame as just some sweaty, gassy humans.

The refinery outside of Midland was only a short hop by air from where we'd been picked up. It seemed like we'd just gotten settled in when the pilot came on the intercom with a warning that we were only 15 minutes out. I worked my way forward to peer through the cockpit windshield, surprised when I could see the lights shining brightly across the dark desert. It looked like the house that gets decorated at Christmas time by the guy with way too much time on his hands.

There was a light everywhere. Hundreds of them, maybe even thousands. And every single one of those bulbs would be a beacon to any infected.

"Hey, Zemeck," I called my friend over. "You guys got detailed to hold the field and refinery, right?"

"Yeah. Why?" He asked, stooping to peer out the cockpit at whatever I was looking at.

Transmission

"You need to get those damn lights turned off. The males are blind, but the females can see like a fucking hawk. You got enough problems without attracting every woman for miles around." I said.

"We're Marines. Can't help it if the ladies are attracted to us." He said in a loud voice with a snide grin on his face. Everyone in the aircraft heard him, and a chorus of oorah's broke out.

"Sorry, couldn't help myself." He said when they quieted down, sounding anything but sorry. "That's on my list. Had to divert to come save some dumb grunt's ass that got lost and haven't had time to take care of it." He said in a quieter voice. "We've fought small groups of them, and of course ones and twos, but haven't tried to hold against a large body of infected. You?"

"Yes," I said, thinking about Murfreesboro. "They're about impossible to hold back once they get into a herd. If you build a wall, they'll pile up on top of each other until they reach the top. You can delay them for a while, but the only way to stop them is to kill every last one of them."

Zemeck knew me well enough to understand I wasn't exaggerating or talking out of my ass. He met my eyes and nodded, concern creasing his forehead.

"Where'd you try to make a stand?" He asked.

I guess it was plain on my face that I was speaking from memory, so I told him about Murfreesboro. He asked a few tactical questions, not liking the answers I gave him.

"Can we hold the refinery?" He finally asked, straight out.

"No," I said. "Not if one of the herds shows up and all you have are a few hundred ground troops. They don't get tired. Don't get frightened. Could care less about how many loses they are taking. You'll run out of ammo long before you run out of targets; then they'll breach your defenses and..."

"Yeah, I got it." He said, looking back out the windshield at the refinery lights. "So what do we do?"

"If I were you, I'd be asking the Air Force to start bombing the shit out of the herd that's approaching. Thin them out some. I'd also look at putting some of my guys in Hummers out in the desert to draw them off. Lead them away. I don't know if that will work or not, but it's all I've got." I said.

He nodded, and we moved back to our seats as the pilot transitioned to hover and brought us in for a landing. The rear ramp dropped, and I held my group back so the Marines could make a quick exit. When the squad was clear of the door I stepped out into the night air, Dog following because that's what he does. Zemeck was waiting for me, looking at the massive collection of pipes and tanks that turned crude oil into gasoline and diesel.

"Don't want to hang around for a bit, do you?" He asked jokingly. He knew I would if I could.

"Matt," I paused until he was looking at me. "Remember what I told you. Have an exit plan. You and your Marines are more valuable than a refinery. I know you don't like the idea of running any more than I do, but this isn't a normal enemy. They won't stop until every last Marine is dead. When they breach, you get your asses out of here. When I get to Tinker, I'll see what I can do about getting you some air assets to assist."

He nodded, turned and took my hand. "Take care of yourself. Hope whatever's going on with these Russians works out."

"Me too," I said, turned and climbed back into the Osprey.

Dog bounded up the ramp, and I shouted to the pilot that we were ready. A moment later the ramp closed, then we were lifting off vertically.

"You OK?" Rachel asked, slipping her arm through mine and resting her head on my shoulder.

"Fucking ducky," I said. "Pretty sure I just said goodbye for the last time to a friend."

Dog picked up on my mood and rested his chin in my lap. Rachel didn't have anything to say and settled for just being close. I put my hand on Dog's head and scratched his ears as we transitioned to horizontal flight and headed north to Oklahoma.

Transmission

42

Roach screeched to a stop outside the barrack where Katie and the rest of her party were housed. Unclipping a radio microphone from the dash, he made an emergency call on the Security Forces frequency, alerting the dispatchers that the fence had been breached and infected were inside the perimeter. 10 seconds later sirens began wailing all across the base. Civilians stood looking frightened, unsure what to do.

Jumping out of the Humvee he ran inside the large building. Finding her should be easy. In the military, every room in every building is numbered, and he knew which room she had been assigned. But when he got there, the door was standing partially open, and the room was empty. Feeling the time pressure, he started going down the hall, opening doors without knocking, looking for her.

Frightened women asked him what was happening, but he ignored them and kept searching. As he was about to open another door, Katie came around a corner at the far end of the building. Moving fast, she was rubbing her long hair with a towel and was barefoot. A robe was cinched loosely around her waist, her free hand holding it closed across her breasts as she ran down the corridor.

"Mrs. Chase," Roach called as she approached.

"Yes?" Katie slowed, pulled the robe tighter across her chest and eyed him up and down. It made him nervous when she did that. There was something about the woman that made him feel like she could see what he was thinking.

"I'm Captain Roach. We met when you arrived. I'm here to take you to your husband." He said in a rush.

Katie came to a complete stop, the towel dropping through her fingers and falling to the floor. "What did you say?"

"Your husband, John. He's back in the Army, a Major now, and we just realized who you are. I talked to him on a satellite phone about half an hour ago. He's at an Army post a short flight away and has asked that you be brought to him." Roach had practiced the line in his head and was happy with how it sounded when he spoke it.

"The Army? He's alive?" She took a step toward him, and for half a second Roach thought she was going to collapse.

Transmission

Tears welled up in her eyes and began pouring down her face. She forgot all about modesty and raised her hands to her face, the robe parting and revealing her nudity. Roach caught his breath at the sight of her body but forced himself to keep playing the part and not get lost in his fantasies and desires.

"Ma'am. We have to go now. There's a breach in the fence, and I've got a helicopter standing by to take you to your husband." Roach added what he thought was just the right sense of urgency to his voice and body language. Katie nodded, realized her robe was open and pulled it closed and tightly cinched the belt.

"Let me get dressed." She said and started to dash towards her room. Halfway there she stopped so abruptly that Roach, who was following, nearly ran into her.

"The children." She said an anguished look on her face. "I can't leave them if there's infected coming."

"Ma'am, there are 15,000 Soldiers, Airmen and Marines on this base right now. No disrespect, but there's nothing you can do to protect the children that they can't. Now, we need to go before the Army moves your husband again and we can't find him." Roach improvised the last part, but it was what was needed to get Katie moving again.

Nodding, she ran into her room and shoved the door closed behind her, the latch not catching. The heavy, steel door slowly swung back open a foot before stopping. As soon as she was inside, Katie had stripped off the robe. Roach stood in the hall, mesmerized by her naked form as she grabbed clothing and dressed as quickly as she could.

He turned before she realized he was watching her, playing the part of a man guarding a woman's modesty. A moment later she stepped out next to him, a holstered pistol on her right hip, boots, and socks in her hand.

"I'll put them on in the car," Katie said when he looked at what she was carrying. "Let's go."

Roach led the way outside, and moments later they were in the Hummer and heading for the flight line. Katie finished dressing, sat up and looked around at a speeding truckload of Marines headed for the fence breach.

"Where's he been? How the hell did he wind up back in the Army?" She asked, looking at Roach.

Transmission

"I don't know ma'am. Like I said, we just matched your name with his a couple of hours ago. When your names matched, the system popped up a notice that he was close, so I gave him a call to make sure there wasn't an error with the names. I was able to send him the picture we took of you to verify we were talking about the right person." Roach was pleased with how well he was making it up on the fly.

"Where are we going?" She asked. "Couldn't he come here?"

"Ma'am, again, no disrespect intended, but were you married to him when he was in the Army?" Roach tried to deflect the questions while he drove.

"Yes, I was. And you're right. I know how the Army works. Sorry, Captain. I had given up on him. I was sure he was dead. Or one of the infected." Katie started crying again, tears flowing for a couple of minutes as she fought to get her emotions under control.

It didn't take long to reach the flight line. As they approached the Pave Hawk, he could see Tillman standing next to the helicopter. He scanned the area with his eyes but didn't see anyone waiting for him. The hangar doors were closed, and Roach worried that there was a squad of cops waiting inside to come charging out and arrest him, but he was out of options. Not trying for the helicopter would be a certain death sentence. If nothing else, there were cameras that had recorded him tearing a hole in the fence.

Approaching the aircraft, Roach patted his left pocket to ensure the law enforcement grade Taser was still there. Satisfied when he felt its bulk, he turned the wheel and came to a stop 30 yards from the big helicopter. Tillman had climbed into the cockpit when he had seen Roach approaching and already had the engines running, the large rotor just starting to spin up.

"Here's our ride," Roach said, killing the engine and getting out of the Hummer.

Katie jumped out on her side and ran to keep up with Roach. He knew this was a critical moment. If she sensed anything was amiss, he wouldn't get away cleanly with her. Action and movement were on his side, though, keeping her from thinking too much if she had to hurry.

They reached the side door of the helicopter, and Roach stepped aside for Katie. She smiled her thanks and moved past him, reaching for the edge of the door to help pull herself inside. As soon as her back was to him, Roach pulled the Taser out of his pocket, aimed at the back of her neck and fired. Two small,

Transmission

metal darts trailing thin wires shot out and embedded into her skin and delivered 775,000 volts of electricity. Katie stiffened, then fell to the ground.

Roach scooped her up and tossed her into the helicopter where he quickly restrained her with flexicuffs around her wrists and ankles. Slamming the side door shut he shouted at Tillman to get them in the air.

"What the hell are you doing?" Tillman shouted as they flew over the perimeter fence, less than 50 feet in the air.

"Worry about your wife, Captain," Roach said, displaying the transmitter to the pilot. The man swallowed nervously and looked like he wanted to say more, but kept his mouth shut.

"Here's where we're going." Roach passed him a small piece of paper with a set of coordinates written on it in a hasty hand.

Tillman gained a little altitude so he could enter them into the computer without having to worry about flying into a tree or utility pole. A couple of moments later a large screen in the cockpit refreshed and displayed a pulsing red dot on a map. The pilot entered a few commands and the system generated a flight plan based on their current position. He swung the Pave Hawk onto the new heading and turned to shout to Roach.

"Nav says we're 48 minutes to destination."

Roach nodded and sat down on the vibrating deck next to Katie. She was conscious, but her nervous system was still so scrambled from the Taser's shock that she couldn't move or speak. Looking down at her, Roach reached out and placed his hand on her hip. Slowly, he began tracing the curves of her body, moving his hand up across her flat stomach and caressing her breasts. He had his leverage.

Transmission

43

The sun was just starting to peek over the horizon as we crossed the southern Oklahoma border. I was trying to sleep, but failing miserably. Part of me felt guilty for not having stayed in Midland with the Marines. The practical part of me realized that they were well trained and perfectly capable of doing what needed to be done to defend the oil refinery and that if I had stayed, I would only have been another rifle amongst the defenders.

I was half asleep, thinking about dropping everyone at Tinker and having the pilots take me back to Midland when a hand on my shoulder startled me. It was one of the pilots, standing well away as he was getting the evil eye from Dog for disturbing me.

"Sir, there's been a breach at Tinker." He said, taking a couple of steps back when Dog growled. That woke me up. Fast.

"How bad?" I asked, moving Rachel's head off my shoulder and standing up.

"Bad enough." He answered, taking another step back when Dog moved to stand with his shoulder against my leg. "What I've gotten so far is that it was sabotage. Someone damaged the fence, and the infected started pouring in. They still haven't gotten them under control."

"Take me to your radio," I said, following him back to the cockpit after telling Dog to stay with Rachel.

In the cockpit, I nodded to the Marine Captain in control of the Osprey and accepted the headset that was handed to me. Reaching out, I dialed in the frequency that Blanchard used for operational control of the Army personnel that were on the base. After a couple of tries, he answered, alarm sirens blaring in the background.

He quickly filled me in on the situation at Tinker, and then asked about the status of my mission. We weren't on a secure channel, so I didn't give him any details other than to say it had failed. I promised a full debrief on my arrival. We signed off, and I returned to the back of the aircraft after thanking the pilots for use of their radio.

Rachel, Irina, and Igor were awake, all looking expectantly at me when I sat down. Dog thrust his head into my lap and gently wagged his tail.

"They've had a breach in the perimeter fence at Tinker. Intentional sabotage. Several

Transmission

thousand infected made it onto the base before enough defenders arrived to push them back and repair the break. It's a mess right now. Infected everywhere. We're coming into a hot LZ."

Rachel nodded and began checking her weapons. Irina translated for Igor, and he also made sure he was ready to fight. I followed suit, and when everyone was satisfied they were ready, I headed back to the cockpit. I wanted a good view of the base as we came in.

The pilots had the frequency being used by the defenders on speaker and it sounded like there was a hell of a mess down there. One Air Force unit was cut off and running low on ammo, under constant attack by a large group of females. They were sounding desperate, but a squad of Marines arrived before they fell. I heard several more calls from units in trouble, some of them not getting help until it was too late. I shook my head and gritted my teeth. Whoever had breached the fence line needed to be flayed open and staked out for the infected to feast on.

We came in over part of the city, threading the needle to avoid the helicopters Tinker had put up to help battle the infected. Flying directly over the main gate, the pilot made a sharp turn to follow a runway, transitioning the engine nacelles to vertical flight as we passed over a huge parking lot full of civilian vehicles.

A couple of yellow school buses caught my eye, reminding me of Betty and the kids I'd run across in Tennessee. I knew they'd escaped Murfreesboro, but had no idea if they'd made it across the Mississippi in the final evacuation. Starting to turn back to the front, a vehicle caught my eye, and I looked closer.

It couldn't be. It wasn't possible. It had to be another truck that just happened to look like mine. Ford sold something like 30,000 F-150s a year, right? I pushed closer to the cockpit glass and stared. Same aftermarket, oversized wheels, and tires. Same third party winch bumper on the front. Fuck me if that wasn't my truck!

"Get us on the ground now!" I shouted to the pilot, startling him.

"Sir, we're not cleared for this area..."

"I don't give a flying fuck what we're cleared for. Set us down now, Captain!" I said, glaring at the man.

He stared back at me for half a second, then shrugged his shoulders and brought us down. I was already in motion for the back of the Osprey, hitting the switch to lower the ramp as I ran. The ramp came down, locking into place while we were still in the air. I didn't give a shit, running out onto it and leaping the final six feet to the ground.

Transmission

Somehow I maintained my balance, turning and breaking into a sprint for the parking lot. A few moments later Dog fell in beside me. I didn't bother to glance over my shoulder to see if everyone else was following. Right now I didn't care.

Reaching the parking lot, I raced around a Buick and nearly ran into a female's embrace. I was running with my rifle up and just shoved the muzzle into her throat and pulled the trigger without breaking stride. Dog leapt at another one, taking a few seconds to kill her before he was back by my side.

Ahead, four males stumbled out from between the two school busses. Letting my rifle drop I drew my Kukri and sped up. Running hard when I reached them I slashed my way through, dropping two of them with severed spinal cords. I swung hard enough to decapitate the third one, his head tumbling into my path and nearly tripping me. Dog took care of the last one, then we rounded a corner, and I skidded to a stop at the front of the truck.

It looked exactly like my truck, only a hell of a lot more battered. There wasn't much of the body that wasn't dented or scraped. As I walked around the passenger side, I noted half a dozen bullet holes in the sheet metal. It had the same bed cover. Then I reached the back and looked for the license plate. It might have been there if the whole rear bumper wasn't missing.

Rachel ran up with Igor and Irina right on her heels. "What's wrong?" She asked, rifle up and ready.

"This is my truck!" I slapped a hand against the tailgate.

"What?" Rachel took her attention off scanning the parking lot for infected and focused on me. "What are you talking about?"

"My goddamn truck!" I said. "It was in my garage in Arizona when I got on a plane to Atlanta. Now it's here. That means Katie's here!"

Rachel looked at me with a shocked expression on her face, then turned to survey the beat up truck. "Are you sure it's yours?"

I looked down at where the license plate should be, then remembered another way to remove all doubt. Striding around to the driver side door, I looked at the external keypad that would unlock the truck, trying to remember a code I never used. I always used the unlock button built into the key.

"What are you doing?" Rachel asked after a few seconds of me staring at the door.

Transmission

"Trying to remember," I said, finally reaching out and punching in the code. The door locks thunked into the open position, and I grabbed the handle and opened the door. Reaching inside, I fumbled around in the center console until I found what I was looking for. Pulling it out, I unfolded the registration with my name and address on it and held it out for Rachel to see.

"My goddamn truck!" I said, feeling real hope for the first time in what seemed like forever. "Now, where the hell is my wife?!"

Dirk Patton

Continue the adventure in [Days Of Perdition: V Plague Book 6](), available now from Amazon!

Printed in Great Britain
by Amazon